MURDER
in the
BELLTOWER

BOOKS BY HELENA DIXON

HELENA DIXON
MURDER
in the
BELLTOWER

Bookouture

Published by Bookouture in 2021

An imprint of Storyfire Ltd.
Carmelite House
50 Victoria Embankment
London EC4Y 0DZ

www.bookouture.com

ISBN: 978-1-80019-059-7
eBook ISBN: 978-1-80019-058-0

Murder in the Belltower is dedicated to my grandson, Isaac William Griffin, who made his appearance during the writing of this book.

Torbay Herald – December 1933

Substantial Reward Offered for Information

A reward of £100 is offered for information leading to the arrest or conviction of anyone involved in the disappearance and subsequent death of Mrs Elowed Underhay on the 11th June 1916 or thereabouts. Mrs Underhay was last seen alive in the vicinity of the Glass Bottle public house in Exeter. Her remains were sensationally discovered interred behind a false wall in the cellar of the Glass Bottle following a fire at the premises a few weeks ago. The body of Mr Denzil Hammett was also discovered, having been most brutally murdered, in an upstairs room. Information regarding the whereabouts of Ezekiel Hammett, former landlord of the Glass Bottle, who is wanted on suspicion of murder, is also desired. Exeter Police advise that Ezekiel Hammett should not be approached if sighted as he is believed to be dangerous and desperate. Anyone with information may apply in confidence in the first instance to Captain Matthew Bryant, Torbay Private Investigative Services, Fleet Street, Torquay or to Miss Kitty Underhay, The Dolphin Hotel, The Embankment, Dartmouth.

CHAPTER ONE

December 21st, 1933

The weak wintery morning sun barely made its way through the leaded panes of the large bay window of Kitty's grandmother's salon in the Dolphin Hotel, Dartmouth. A small Christmas tree scented the room with the heady note of pine and a series of festive cards depicting robins and snowmen adorned the mantelpiece.

'I'm so pleased your mother has agreed to allow you to accompany Kitty to Enderley Hall, Alice,' Mrs Treadwell said.

The young, red-haired maid beamed at her employer. 'Christmas is more a time for the young ones, Mrs Treadwell, and our Dolly is of an age now to be more help to Mother.'

Kitty suspected that her grandmother knew full well that Alice's mother might have been persuaded in her decision by the large joint of ham that Kitty had sent round to the Millers as an early Christmas gift. Alice was the eldest of eight children and money was tight in their household.

'Now, Kitty darling, you have remembered all the presents you planned to take for your aunt and uncle and everyone else at Enderley?' Kitty's great-aunt Livvy asked, eyeing the carpet bag filled to the brim with wrapped and beribboned parcels.

Kitty laughed. 'Yes, I have spare gifts for the other house guests too, plus presents for the staff who were so kind to me on my visit in the summer and even a new ball for Lucy's dog, Muffy.'

Her grandmother and great-aunt laughed.

'Then I think you have everything.' Her great-aunt kissed her cheek and Kitty caught the soft scent of violets from the perfume Livvy always wore. 'Have a wonderful time, my dear.'

'Grams, are you quite sure that you and Aunt Livvy don't mind me spending Christmas at Enderley?' Kitty turned to her grandmother who was seated sedately beside the fire, her grey hair neatly coiffed and her pearls in place around her throat. She couldn't help feeling a little guilty that she and Alice were swanning off for a country house Christmas so soon after the long-delayed funeral for her mother.

The funeral had been emotional and well attended by their many friends in Dartmouth who remembered Elowed. At least they now had a place to grieve and some sense of closure after such a long period of uncertainty.

'Quite sure,' her grandmother said firmly. 'We shall be perfectly fine. We have a nice quiet Christmas planned. Millicent Craven is joining us for Christmas dinner, and we have quite a few social events planned with the gals.'

Kitty was privately rather relieved not to be spending Christmas Day with Mrs Craven, something she guessed that her grandmother knew perfectly well. Mrs Craven, the formidable former mayoress of Dartmouth, had never been overly fond of Kitty or her mother.

'Besides, it will be nice for you and the dashing Captain Bryant to be able to spend Christmas together.' Livvy winked and smiled mischievously.

Kitty blushed and shook her head in disapproval at her aunt's nonsense. She was still adjusting to the idea that she and Matt were now officially walking out. 'We should go downstairs, Alice; Mr Potter will be here with the taxi at any minute to collect us.'

The bulk of their luggage was already in the lobby. Alice finished checking that they had the rest of their things as Kitty donned her new navy hat with red festive trim, matching wool coat and red kid gloves. Alice sported a pretty green and red Christmassy brooch on her lapel and carried a new black handbag to match her outfit.

They should arrive at Enderley Hall in time for lunch and Matt would join her in the evening. He had been at his parents in London for a few days and had some things to attend to at his office in Torquay before he would be free for the holiday.

Her grandmother and great-aunt accompanied them downstairs. Mary, the young receptionist, was already overseeing Mr Potter as he stowed their bags in the boot and on the rack at the rear of the taxi.

'Have a wonderful time, darling. Give my regards to Lord and Lady Medford and of course dear Lucy. And please, I beg you, no more murders.' Her grandmother kissed her goodbye as Alice hopped onto the back seat of the taxi and settled the last small pieces of their luggage.

'I'm sure we shall have a marvellous time. And I assure you, I really do not go about the county hoping to stumble upon murders,' Kitty said with a smile. She turned and kissed her great-aunt farewell.

'Don't worry about us. Just enjoy yourself and give my regards to your young man,' Livvy whispered.

'You are incorrigible.' She smiled at the elderly woman, so much like her grandmother in looks but with a more informal sense of style.

Kitty climbed into the back of the taxi next to Alice and Mr Potter closed the door before taking his place at the wheel. She gave a last wave to her great-aunt and grandmother as the black car pulled away and set off through the streets of Dartmouth, out up the hill past the naval college and on towards Exeter.

As they drove further away from Dartmouth the sun gave up its feeble attempt to break through the heavy, leaden clouds and retreated, leaving behind a forbidding gunmetal grey sky.

Alice appeared happily engaged in watching the bare fields and stone walls flashing by so Kitty settled back in her seat, appreciating the warmth of the red tartan travel rug tucked around her legs.

Lucy hadn't said much about who else would be in the house party for Christmas. She'd mentioned a distant cousin of Lord Medford's who she said came every year. Kitty couldn't help but feel slightly nervous about her impending stay, despite her affection for her cousin and her family. Her previous visit during the summer had almost proved fatal for both herself and Lucy.

'Are you all right, miss?' Alice asked.

'Yes, I'm fine. I was just thinking about our last visit to Enderley,' Kitty replied. She hoped Alice wasn't feeling nervous or having second thoughts about accompanying her.

Alice frowned. 'That was a bit of a to-do in June, wasn't it?' She shuddered. 'Gives me the goosebumps thinking about it, such wicked goings on. It'll be good to be there for something nice this time. You and Miss Lucy can spend more time together and what with your Captain Bryant being there too, well, it's just right for romance, I reckon.' The young maid flashed her an impish smile.

'Alice!' Kitty reproved her companion but couldn't help smiling as she did so.

The girl smirked and turned her gaze back to the views of the countryside passing by the car window.

Matt had said he would bring any responses to her advertisements in the local newspapers for information of her mother with him. She had only received a couple of letters at the hotel. Neither had contained any new or relevant information regarding the circumstances of her mother's disappearance and subsequent murder. Let alone how Elowed had come to be buried in a subterranean passageway beneath an unsavoury public house in Exeter.

A shiver trickled along her spine as she recalled the events leading up to her discovery of her mother's remains after so many years of searching. Now, the one man who probably knew something of what had happened that June day in 1916 was on the run. Ezekiel Hammett was suspected of murdering his half-brother, Denzil, and setting fire to the Glass Bottle public house in order to cover his tracks.

There was a countrywide manhunt for him, his description had been widely circulated, but as yet he had not been apprehended. Inspector Pinch, the Exeter policeman in charge of the case, was convinced he had escaped abroad. Kitty was not so certain. He was known to have a lot of criminal underworld connections in and around Exeter who could be sheltering him.

Her friend, Father Lamb of the Sacred Heart Church in Exeter, had promised to keep her informed of anything he heard, aided by two young street urchins. The young brothers had been instrumental in running errands and passing on news when she had been searching for her mother.

Kitty had sent Christmas presents to them via the good Father. She hoped the scarves, socks, gloves and sweets would make a nice Christmas surprise, along with the small sum of money she had sent to their mother. She had also gifted Father Lamb a nice bottle of Madeira. The priest had been right when he had said that the quest to find her mother was ended but now there were a whole lot of new questions that needed to be answered.

They had passed the outskirts of the city now and were heading along the country roads towards the small village of Newton St Cyres and on to Enderley Hall. Before long they were turning into the long driveway past the small white painted gatehouse that marked the entrance to the estate. Kitty averted her gaze from the burnt out remains of a large oak tree where the man who had tried to kill her in the summer had met his end.

'Cor, miss, I'd forgot how big Enderley Hall is,' Alice remarked, her gaze fixed on the building ahead.

The large red-bricked building with its deep-set leaded windows loomed in front of them. The exterior was as forbidding as she recalled from her last visit. Smoke drifted upwards to meet the angry grey sky from the multitude of chimneys. The trees near the house had shed most of their leaves exposing the huge untidy rook nests perched high up in the bare branches.

Mr Potter swung the motor car around on the gravel at the front entrance and pulled to a halt. As on her previous visit, the large oak front door of the hall opened and Muffy, a small dog of indeterminate parentage, capered towards the car followed by the stately figure of Mr Harmon, the family butler. Her cousin Lucy, wasn't far behind, her neat figure clad in a tweed suit matched with an emerald green sweater.

'What perfect timing, Kitty darling. Lunch will served in a few minutes.' Her cousin beamed at her and swept her into an affectionate embrace as soon as she exited the car. 'Come on in out of the cold.' Lucy hustled her into the large hall where a uniformed maid relieved her of her coat and hat. Kitty and Lucy had grown very close since their first meeting in the summer and the warmth of her welcome immediately made Kitty feel more at home in the large house.

Kitty left Alice to deal with the luggage, assisted by the house staff. She knew her maid would be well looked after, and Alice revelled in the temporary promotion from her usual employment as chambermaid at the hotel.

'Come through to the drawing room. Mother is with Miss Hart, you must meet her. She's Mother's new companion. After we lost darling Nanny Thoms, Mother needed someone else to boss around and thank heavens Miss Hart took the job. Although, between us, I'm not sure how long the arrangement will last.' Lucy hooked her arm companionably through Kitty's while Muffy trotted on ahead of them, her paws clicking on the black and white marble tiled floor. 'Cousin Hattie has already arrived; she always comes early. I think Father is bringing more guests back with him this afternoon when he returns from London.'

Her aunt was seated beside a blazing fire in the elegant drawing room that overlooked the terrace running along the back of the house. A small, thin, elderly woman with untidy hair was seated opposite her. Christmas cards stood on the Italianate marble fireplace to either side of the large golden gilded clock.

'Mother, look who I've found,' Lucy sang out as they entered the room.

'Kitty my dear, how are you?' Her aunt rose and kissed her cheek. 'Just in time for luncheon.' The faint scent of her aunt's lavender perfume tickled her nose. Lady Medford surveyed her keenly. 'You still look a little pale, my dear. No wonder at it after making that terrible discovery and having to attend the inquest and your poor mother's funeral. I doubt that my useless brother was much support to you. I know he's my brother but, well, he really is the limit.'

Before Kitty could reply to her aunt's remarks about her father, the drawing room door reopened, and a tall, skinny man dressed in slightly shabby clothes carrying an open book in his hands entered the room. He stopped short and peered over his black round-framed spectacles when he realised there was someone new in the room.

'Oh, Kitty, I forgot, this is Simon Frobisher, he's a botanist. Simon, this is my cousin, Miss Kitty Underhay.' Lucy waved airily in the man's direction.

'Oh, yes, um, nice to meet you, I'm sure.' The man extended his hand. His handshake was rather limp and damp, Kitty decided, not unlike the man himself. He looked to be in his early thirties, a similar age to Matt, but where Matt had a slightly dangerous air, Simon exuded a sense of apology.

'Simon is staying here to use the library, researching for his new book. And this is Miss Hart, mother's companion,' Lucy completed the introductions.

'Delighted I'm sure.' Miss Hart had a hushed, breathless, genteel little voice.

'I expect the gong will go in a moment.' Lady Medford consulted her small gold wristwatch.

Just as she spoke the sonorous tones of the dinner gong sounded from the hall.

'Where is Hattie?' Lady Medford demanded irritably. 'Forgive me, Kitty dear, but that woman will be late for her own funeral.' She led their small party along the hall to the formal dining room. Only one end of the long polished dark wood table was formally set with china, crystal and starched white linen. Miss Hart fluttered helplessly behind Lady Medford like a confused duckling following a stately swan.

They had all taken their places at the table when a plump older lady festooned in pink chiffon drapery, who Kitty presumed must be Hattie, appeared rather breathlessly in the doorway. 'Oh, dear Hortense, I'm so sorry. I was in my room and lost track of the time.' She slid into her seat with Lady Medford glaring at her.

'Really, Hattie, you know what time we eat luncheon.' Lady Medford nodded at the maid to commence serving.

Colour climbed even higher in Hattie's already florid cheeks. 'Yes, I know, Hortense, but I was visited by the muse and simply had to make some notes before it all vanished.' Hattie waved a plump arm in the air causing her many bracelets to jangle and the maid to almost spill the consommé.

Lucy performed the introductions and added, 'Hattie is a poet.'

Kitty caught the warning glint in her cousin's eye.

'How lovely,' she murmured.

This appeared to be the appropriate response as Hattie smiled graciously at her and Kitty detected Simon breathing a sigh of relief into his soup.

'Perhaps I can share some of my art at the soirée this evening? I'm sure everyone would enjoy some cultural activities?' Hattie enquired, looking hopefully in Lady Medford's direction.

Kitty thought she detected a flicker of alarm cross her aunt's patrician features. 'A kind offer, Hattie, but we shall have to see when Lord Medford arrives with the rest of the house party. They may not be of an artistic bent.'

'Do we know who is coming yet, Mama?' Lucy asked.

Lady Medford frowned. 'Some Americans and an Austrian count and his sister, I believe. You know how your father gathers people for Christmas. Oh, and your young man, of course, Kitty.'

It was Kitty's turn now to blush at the reference to Matt as her young man. It had only been a few weeks since they had agreed to take their relationship beyond mere friendship. He had been a rock of support during the inquest, which had thankfully been held in private. Her uncle had persuaded the coroner that it would be better given the time span since her mother had gone missing.

Her father had returned briefly from America in time to attend the funeral, spend a couple of days with her, and had then caught a ship back to New York where he now resided. A decision that had been welcomed by her grandmother and by his sister, Lady Medford. Edgar Underhay did not have the best of reputations. Nevertheless, Kitty had been pleased to see him.

'Ah, young love.' Hattie sighed, her eyes becoming dewy and luminous at the idea.

Fortunately, as far as Kitty was concerned, the maid began to clear the empty soup dishes before Hattie could expand on whatever she had been about to say.

'Am I right in thinking that Matt was calling in at his office, Kitty, before coming here?' Lucy asked.

'Yes, he's been away visiting his parents for a few days and he wanted to check his mail and clear his desk before the New Year.'

Kitty looked approvingly at the steak and kidney pudding that had been placed before her.

'Perhaps someone might have applied for the reward. There might be some new information if people have sent it to Matt's office instead of the Dolphin.' Lucy's face brightened at the prospect as she made the explanation to the rest of the table.

Simon dragged his attention away from his potatoes and the book on herbs of the eighteenth century that lay tantalisingly closed next to his side plate. 'Reward?'

Lucy explained that Kitty hoped someone would come forward with information leading to the discovery of what had happened to her mother all those years ago. The occupants of the dining room listened silently as Lucy explained about the fire at the Glass Bottle and Kitty's subsequent discovery of her mother's remains.

'The inquest found that she had died from a head injury. I hope to try and get some answers to what may have occurred and who was responsible.' Kitty placed her cutlery down, her appetite deserting her for the last few forkfuls.

'Oh dear,' Miss Hart fluted. 'How dreadful, and this man is on the run, this Hammett fellow?' She clutched nervously at her jet bead necklace, her gaze darting into the shadowy corners of the large room as if she suspected he might be lurking there ready to pounce.

Lady Medford cast a scornful glance at her companion. 'Really, Miss Hart. I expect he has long gone from the area. I'm quite sure we shall all be perfectly safe in our beds. Now a change of subject, if you please, to something more congenial. I'm sure my poor niece would rather not dwell on such a disturbing topic.'

Kitty smiled gratefully at her aunt as Miss Hart gave a rambling apology.

CHAPTER TWO

Matt arrived at his office in Torquay shortly after lunch. He parked his Sunbeam motorcycle in the street and hurried up the short flight of stairs to the first floor. The company that shared his landing had already closed for the Christmas holiday.

He shivered as he unlocked the door. His private investigative business was not yet established enough to employ any help, so the office had been closed whilst he had been in London visiting his parents. A pile of post lay on the mat and he scooped it up, carrying it through to place it on his desk.

It looked as if there was a mix of advertising flyers, a couple of envelopes that he suspected contained Christmas cards, and a few letters. Matt tugged off his leather motorcycle gauntlets and blew on his fingers to warm them up. It wasn't worth spending time lighting the fire as he wanted to finish up quickly and get off to Enderley. The shoulder he had injured during the war was already aching and it would no doubt be worse by the time he got to Kitty.

Matt placed the flyers in the grate with the kindling ready for the next time he was back in the office. The Christmas cards were from his immediate neighbours. The firm making dentures that shared his landing and the gentleman's tailoring establishment downstairs.

He tucked the letters inside the inner breast pocket of his leather greatcoat. If they were new clients, he could telephone them or write when he reached Enderley. If they were claimants for the reward, then he would open them with Kitty.

Satisfied that everything else appeared to be in order he was about to collect his gloves ready to leave when the black telephone on his desk began to ring.

'Hello, Torbay Private Investigative Services, can I help you?'

'Captain Bryant?' It was a male voice with a clipped air of authority.

'Speaking.' He didn't recognise the speaker.

'One moment, sir, I have someone here who wishes to talk to you.'

Matt frowned as he waited for the other person to come on the line. His curiosity was definitely aroused.

'Bryant?'

Matt moved the receiver a good inch away from his ear. He knew that voice all too well. His former employer had the telephone skills of a bull elephant and seemed to believe it was necessary to shout in order to make himself heard.

'Sir, good afternoon. What can I do for you?' He knew that Brigadier Remmington-Blythe would not be calling merely to wish him a merry Christmas.

'Got a ticklish situation, Bryant. Glad I caught you. Understand you're spending Christmas at Enderley Hall?' the brigadier boomed.

'Yes, sir.' He waited for the officer to fill him in wondering how the brigadier had discovered his plans. This did not bode well.

'Good, good. Medford is a sound chap, did lots of good stuff during the war. He's got some people staying with him for Christmas. We, and he, suspects one or more of them may be a wrong'un. Could do with another pair of eyes and ears to sort it out.'

Matt sighed. It looked as if his plans to have a nice, peaceful Christmas with Kitty were about to be upended. 'But, sir, you're aware that I no longer work for the diplomatic service.' And there had been good reasons for that decision.

He lifted the receiver a little further from his ear as an incoherent spluttery roar came out of the receiver. 'You're still bound by the Official Secrets Act, Bryant, as is Medford. This is a simple observation job. It won't disrupt your Christmas. Watch what goes on and report back anything that seems out of order. Understand you're a private investigator now, so think of this as a small job. Submit an invoice to the department, you'll be reimbursed for your time.'

'Is there anyone or anything in particular I should be observing, sir?' Matt resigned himself to the inevitable. Besides which, his curiosity was piqued by the unusual request. This had to be something important, something to do with national security if the brigadier was involved.

'Medford will fill you in when he sees you. Better you know as little as possible, fresh eyes and ears. Don't want to tip the bounder off before the trap is sprung. It could get a bit tricky, dangerous even,' the brigadier boomed.

'Very well, sir.'

'Good show. And not a word to anyone. Anyone at all. Hush-hush.' The phone went dead as the officer rang off.

Matt replaced the handset, his mind racing. The house party at Enderley was to be no normal Christmas party then. It looked as if Lord Medford had been persuaded to use the occasion to entrap a potential enemy of the country. A potentially dangerous enemy. Even worse, the restrictions placed on him by the Official Secrets Act meant he couldn't say anything of this to Kitty.

*

With lunch completed, the occupants at Enderley drifted back to their various employments. Simon Frobisher disappeared into the library and Hattie back to her room.

'Lucy my dear, I have a small errand for you and Kitty.' Lady Medford glared at Muffy as the little dog emerged from beneath the dining table licking the remains of steak and kidney pudding gravy from her whiskers.

'Of course, Mother, what would you like us to do?' Lucy asked.

'I have a nice evergreen wreath prepared for Nanny Thoms' grave. Golightly placed it in the orangery this morning. Would you and Kitty be so kind as to take it to the churchyard? While you're there can you check the church flowers too. Those dreadful women have been fighting again and the vicar does absolutely nothing to sort it out. Really, it's a disgrace. If things don't improve, I shall be forced to write to the bishop again.'

'Very well, Mother. Are you up for it, Kitty? It's not far. The church is just outside the boundary wall of the estate and Muffy could do with a walk.'

Kitty was feeling rather full after a generous helping of stewed apples and custard for her dessert, so a walk sounded just the ticket. Plus, she now wanted to know about the flower wars at the church. It all sounded rather humorous. 'Of course, I'll just run and change my shoes.' She smiled at her aunt and cousin and headed for the large oak staircase with its splendid painted mural that ran from the foot of the stairs and along the landing.

She knew her aunt had given her and Alice the room they had shared during their last stay at the Hall so had no trouble finding her way.

Alice was already busy unpacking her case and sorting out her clothes. The room was a charming one, decorated in a soft floral pink. A fire burned brightly in the grate and the maid's bed was screened off in a small side room.

'I need to change my shoes, Alice. Lucy and I are walking to the church.' Kitty looked at the open door of the wardrobe.

'Your brown brogues are in the box there, miss. Better take your thick scarf, it's turning proper cold out there now. Cook reckons as we could have snow for Christmas.'

Kitty smiled at the mention of Cook. 'I trust she gave you a good lunch. Is she still reading the tea leaves?'

'Oh yes, miss. I had steak and kidney pudding, lovely it was. Yes, she read Mr Golightly the gardener's cup for him this morning. Said as he would have a shock coming his way.' Alice giggled as she took Kitty's brogues from their box and passed them to her.

'I bet the shock will be when he has to part with some of his hot house treasures for my aunt's festive tables.' Kitty smiled back as she eased her feet into her shoes and tied the laces.

'He was already in a bad mood, said as someone had been messing with the lock on the gardener's hut. The one down by the lake.' The smile slipped from Alice's face and she shuddered. 'He keeps a good eye on that place now after what happened here in the summer.'

'Probably a vagrant passing through looking for a bed for the night,' Kitty reassured her.

Alice frowned as she picked up Kitty's discarded patent Mary Jane's and set them neatly aside for cleaning. 'That's what Cook said. Best take your red scarf, miss.'

'Thank you, Alice.'

Kitty slipped the scarf around her neck and ran lightly back down the stairs to collect the rest of her outdoor things from the large cloakroom just off the hallway. She had almost finished adjusting her hat when Lucy reappeared clad in a smart burgundy coat with a fur collar and matching hat. She had a large wicker basket over one arm. Muffy, as always, was at her heels.

'I virtually had to prise this wretched wreath out of Golightly's hands. He said Mother had been moving some of the plants he was preparing for the house for Christmas.' Lucy squinted at the wreath.

Kitty turned away from the mirror, satisfied her neat navy hat with its scarlet band was now straight, and smiled at her cousin.

'Gardeners are a rum lot, aren't they? Come on, you can show me the church and tell me about this to-do with the flower ladies.'

Lucy smiled back and the two girls set off through the front door before turning away from the main drive to take a gravel path running past the tennis courts.

'We escaped just in time. Cousin Hattie was making noises about accompanying us,' Lucy said.

Muffy raced ahead of them, her tail wagging happily.

'I take it the poetry is rather a trial?' Kitty asked delicately.

Lucy released a peal of laughter. 'Darling, it's ghastly and she will insist on inflicting it upon us all. Her singing is even worse. Oh, do tell Alice to make sure she locks your room when you aren't there. Hattie is like a magpie. If it's bright and shiny it finds its way into her handbag. Last Christmas Mr Harmon had to send Gladys to search her room before we ran out of teaspoons.'

'Thank you for the warning. She certainly seems quite a character.'

'There's no harm in her really. Just rather lonely, I think. She spends her year flitting between one family member and another.' Lucy slipped her free arm through Kitty's as they took another turn along a path Kitty hadn't seen before that led towards the stone wall bordering the estate grounds.

'Aunt Hortense didn't sound very keen on the vicar, is he new?' Kitty asked as Lucy whistled for Muffy to come out of the evergreen shrubs that bordered the path.

'Reverend Crabtree came at the end of September when Reverend Kiddlington retired. Honestly, he's awful, no one likes him. I sometimes wonder if he's even a proper vicar. You'll see what I mean when you meet him. But as to the flowers, well the ladies' groups have always been a bit at odds. Mrs Baker has usually had the last say on everything. She reminds me rather of your grandmother's friend, Mrs Craven. Then this new lady moved into the village,

Mrs Tabitha Vernon, she's a retired music hall star and she joined everything. By the end of October she was on all the committees and has ousted Mrs Baker completely from a few of them. Since then they have argued over everything: the flowers for the church, the cleaning rota, the Christmas bazaar, the children's play.' Lucy paused for breath and shook her head. 'Kitty, you would be astonished at the skulduggery involved.'

Kitty smiled at her cousin's indignation. The path had narrowed as they had neared the estate wall. It was bordered now on both sides by laurel bushes and some other rather sad and dark-looking shrubs, which had lost most of their leaves. She was glad she had changed her shoes as the path was muddy now in places. The darkness of the afternoon gave it an air of foreboding and it was not a route she would have cared to walk on her own.

Eventually they halted in front of a small wooden door painted green that was set into the rough stone wall. Lucy delved in her coat pocket and produced a large iron key.

'Father keeps the gate locked to deter vagrants and poachers. The key is kept in the cloakroom should you ever need it, near the spare galoshes and mackintosh coats.' She unlocked the door and they walked through into a narrow lane. Lucy locked the door behind them and slipped the key back into her pocket.

The trees on either side of the road were bare of their leaves and leaned towards each other forming a tunnel. Sodden and tattered fronds of bracken filled in the space beneath the trees, along with large clumps of evergreen rhododendrons that had clearly escaped the confines of the estate. Muffy pattered on ahead as they continued to walk.

'The church is just along here. The villagers have a separate road coming up from the village past the vicarage and Miss Plenderleith's cottage. She's very friendly with Miss Hart. Father had this route put in for the estate workers and the servants. It saves going all the way round down the drive and through the main gate,' Lucy explained.

The church was ahead of them now, a small square construction with a tower built out of honey coloured stone. A low stone wall surrounded the churchyard with the entrance via a lychgate set between two yew trees.

The wind blew, sending long-dead leaves skittering past their feet and causing the naked tree branches and the shrubs to rustle. Kitty suddenly had the eerie sensation they were being followed, watched.

They walked through the gate and Muffy paused as if picking up Kitty's feelings.

'What is the matter, silly dog? Come on, this way,' Lucy encouraged as they walked around the church towards the newer gravestones on the far side.

Nanny Thoms' grave was marked with a simple white marble headstone. Kitty helped Lucy to remove the dead flowers from the small stone urn and they placed the new wreath on the grave.

'You must miss her so much.' Kitty hugged her cousin. Nanny Thoms had cared for Lucy since she had been small and had then gone on to be companion to Lady Medford.

'We all do, especially Mother. Miss Hart appears a pleasant enough woman, if rather a snob, but she isn't my darling nanny.' Lucy dashed a tear from her eye with a gloved finger. 'Come on, let's go and check the church and then we can go back to the Hall for tea. I'm parched.'

'Is the church open?' Kitty asked.

'There should be someone here. It's normally the time the village ladies come to clean the brasses and arrange the flowers,' Lucy said as they turned to retrace their steps along the path.

Ahead of them Muffy had paused once more. Her tail was down, and a low, deep growl came from her throat. Her attention was fixed on a densely wooded spot beyond the boundary.

'Muffy?' Lucy frowned. 'What's the matter? Is it a fox?'

Kitty looked around trying to see what had alerted the dog. It was unlike Muffy to growl, she was normally a very sweet, lovable hound. At first, she couldn't see anything, and she was about to say so to her cousin when she heard what sounded like a twig snapping to her left. She turned and thought she caught a glimpse of something or someone in the bushes outside the churchyard.

'Lucy, let's go into the church.' She kept her tone even not wanting to alarm her cousin. She kept an eye on the shrubbery where she thought she'd seen movement while they started towards the sanctuary of the building.

Muffy was apparently satisfied that she had successfully defended her mistress and resumed her investigation of the churchyard.

Lucy's brow was still furrowed. 'How very odd. Muffy is usually fine when we're here. She must have seen a fox. They do get bolder at this time of year.'

Kitty was still uneasy, sure that it had been a human watching them and not a woodland creature.

They walked back into the older part of the grounds. The gravestones here were covered in moss and many leaned drunkenly at odd angles where they had sunk over time into the soft earth. They were almost at the large arch-shaped wooden door of the church when Kitty spotted something that caused her to halt in her tracks.

'Lucy, that stone there.' She left her cousin's side to take a closer look, a sick feeling of fear mixed with excitement as she read the name on the stone.

'Hammett,' Lucy read. 'Why, that's the same name as the man who killed his brother at the pub. The one who might know something about what happened to your mother.' Lucy looked around the graves, wandering between the stones. 'There are several of them here. Perhaps it's a local family or it could just be a coincidence. How odd, I've never noticed the names before.'

'Perhaps.' Kitty wondered if there were any Hammetts still in the area. Maybe it was a coincidence, they might well be all long dead or no relation to Ezekiel. She shivered and hoped that it was simply a common name.

'Some of the servants might know or the ladies cleaning in the church. Cook, perhaps, she's from the village,' Lucy suggested.

Despite herself, Kitty felt unnerved by the discovery, especially with the suspicion that she and Lucy had been followed to the church. The events of the past year had taught her to think more like Matt, and now, like him, she didn't trust coincidences.

CHAPTER THREE

The church was indeed open, and Kitty was relieved to discover that two pinafore-clad older ladies were hard at work inside. The one closest was vigorously sweeping the stone flagged floor, whilst the other lady was polishing the brass as if her life depended on it. The air smelled of polish, dust and pine.

'Good afternoon, ladies,' Lucy said as Muffy pottered off to investigate the oak pews near the front of the church.

'Afternoon, Miss Lucy. If you'm wanting the vicar he's in the bell tower with the verger. Says there's something up with the bell.' The brass polisher didn't pause in her task as she imparted this piece of information.

'Oh no, that's quite all right. I came to show my cousin the church and Mother asked me to see if you had everything you needed for the flowers. You are very welcome to take greenery from the estate to decorate the church should you require more.' Lucy smiled at the women as Kitty looked with interest at her surroundings.

It was a small church, the interior painted in cream with various marble plaques on the walls commemorating the lives of past members of the Medford family and other local dignitaries. Above the altar was a fine stained-glass window featuring Mary and the Christ child and Kitty assumed the church was probably dedicated to Mary.

At the rear of the church near where they had entered was a painted wooden marker post headed 'Raise the roof' marked with various cash amounts with the target at the top. She guessed the vicar must be attempting to raise funds for repairs. She'd often seen similar indicators in St Saviour's in Dartmouth whenever something needed renewing.

'That's very kind of her ladyship, but Mrs Baker said as she had everything in hand. That's if that Mrs Vernon don't come upsetting the apple cart again. Just look at what she's done to the nativity scene.' The woman indicated towards a large wooden model of the stable lined with straw that was set up near the stone font at the front of the church.

'Only gone and chucked the proper one away she has. Said it were a load of old tat. Mr Gibbon made the old one when he were an apprentice, been good enough for the last thirty years it has. Tat indeed. And she's gone and redone baby Jesus.' The wielder of the broom sent a cloud of dust up into the air.

Kitty privately thought it looked rather splendid. The figures of the holy family were finely carved and painted and the animals looked very well done. She surmised these ladies must be friends of Mrs Baker and that the changing of the nativity set therefore was a heinous crime in their eyes. The new scene looked nice with a selection of carved wooden animals, angel, shepherds and kings. Baby Jesus was not yet in the crib. No doubt he would appear on Christmas morning in time for the service. If he hadn't been kidnapped.

'Well, the greenery does all look very lovely,' Lucy said diplomatically.

The pine scent seemed to be emanating from the fronds mixed with the boughs of holly and ivy placed along all the stone sills of the church. At the end of each pew a small paper cone of what seemed to be sheet music held a small arrangement in festive green with red berries.

'There's some of us that still values tradition,' the broom lady remarked with a sniff.

'Unlike some as want everything all glittering like it was on the stage. 'Tis a church, not a circus, and so I said to her.' The polisher glowered darkly at the piece of brass she had just completed.

Lucy exchanged a meaningful glance with Kitty and Kitty was not at all surprised that the verger and the vicar were hiding in the bell tower.

'The church looks very old. I noticed some very aged stones on our way in. Some of them were for a family called Hammett. Are there still some of that family living locally, do you know?' Kitty asked. The women were local and had obviously lived in the area for a long time, judging from their knowledge of the nativity set's history.

The woman with the broom straightened and looked at her companion. 'Old Mrs Hammett died a few years back, them's her family graves. The rest of her family come from near Crockernwell up on the edge of the moors. Right load of rogues they am. Stealing sheep and such.'

'Anything that wasn't nailed down you mean,' her companion agreed.

Kitty's sense of unease deepened. 'You may have read something in the newspapers a few weeks ago about a man called Ezekiel Hammett who is suspected of murdering his half-brother Denzil and committing arson to try and hide the crime?'

She now had the full attention of both women who eyed her with beady curiosity.

'I wondered if he might be part of the same family?' Kitty asked.

'Not seen Ezekiel Hammett in the village since old Mrs Hammett died. Her side was respectable, and I think he only came to see if her had left him anything. Most of the family is long gone but I think they still has a farm near Crockernwell. Right rogue is Ezekiel, always said as he would come to a bad end. If he killed his brother, the way it said he had in the newspapers, then hangings too good for him,' the broom lady declared firmly.

'Now then, ladies, that is hardly a Christian attitude, especially during this blessed season.'

Kitty was startled to see the owner of the oily male voice emerging from the shadows of a narrow doorway to the side of the altar, which she presumed was the entrance to the bell tower.

Reverend Crabtree was a short, thin man in his mid-fifties, his black hair was on the long side and slicked back with an unpleasant smelling pomade.

'Reverend Crabtree, may I present my cousin, Miss Kitty Underhay,' Lucy said as Kitty's hand was seized by the vicar in an uncomfortably tight grip.

The hairs on the nape of her neck prickled and she was relieved she was wearing gloves.

'Miss Underhay, I've heard so much about you. The business with your mother, very sad my dear, very sad.' Reverend Crabtree had a curious way of not looking directly at a person when he spoke, instead addressing a spot somewhere over her left shoulder.

'Thank you, yes, it has all been very distressing.' Kitty extricated her hand.

'All finished, ladies?' The vicar turned his attention to the two women who had rapidly packed up their things and slipped on their coats while he had been speaking to Kitty.

'Mrs Baker is coming in a bit to finish off the decorations,' the broom lady said.

'Actually, we should be leaving too, Kitty. Mother will be expecting us to return in time for tea,' Lucy said and called to Muffy, who was busy sniffing all around the font.

'Please give my regards to your parents, Miss Medford. I'm looking forward to attending the evening party at the Hall. Most generous of them to invite us all.' The vicar's lips twisted upwards in a smile.

Kitty couldn't help contrasting the obsequious charms of Reverend Crabtree with the friendly openness of Father Lamb. She couldn't imagine anyone finding comfort from Reverend Crabtree in their hour of need.

'Of course. Muffy, do come here!' Lucy summoned her dog once more and they made their way out of the church into the cold, gloomy air of the churchyard.

Kitty was relieved to be returning to the Hall. It was already getting dark and the route back along the lane and through the gate looked even less inviting than it had when they had arrived. Even Muffy appeared more subdued, trotting along at Lucy's side as they re-entered the estate grounds.

Thankfully, although she kept a sharp lookout, there was no sign of anyone watching them and Kitty started to wonder if she had imagined it.

'You see what I mean now, Kitty darling, about the vicar and the feuding over the flowers and the church. It's all quite ridiculous. The nativity set was an old grubby thing. I rather expect it fell to pieces or the mice ate it.' Lucy shivered and hitched the wicker basket further along her arm. 'Gosh it's cold. I hope Mother has got the fire roaring, I can't feel my toes.'

As they drew nearer to the house Kitty saw a motor car, a sporty, shiny red model, was parked near the front door and Mr Harmon was supervising the footmen in the unloading of a considerable amount of luggage.

'That's not Father's car. It must be some of the guests. What a lot of bags,' Lucy murmured in Kitty's ear.

They hurried inside and left their coats and hats in the cloakroom, and Lucy carefully replaced the gate key on its hook. Kitty paused in front of the mirror to fluff up her short blonde curls. There was no sign of Matt's motorcycle on the gravel driveway and she wondered what time he would arrive.

Her aunt was entertaining in the drawing room it seemed. Kitty heard the murmur of voices through the partly open door as she and Lucy approached. Muffy had already found her way inside and as they entered was disappearing behind one of the low chintz sofas with a biscuit in her mouth.

Miss Hart was fussing over the tea trolley and Hattie appeared to be deep in conversation with the new arrivals.

'Ah, Lucy, Kitty, there you are. Count Vanderstrafen, may I present my daughter, Lucy, and my niece, Miss Kitty Underhay. Girls, Victor and his sister will be staying with us for Christmas,' Lady Medford announced as the count rose to his feet and bowed, first over Lucy's hand and then Kitty's.

He was a tall, good-looking man of about thirty-five with fair hair and bright blue eyes. 'I am delighted to meet you both. May I present my sister, Juliet.'

Juliet Vanderstrafen was almost as tall as her brother and looked to be about five years his junior. Her hair was as fair as Kitty's but longer and styled in a simple chignon at the nape of her neck. Like her brother she was simply and expensively dressed.

'It is lovely to meet you both. My brother and I are very much looking forward to seeing a traditional English Christmas.' Her English, like the count's, held only the trace of an accent. Kitty thought she could easily pass for one of Alice's film stars. There was an air of almost ethereal loveliness about her pale features.

'Oh dear, I think we need more cups. Shall I ring for Mrs Jenkinson, Lady Medford?' Miss Hart was still dithering about with the trolley. Kitty could see how Muffy had managed to steal a biscuit.

'I'll do it, Miss Hart.' Lucy tugged on the embroidered bell pull at the side of the fireplace as her mother stifled an impatient sigh.

Mrs Jenkinson had clearly anticipated the need for fresh tea and more cakes as a maid swiftly appeared and replenished the trolley. Lucy took over hostess duties and Miss Hart fluttered to a halt in the chair next to Lady Medford.

'So you are Austrian, Count Vanderstrafen? Such a cultured people, so musical,' Hattie said.

'Please, you must call me Victor. Thank you, yes, my country is indeed famous for its music. You are a music lover yourself?' he asked.

Lucy's eyebrows raised slightly in alarm at this seemingly innocent question.

'Music, poetry, painting. Yes, my dear, I am positively immersed in culture. I have been told many times that I have a good operatic voice. Perhaps we shall be able to enjoy a musical evening during your stay. My cousin has a very fine grand piano in the music room.'

'I am sure that sounds delightful,' the count said in a polite tone.

Kitty judged from Lucy's expression that this was unlikely to be the case.

'Kitty, do you sing, my dear, or play an instrument?' Hattie turned to Kitty.

'I, um, I can play a ukulele,' Kitty faltered. Somehow she didn't think this would count as culture, especially as the songs she knew were a little on the bawdy side as Mickey, her maintenance man at the hotel, had been her tutor.

Her cousin turned what sounded like a giggle into a cough as Hattie lost interest in Kitty's lack of accomplishments.

'Juliet is a very good singer also.' Victor smiled at his sister.

Faint colour rose highlighting Juliet's high cheekbones. 'My brother is flattering me, I assure you,' she said.

Kitty settled back in her seat and took a sip of tea from the delicate china cup that Lucy had handed to her. A wave of tiredness washed over her as she half-listened to the various conversations swirling around her.

The heat from the fire was thawing the cold from her toes. Lucy perched on the arm of the chair next to her.

'The count is a bit of a dish, isn't he?' Lucy whispered. 'Shame you're spoken for, Kitty.'

Kitty smiled at the cheeky twinkle in her cousin's eyes. 'What about you?' she asked. 'Is Rupert no longer on the scene?'

Rupert Banks and his sister, Daisy, had been guests at the house party in the summer. Lucy had refused his proposal of marriage, believing at the time that his attentions were just harmless flirtation, but Kitty was certain they were still seeing one another.

'Daisy and Aubrey are at Thurscomb House with Rupert for Christmas. I said I would visit with a party in the new year.' Lucy blushed.

'Oh yes?' Kitty grinned.

'Well, we shall see.' Lucy drained her tea and held out her free hand to take Kitty's cup away too.

Kitty refrained from teasing her cousin any further. Perhaps the new year might bring a wedding. She knew her uncle would not object to the match now Rupert's communist sympathies appeared to have abated somewhat. Her aunt, however, might require a little more persuasion despite Rupert's wealth and elevation to the peerage. His liberal sympathies had not impressed Lady Medford.

With tea dispensed with, the Vanderstrafens retired to their rooms while Hattie went off to the music room to check that the piano was in tune. Mr Frobisher it seemed had taken his tea in the library where he was still making notes from Lady Medford's extensive collection of rare books.

Kitty decided to follow the Vanderstrafens' example and retire to her room for a nap before dressing for dinner. She was concerned that Matt had not yet arrived at the Hall. She hoped his journey to Torquay had not been too arduous and that nothing had occurred to detain him.

When she reached her room, she discovered Alice seated beside the fire busy with her sewing basket. The girl's auburn hair was escaping the confines of her starched frilly lace cap and she was deep in concentration. A small table lamp cast a gentle yellow glow over the scene and the radio played softly in the background.

'Oh, Miss Kitty, I wasn't expecting you back up here just yet.' Alice leapt to her feet placing the skirt she had been mending to one side as soon as she heard the door open.

'It's quite all right, Alice. I shan't disturb you. I thought I might just rest for a while before dinner.'

Alice looked concerned as Kitty took a seat in the other fireside chair and started to unlace her shoes. 'Can I get you anything, miss? You look quite pale.'

'I think I'm just a little tired. I haven't been sleeping terribly well and the journey seems to have worn me out.'

Alice switched off the radio and knelt to collect Kitty's shoes, her brow wrinkling at the mud splashes marking the toes. 'I expect it was the walk in the fresh air too, miss. Is it far to the church?'

'It's quite a way, even with the shortcut through the estate grounds. And it's not a route I would care to take alone as it's quite eerie under the trees. Even Muffy was spooked at one point, as if someone was following us. Ridiculous, I know.' She wriggled out of her tweed skirt and scarlet sweater.

Alice had turned back her bed so she could jump beneath the covers. The maid tucked her in. 'Have yourself an hour, miss, then I'll bring you a nice cup of tea before you have your bath to change for the evening. I expect Captain Bryant will be here by then.'

'I hope so. It's cold out there and I confess I'm worried there may be ice on the road.' Kitty yawned and closed her eyes.

*

It was dark when Matt finally pulled his Sunbeam to a halt on the drive outside Enderley. His shoulder ached from the long journey in the freezing weather. The last part had been especially trying with patches of ice on the narrow unlit lanes. A puncture just outside Exeter had caused him to be delayed still further. Even so, he still preferred the freedom of his motorcycle over the confines of a motor car any day due to the claustrophobia he still suffered since his time in the trenches.

He unfastened his leather bag from the back of his motorcycle and rang the bell.

'Captain Bryant, welcome, sir. We were becoming concerned.' Mr Harmon took his bag and stepped aside to allow him into the cosy warmth of the brightly lit hall. A Christmas tree stood at the foot of the great stairwell awaiting decoration and ivy garlands now festooned the polished oak balustrades.

'If you would care to follow me, sir, I'll show you to your room. Dinner will be served in fifty minutes.'

Matt followed the butler's stately figure up the stairs and along the landing. 'Her ladyship has given you the same room as your last stay, sir. I trust this will be satisfactory?'

'Thank you, Mr Harmon.' Matt followed the man inside the large bedroom. It was comfortably furnished in muted autumnal tones and a fire burned in the grate, greeting him with a welcome heat after his long hours on the road.

'Will you require any assistance to dress, sir?' Mr Harmon deposited his valise on a small stand next to the walnut veneered wardrobe.

'No, I'll be quite all right. Thank you.' Matt was used to managing for himself. He hadn't kept a valet or manservant for many years.

'Very good, sir. Pre-dinner drinks are in the drawing room.' The butler withdrew and Matt went to stand beside the fire before attempting to remove his coat, cap or gloves. The thought of a pre-dinner drink, hopefully with Kitty, was most attractive. He was curious to meet his fellow guests and to discover from his host exactly what this delicate observation job was all about.

He hastily bathed, the steam from the hot water helping to thaw his frozen limbs, and changed before heading to the drawing room.

He glanced at his watch as he reached the hall. Ten minutes until Mr Harmon was due to sound the gong for dinner.

The drawing room was abuzz with chatter when he entered. A uniformed maid was circulating with a silver tray of drinks. He spotted Kitty immediately in her dark red satin gown standing with Lucy near the curtained French doors. She had a glass in her hand and was laughing at something her cousin must have said.

She turned his way and smiled when she saw him, her delicate face lighting up. Lady Medford was talking to a tall, thin bespectacled man in a rather shabby dinner suit. An elderly woman, clearly her companion, hovered at her elbow.

A plump, older lady was seated on an armchair talking in an animated fashion to Lord Medford who was standing to the side of the fireplace with another well-dressed older couple. His host nodded in acknowledgement of his arrival. Matt accepted a drink from the maid and made his way towards Kitty.

'I was starting to fret. Did something happen to delay you?' Kitty asked as he bent his head to kiss her cheek.

'Bad weather and a puncture just outside Exeter.'

'Oh no, what rotten luck,' Lucy sympathised as he greeted her. 'When did you arrive?'

'Less than an hour ago. I think I'm still thawing out.' He took a sip from his drink. 'Tell me who everyone is.'

Lucy and Kitty gave him a rapid introduction to the other occupants.

'The lady and gentleman with Papa are the people he brought with him from London, Delilah and Cornelius Cornwell. They're American, and keen to see an English Christmas, like our other guests. Mrs Cornwell was unwell, and they missed their sailing back to America, so Papa invited them to spend Christmas here,' Lucy explained.

'Are there more guests?' Matt asked. It seemed as if there would be quite a few people at Enderley for Christmas.

'Just two more,' Kitty said. Before she could tell him anything further the door to the drawing room opened once more and two people entered who Matt hadn't seen for almost two years. Victor and Juliet Vanderstrafen. His gaze tangled with Juliet's and it hit him like a punch to his solar plexus. Something flittered across her delicate features; recognition, alarm.

Her gaze shifted almost imperceptibly to Kitty, standing at his side and then back. He was taken straight back in time to Alexandria; the heat, dust and flies. He had been at a low point in his life, both with work and his personal life.

No wonder the brigadier had said the matter was sensitive, but surely he hadn't known about his connection to Juliet or suspected the Vanderstrafens of something undesirable? Or had he?

Matt became aware of someone speaking. Lucy? Kitty? Victor had his ice-blue gaze fixed upon him. There was little love lost between the two of them. Victor was protective of Juliet and had disliked her friendship with Matt although he always strived to hide it well.

Outside in the hall the gong sounded for dinner and people began to move.

'Matt? You know her, don't you? Juliet?' Kitty's hand was on his arm.

He tore his attention away from the tall, slender blonde in the gold dress back to Kitty.

'Yes, we've met before. Come on, we'd better go in for dinner.'

CHAPTER FOUR

Kitty permitted Matt to escort her into the dining room and took her place at his side at the dinner table. Unlike the informal luncheon setting, the table now groaned under the weight of silverware and crystal, all glittering under the light from the elaborate chandeliers. Festive centrepieces of holly red berries and pine cones adorned the snowy white table linen.

Matt's reaction to seeing Juliet Vanderstrafen enter the drawing room had been strange. It was clear, at least to her, that there had been something in the past between them. She ate her first course without any awareness of what she was eating. All her anticipated pleasure in Matt's arrival seemed to have fizzled away like a failed firework, leaving her flat and disappointed.

Alice had assisted her to dress for the evening, selecting one of Kitty's newer gowns in her favourite colour, aware that she had wanted to impress Matt when he arrived. Instead he appeared preoccupied and silent, taking sly peeks at Juliet Vanderstrafen when he thought no one noticed.

'So what is it you do exactly, Captain Bryant?' Hattie was seated opposite them beside Simon Frobisher.

'I'm a private investigator.' Matt took a sip from his wine glass.

'How very exciting, and what does that involve? Is it all divorces and scandal, or murder and mayhem?' Hattie's clarion voice had attracted the attention of some of the other diners.

Matt smiled politely. 'Theft and fraud mainly, although Kitty and I have been caught up in more than our fair share of murders this year.'

Hattie's knife clattered against her plate. 'Oh my goodness. Murder!'

'You are a private investigator now? You left the service?' Victor's cultured tones cut into the conversation.

'Yes, I left some time ago. I decided on a change of career.'

Kitty detected a hint of frostiness in Matt's reply. Victor and Matt didn't care much for each other, interesting. She was prepared to bet her last shilling that the ice-cool Juliet was probably the source of their friction. Victor gave her the impression of being quite a possessive brother.

'I wouldn't have thought there would be that many murders in a sleepy county like Devon?' Simon Frobisher ventured.

'Kitty seems to find them out,' Lucy said.

Victor turned his attention to Kitty. 'You too are an investigator?' His question held a slightly derisive note, which instantly irritated her.

'No, I'm a hotelier, but I have assisted Matt with a few of his cases.' She returned his gaze.

She saw a flicker of what appeared to be amusement in his eyes at her response and it nettled her. 'I take it that you and Matt know each other?' she asked.

'We have met before some time ago,' Victor said. 'Alexandria, I believe, when we last saw you. It was a difficult time.'

'Yes, I think you may be right.' Matt placed his cutlery down on his plate.

'Oh that is so swell. We were in Alexandria a few years ago too, weren't we, honey?' Mrs Cornwell remarked to her husband.

'Sure thing, sweetie, we've travelled quite a lot. My work takes me all over.' Mr Cornwell beamed around at his fellow diners as if seeking their approbation of his journeys.

'Oh to travel. I have always wanted to visit Egypt. Such a romantic place. A cruise along the Nile, a trip to the ancient temples and to see the great pyramids.' Hattie wafted her arm around jogging Simon's elbow.

'Perhaps you may go some day,' the count suggested courteously as the maid moved in to remove their empty plates, ready to replace them with their desserts.

Kitty noticed that Juliet had remained silent throughout this exchange, toying with her fork and eating very little of the roast lamb on her plate. The other couple at the table had mainly been engrossed in conversation with her aunt and uncle apart from the mention of Egypt.

Kitty hadn't spoken much to the American couple beyond pleasantries. Mr Cornwell, 'call me Corny', was a bluff American in his mid-fifties, well dressed and inclined to be loudly delighted with everything. His wife, Delilah, was a thin woman of a similar age with carefully arranged dark hair and an assortment of diamonds, which flashed and caught the light as she moved.

Like her husband, she appeared to be interested in experiencing a traditional English Christmas.

'I was just so disappointed that we missed our ship. I was very ill, you see. Then, Lord Medford suggested we spend Christmas here in this fabulous house. So very kind.' Delilah smiled at Kitty's uncle.

Dessert consisted of a rather delicious trifle. Kitty forced herself to do it justice. Once dinner was over, she intended to try and take Matt to one side and establish what exactly was going on with the Vanderstrafens.

She knew from her stay at Enderley Hall during the summer that her aunt and uncle liked to follow a traditional pattern after dinner, with her uncle taking the men for port and cigars in the library. Her aunt would entertain the ladies, meanwhile, with coffee back in the drawing room. Perhaps she might be able to draw Juliet on her connection with Matt while he was enjoying her uncle's postprandial entertainment.

Kitty's plans were somewhat thwarted by Hattie attaching herself firmly to her side as they exited the dining room. She glanced around hoping Lucy might come and rescue her, but her cousin had disappeared, presumably to collect Muffy from the kitchen.

'You must come and sit with me as I insist upon hearing more about these murders. It's so thrilling.' Hattie steered her towards the sofa, seating herself down and coyly patting the vacant cushion next to her. Kitty was left with no option but to accompany the woman.

Mrs Cornwell was seated beside Lady Medford, with Miss Hart presiding somewhat uselessly over the coffee pot. Juliet Vanderstrafen had slipped away to the other side of the room to leaf through the selection of gramophone recordings.

Kitty suppressed a groan of frustration.

'Now, tell me all the details. How very exciting for you.' Hattie's eyes gleamed.

'I assure you it's really rather dull. The police do most of the work. It is their job after all.' Kitty had neither the desire or the intention to go into details with Hattie about the various cases she and Matt had been caught up in. Reliving incidents where either she or Matt, or both, could have been killed was not conducive to creating a good festive atmosphere.

Hattie was a little deflated by her reluctance to talk. 'But, my dear, you must have seen some things. You know, bodies? I find it all terribly fascinating. I've often thought I would make a good detective. Or perhaps I should turn my hand to writing one? I've often thought they must be quite easy to do.'

Rather uncharitably, Kitty thought that in a fictional murder Hattie would be the ideal first victim. She spotted Miss Hart wobbling towards them bearing two delicate china coffee cups on their saucers.

'Miss Hart, how thoughtless of me, I should have come to help you.' Kitty jumped up and retrieved the cups, passing one to

Hattie. 'I'll take this to Miss Vanderstrafen if you like, I don't feel ready for coffee yet myself.'

Miss Hart seemed a trifle startled at Kitty's offer to help but smiled happily at her. 'Thank you, Miss Underhay, most kind of you.'

Kitty crossed the room to where Juliet was now seated on a low hide chair with chrome arms beside the gramophone.

'Miss Hart has dispatched me with coffee.' Kitty proffered the cup to Juliet hoping that the other girl hadn't heard her volunteering to bring the drink across.

'Thank you, that is most thoughtful of you.'

Kitty noticed a faint tremor in the girl's hand as she accepted the cup.

'Have you found any good music? My cousin has a very varied selection,' Kitty asked, nodding towards the pile of recordings.

'Yes, she does. An interesting choice in music of all kinds.' Juliet looked slightly discomfited by the question and Kitty wondered if the girl had really been looking through the collection or if she had used it as an excuse to escape making conversation with the rest of the party.

'Your brother said you had met Matt before in Alexandria, it must be quite a surprise to see him again here at Enderley?' Kitty dropped down on the chair opposite Juliet's. She deliberately kept her tone friendly and gossipy as she too busied herself looking at Lucy's collection of recordings. She had noticed from Matt's reactions that he had had no idea that Juliet would be at Enderley, but she wondered if that were true of Juliet. Had she known that Matt would be here?

Juliet leaned back in her chair, her wide blue eyes betraying a hint of amusement that called a faint flush to Kitty's cheeks. 'If you wish to know, did I know if your boyfriend would be here? The answer is no. I did not know. I last saw Matt two years ago in Alexandria as my brother said.'

The door to the drawing room opened and Muffy scurried in, tail wagging as she headed to investigate the trolley. Lucy followed hot on her heels.

'The wretched dog stole a bauble from the tree in the servants' hall. I was terrified it would shatter and she would not give it up.' Lucy came to sit with Juliet and Kitty. 'Music, marvellous. What shall we have on?'

Her cousin selected a recording by one of the big bands and placed it on the gramophone. Music filled the room as Lucy sat back down again. 'I daren't have it on too loudly or Mother will complain that she can't hear the conversation.' She smiled at Kitty.

The door opened once more, and the men filed in to join them. Her uncle and Mr Cornwell went to sit with their wives. Simon Frobisher was accosted by Hattie and Matt and the count made their way to the gramophone.

'May we join you, ladies?' the count asked as he drew out a silver monogrammed cigarette case and proffered it around.

'Of course,' Lucy said.

Only Juliet accepted a cigarette, fixing it into a slender ebony holder that she produced from her gold evening purse. Her brother lit her cigarette and then his own.

Kitty peeped up at Matt. She thought he still seemed distracted.

'Your father was explaining that the house will be finished with the decorating for Christmas tomorrow and there is to be a drinks party in the evening?' Victor turned to Lucy.

'Yes, we all lend a hand at placing the remaining greenery about the place and the tree that goes in here we decorate ourselves. We have a family tradition that guests in the house design an ornament for the tree. It's rather fun and all looks very festive when it's finished. Dinner will be early and then Mother has invited some of the people from the village for drinks and nibbles. Another one of the traditions of the house,' Lucy said.

'That sounds most interesting. You think so, Miss Underhay? Do you also have this kind of tradition?' he asked.

'The hotel stays open for resident guests only over Christmas.' Kitty was unsure of the purpose of his question unless he was trying to see if she had been telling him the truth earlier.

'What about you, Matt? How do you usually spend Christmas?' Lucy asked.

The corners of his lips quirked upwards. 'Most years I've been abroad, but generally I accompany my parents to visit various aged relatives in the North of England.'

Lucy gave a mock shudder. 'That sounds rather grim.'

'Hence my gratitude at being rescued by your parents' kind invitation.' Matt smiled, and his gaze locked with Kitty's.

'You won't be so grateful when you meet the guests Mother has invited for drinks tomorrow,' Lucy said. 'In fact, Matt, you and Count Vanderstrafen may be forced to step in and referee.'

'I don't understand?' Juliet blew out a thin stream of cigarette smoke and frowned at Lucy.

'I don't know what it's like in Austria but sometimes in English villages there can be a great deal of rivalry over quite trivial things,' Lucy explained.

'Who is coming tomorrow?' Kitty asked. She knew that Reverend Crabtree had accepted an invitation.

'Reverend Crabtree, Miss Plenderleith – who is Miss Hart's particular friend and secretary of the Parish council – Mrs Baker, and Mrs Vernon. I think that's everyone.' Lucy ticked off the guests on her fingers.

'It sounds most interesting,' the count said politely.

The music finished and Lucy jumped up to change the recording for another one of dance band music.

'If you will excuse us, Miss Medford, Miss Underhay, my sister and I are going to retire early. It has been a long day travelling and my sister has delicate health.' Victor gave a short courtly bow in their direction and looked at his sister.

Juliet immediately extinguished her cigarette and stood ready to follow her brother. 'Yes, thank you for a pleasant evening. I'm sure tomorrow will be very entertaining also.'

Kitty noticed her quick glance in Matt's direction when she thought her brother wouldn't notice and bile churned in her stomach.

Normally Kitty prided herself on her even temperament and lack of jealousy, but something was going on and she was determined to get to the bottom of the puzzle.

'Muffy! Drop that!' Lucy leapt up as her errant dog headed for the door carrying what appeared to be one of Hattie's chiffon scarves.

Matt took Juliet's place on the seat opposite Kitty.

'This has been quite an interesting day.' Kitty adjusted her posture in her seat so she could observe his features in the lamplight.

'Yes.' Matt looked at her.

'A surprise for you, meeting the count and his sister again?' Kitty tried to sound casual.

'Yes.'

Kitty narrowed her eyes at his monosyllabic responses. 'The count seemed quite cool towards you, I thought. Do you two not get on?'

Matt sighed. 'There were things that happened back then in Alexandria that made things a little awkward between us. The count is the kind of person who doesn't care for many people.'

'Except for his sister,' Kitty said, a bright spot of colour burning now on her cheekbones.

'Yes, he is very protective of Juliet,' Matt agreed.

Kitty could see that Matt was not about to tell her anything more.

'I have some letters from my office. I haven't opened them yet. There could be some information in them about your mother.

I thought we could take a look tomorrow after breakfast,' Matt suggested, changing the subject.

Kitty realised that he looked tired and she guessed the long drive in the cold and dealing with the puncture had triggered the pain in his shoulder again. The shoulder often gave him problems from the many surgeries that had been performed to remove shrapnel from the war.

'That sounds like a good idea.' Perhaps after a night's sleep she might find a way to discover more about what had gone on between Juliet and Matt in Alexandria.

He smiled at her and her heart gave an inconvenient twinge of sympathy.

'I'm going to turn in. I'll see you tomorrow.' Matt stood and bent to kiss her cheek. 'Good night, old thing.' His breath tickled her skin as he murmured in her ear.

*

Matt made his way up the broad oak staircase to where the landing split, one way leading to the gallery and the other to the bedrooms on that side of the house. He knew Kitty was curious about his relationship with Juliet, and he couldn't blame her.

Were the Vanderstrafens the people he was meant to observe, or was it the Cornwells? It could even be Simon Frobisher or, unlikely as it seemed, Hattie. He needed to speak to Lord Medford to find out what he knew and to see if he could give him some kind of clue to the purpose of the mission.

He hated keeping the brigadier's mission a secret from Kitty. She would be bound to think the worst of his friendship with Juliet, but until he knew if she and Victor were above board, he needed to keep both brother and sister close. What started as a straightforward request from his former employer had suddenly taken a complicated turn.

He strolled along the landing towards his room at the far end, suddenly aware that he could hear the muffled sound of raised voices. He tiptoed closer to the sound. Victor was in his sister's room and it sounded as if he were shouting at Juliet.

The combination of the language barrier and the thickness of the doors at Enderley Hall prevented him from making out exactly what was being said but it was clear from the tone that the count was angry. He listened for a few more seconds and gathered that Juliet was pleading in some way.

The voices changed and Matt hurried past just making it inside his room when he heard the door to Juliet's room open, followed by the sound of the count's bedroom door slamming shut.

Matt pulled his black tie undone and unbuttoned his collar. Nothing seemed to have changed since Alexandria.

CHAPTER FIVE

Kitty retired to bed herself not long after Matt had gone up. She hadn't wished to spend the rest of the evening with Hattie or listening to the Cornwells' travelogue of places they had visited during Mr Cornwell's employment as a manufacturer and salesman for a steel company. At least she thought that was what he'd said.

Alice had sensed Kitty's reluctance to discuss her evening when she had returned to the room. She had assisted Kitty into bed along with a couple of hot water bottles and an extra blanket as the night had turned cold. Kitty declined the offer of the large copper warming pan hanging on the wall at the foot of Alice's bed, suggesting Alice might like to use it instead.

The maid woke Kitty the following morning with a cup of tea. The fire was already blazing in the hearth and the room was cosy and warm.

'There was a right old frost last night, miss,' Alice remarked as she drew back the curtains to reveal a landscape touched with white outside the Hall.

Kitty sat up in bed and tugged her warm red dressing gown around her shoulders before collecting the tea Alice had deposited on the rosewood bedside cabinet next to her bed.

'It certainly looks chilly out there.' She took a sip of her drink.

Alice moved around the room to open the imposing wardrobe ready to assist Kitty with her choice of clothes for the day. 'Begging your pardon, miss, was everything all right last night? You didn't seem none too happy when you come upstairs.'

Kitty sighed. Nothing much escaped her friend.

'I suspect I'm just being rather silly. It seems Captain Bryant has met Count Vanderstrafen and his sister before, a couple of years ago in Egypt. I rather get the impression that Juliet and Matt may have been particular friends back then.'

Alice considered this piece of information. 'That's a bit of a facer, miss. Did Captain Bryant seem pleased to see her again?'

Kitty took another sip of her tea and pondered Alice's question. 'He seemed surprised, shocked almost.'

The maid sniffed and started to sort through Kitty's clothes. 'Then I don't reckon as you should worry. He hasn't been looking for her for all these years so she can't have meant that much to him. He's not the fickle kind, Captain Bryant.' She selected the tweed skirt and jacket Kitty had worn yesterday but this time she added a cornflower blue knitted jumper.

Kitty often wondered how someone as youthful as Alice could be so wise, but she knew Alice had lived a very different kind of life to Kitty. She had been forced to grow up more quickly having responsibility in the form of several younger siblings thrust upon her from an early age.

She finished her cup of tea. 'I know I'm being silly, and he did warn me before we decided to try being more than friends that there were things in his past. I just never expected Juliet Vanderstrafen to be one of those things. Matt was devoted to his wife, it's quite a puzzle.' She smiled at Alice.

'This jumper brings out the blue in your eyes, miss. I reckon he'll soon get over the surprise of seeing her again,' Alice remarked briskly.

Kitty hopped out of bed and pulled on her dressing gown ready to head to the bathroom across the landing. She hoped Alice was right. She knew Matt had been deeply in love with his wife and had been greatly scarred by her death even though it had been years ago. Whatever Juliet had meant to him couldn't have been much. Yes, Alice was right, Matt wasn't the fickle kind.

When she arrived downstairs for breakfast, she found the Cornwells already seated at the dining table. Mrs Cornwell was wearing a daring black trouser suit with a dark green silk blouse.

'Good morning, it looks like there's a good frost outside today,' Kitty remarked as she helped herself to scrambled eggs and bacon from the large silver platters on the sideboard.

She took her seat at the table and a maid bought her a glass of orange juice and filled her teacup from a silver teapot.

Delilah Cornwell gave an exaggerated shiver. 'Really, I'm thankful Lady Medford keeps plenty of coal fires in the house. There are radiators too. We've stayed some places where there was sheet ice on the inside of the bedroom windowpanes in the morning. I cannot abide being cold.'

'My aunt dislikes the cold. She has fires in some of the rooms even in summer.' Kitty smiled at the American woman.

'Delilah is the same way, aren't you, sweet pea? Why she doesn't do well in any kind of extreme of temperature.' Mr Cornwell looked fondly at his wife.

'That must have been difficult with all the travelling you both have done?' Kitty said mildly.

'Corny takes good care of me.' Delilah smiled smugly.

'Nothing is too much trouble for my sweetie.' Corny patted Delilah's hand.

Hattie sailed into the dining room swathed in chiffon and headed for the dishes on the side. 'Good morning. Tree decoration today and the first party of the festive season this evening. The frost is so lovely this morning on the trees. Quite inspiring, I wrote a couple of verses before dressing. I shall have a word with Hortense to see if I can perform them tonight.'

'My, that's very creative of you,' Delilah said.

Hattie beamed as she took her place at the table opposite Kitty. 'I've always had a flair for the arts. My dear mother, may God rest her soul, always said I was too sensitive and artistic. She engaged a private drawing master and a music teacher when I was a girl to develop my skills.'

'Goodness,' Kitty remarked. She hoped Hattie's poems would be short ones if she intended reading them at the party.

'Delilah is very talented too. She is regularly invited to give concerts when we're at home. She plays the piano and sings like an angel.' Corny gazed devotedly at his wife and Hattie's expression soured slightly.

'Oh Corny is too sweet. I'd love to hear you sing and play, Hattie,' Delilah said, smiling.

'I feel quite under talented amidst so many clever ladies,' Kitty attempted to defuse the conversation.

She was relieved to see the Vanderstrafens enter. They too made their selection from the covered dishes and took their places at the table, greeting the others politely.

'We were discussing the arts, Count Vanderstrafen. It seems Mrs Cornwell is also a musician and a singer. We shall have quite the little concert party. You said you sang too, Juliet dear?' Hattie waved a piece of toast in the air shedding crumbs in her enthusiasm.

'Yes, a little, although I do not perform in public.' Juliet looked discomfited by Hattie's suggestion.

'A private party is hardly in public. Of course, Mrs Cornwell and myself shall take the principal parts.' Hattie looked at Kitty. 'I don't suppose you have your ukulele with you? Such a shame it would have made quite a diversion.'

Kitty was pretty sure it would have done, especially with the songs Mickey had taught her which seemed to involve a good deal about drunken sailors.

'My dear Mr Frobisher, do come and join us. We are planning an evening of musical and artistic endeavours. Do you have a talent we might use?' Hattie asked as Simon joined them.

'Um, I'm really not a performer at all, I'm afraid.' Simon helped himself to bacon and took the seat next to Juliet Vanderstrafen.

Hattie subsided looking sulky.

Kitty wondered if Matt had already breakfasted. Lucy liked to come down later and her aunt preferred her breakfast on a tray in her room. She finished her eggs and decided to wait in the drawing room for her cousin or Matt to come downstairs. She intended to see if the post Matt had collected would have any fresh information about her mother. She also wanted to see if he intended to tell her more about his relationship with Juliet Vanderstrafen.

*

Matt had indeed risen early. He knew Lord Medford was in the habit of taking an early breakfast before the rest of the house began to stir so decided this might be the best time to speak to him. During the war Lord Medford had worked closely with the government and had developed several new materials to assist the armed forces. Presumably, it was the possibility of more new inventions that had led the brigadier to request Kitty's uncle to invite this mixed party of guests for Christmas.

The servants were just setting up the burners on the sideboard to keep the covered breakfast tureens heated when he caught up with his host in the dining room.

'Morning, Bryant my boy, up with the lark, eh?' Lord Medford said, taking his seat at the head of the table. Matt took a place beside him and they made small talk about the weather whilst Mr Harmon served them both with tea.

Matt waited until the servants had finished their tasks and both he and Lord Medford had loaded steaming plates of eggs, bacon, tomatoes, mushrooms and kidneys before them.

'I was hoping, sir, that you might have a little more information for me from the brigadier,' Matt said.

Lord Medford raised a bushy eyebrow. 'Hmm, I'm not sure what more I can tell you that the brigadier hasn't already said.' He paused to glance about the room as if half suspecting that the velvet drapes at the windows might conceal a spy. 'The fact is, we've very little to go on.'

'Then what exactly is the worry? I assumed it must be a matter of national security.' Matt added pepper to his eggs and started to eat.

'Just so. These are difficult times. You know from your visit in the summer that tensions are high in Europe. In my opinion we are building up to another war. I hope I'm wrong but there are worrying incidents. Nations jockeying for position, spies everywhere.' Lord Medford attacked his egg with a slice of toast.

'In places like Austria, for instance.' Matt remembered all too well Frau Fiser who had been paranoid about being spied upon during her stay at Enderley in June.

Lord Medford patted egg yolk from the corner of his mouth with his napkin before replying. 'Austria,' he agreed. 'But also others. There have been a series of incidents lately. Possibly connected and possibly not. Various pieces of information have found their way into the ears and hands of people they shouldn't have. Countries that have a record of being less than well intentioned towards us. You worked for the diplomatic corps cleaning up messes, you know what I mean.'

Matt frowned. 'And you suspect someone in the house party of being the conduit for the information?'

'The brigadier tested it out with a couple of false planted pieces. They both made their way to different nations suggesting that the culprit is not serving a particular national interest but is selling to the highest bidder. The trouble is we can't catch the blighters at it.' Lord Medford took a draught from his cup of tea.

'What makes you suspect members of the party, sir?' Matt asked.

'The brigadier had a list and shared it with me. We found many of our suspicions tallied so we cooked up this plan to bring them all to the Hall. Frobisher appears totally legitimate. He has the right credentials and a publishing deal for this botany book he's writing, but he has been at three of the houses where information has been leaked. The Vanderstrafens as you know move in the highest circles. They have all the connections and move around. Again, they have been present when these leaks have occurred. They have crossed paths with Frobisher several times, not that there is anything that appears to connect them. The Cornwells are a rum pair. He travels extensively and his wife, Delilah, has some well-connected friends. There's something about him though that I can't quite put my finger on. On the surface it seems he is exactly what he says he is. The brigadier checked him out. Even my own blasted cousin, Hattie, has been at a couple of the houses or parties where the breaches are either known or thought to have occurred.'

'And there are too many coincidences to ignore?' Matt asked. He could see the dilemma. There could be no risk of scandal or of causing offence to any innocent party.

'I'm too close to the thing to catch out whoever is doing this. The brigadier suggested I get everyone here for Christmas and perhaps drop another bit of bait and see which of our fish bites. You've left the service, so they are less likely to worry about you. You can observe the blighters, look for clues. You and Kitty ran that other bounder to ground here in June.' Lord Medford placed his cutlery down on his empty breakfast place.

'The brigadier has insisted that Kitty is kept in the dark about all of this.' Matt was still unhappy about this part of his instructions.

Lord Medford frowned, his heavy brows beetling together. 'With good reason. That's the other thing. Three of the brigadier's operatives have been killed in the last twelve months while this has been going on. Oh, it looked like accidents but whenever it seemed we were getting close then something would happen. Leave my niece out of it. You know she is inclined to meddle if she thinks something is afoot. It's too risky. I agree with the brigadier there and we are both bound by the Official Secrets Act.'

Kitty was not going to like this at all if she found out. Matt could see the brigadier's reasoning and the news that trained government operatives, men like himself, had been killed while this had been going on added a new dimension to the case.

'Is there anyone in particular that you suspect, sir?' Matt asked.

Lord Medford snorted. 'I don't think it's likely to be my cousin Hattie, despite her fondness for acquiring shiny trifles. As for the other blighters, well, the Vanderstrafens, the Cornwells and that Frobisher chappie are all likely contenders.'

'And the bait, sir?' Lord Medford had mentioned that he had a plan to try and lure the suspect out into the open.

'The materials formula we developed when you were here in June has gone into first phase testing. A good many countries would like to get their hands on the results and the formula itself. Obviously, we can't let this happen, so we've made up a good dummy package. Convincing enough to hopefully flush the beggar into the open.' Lord Medford finished his tea and set the cup back on its saucer.

Matt nodded slowly, thinking through his host's plan. 'When do you intend to set this in action, sir? It will have to be handled quite subtly.'

Lord Medford gave him a sharp glance. 'Agreed, we don't want any more deaths. This side of Christmas I intend to hint that the papers and results are here. What we think usually happens is that our man or woman finds a buyer and then steals to order.'

Matt could see that would make sense. There was no point in taking something, with all the risks that were involved, if it was not financially worthwhile. 'So, after you've laid a trail, so to speak, I'm simply to spy and see who may take the bait?'

'Got it in one, my boy.' Lord Medford frowned. 'Just be very careful, Bryant. This chap, whoever it is, has killed already.'

'I'll be careful, sir,' Matt assured his host. He had survived many difficult and dangerous situations in the past. He fully intended to survive this one, and to ensure Kitty's safety too.

To clear his thoughts, he donned his thick overcoat, cap, scarf and gloves and headed out into the grounds. A brisk stroll in the frosty air would hopefully be refreshing before he went in search of Kitty. The frosty ground might also show any footprints in the area around the low stone building in the grounds that Lord Medford used as a workshop. He would have expected any potential spy to have familiarised themselves with the layout of the estate.

On his return to the house Matt was somewhat startled by what sounded like a cat being tortured. He disposed of his outdoor clothing in the cloakroom and peeped in through the door of the music room where he spotted Hattie seated at the grand piano practising her scales.

He winced as she hit a top note and slipped away before she saw him. He really hoped that Lady Medford would stand firm on not allowing Hattie to entertain them over the festive period.

In his haste to escape Hattie's notice he stumbled straight into Simon Frobisher who was skulking near the door to Lord Medford's study.

'Terribly sorry, my dear fellow, I didn't see you.' Matt wondered why Simon was hanging around near the study. He was usually in the library by now, nose deep in a stack of books. At least that was what he had been led to believe.

'Oh, um, my fault, I was deep in thought,' Simon stammered, his cheeks turning a ruddy colour.

'Were you looking for Lord Medford?' Matt asked, curious to discover what Frobisher had been up to.

'What? Oh no, yes, not really, I've, um, misplaced one of my notebooks and wondered if it might have been moved by one of the servants. You know, they may have thought it was Lord Medford's.' Simon stumbled to a halt.

'I believe his lordship has already gone to his workshop. I should try Mrs Jenkinson, the housekeeper. She will probably know if anyone has found your book,' Matt replied. He kept his tone cheery and helpful, determined not to betray his disbelief at such a weak excuse.

Another high note reached them from the direction of the music room and both men winced.

'Thank you, I will. I'll, um, go and find her before Miss Merriweather, um, finishes her practise.' Simon swallowed, his Adam's apple bobbing in his long, skinny neck.

'Good idea. I don't suppose you've seen Miss Underhay anywhere?' Matt asked.

'I believe she went to the drawing room,' Simon said and went on his way, although Matt very much doubted it was to look for the housekeeper.

Kitty was indeed in the drawing room, seated beside the fire leafing through a magazine.

'Hello, have you been down to breakfast?' He took the seat opposite her admiring her neat appearance and soft blue-grey eyes.

'Yes, have you?' She placed the magazine to one side.

'Yes, I was out and about early. I had a very pleasant walk in the grounds before anyone else was stirring,' Matt said.

'I expect that was quite bracing.' Kitty raised a delicate arched eyebrow. Her tone held the same edge of ice as the frost in the garden.

'Very. I have the post with me that I collected from the office. I haven't opened any of it yet so I don't know if there will be anything useful.' Matt felt inside the inner breast pocket of his jacket and retrieved the small bundle of letters.

He watched Kitty's expression change. 'I made a discovery yesterday.' She told him about the names on the gravestones at the church and the information the ladies cleaning in the church had provided.

'There's something else,' she added, and glanced around as if to ensure that no one else might hear her.

He listened with no small amount of alarm at her description of the dog's changed behaviour and her suspicion that she and Lucy had been followed on their way to the church.

'You think it may have been Hammett?' he asked.

She frowned. 'I don't know. It could have been anyone: a poacher, a vagrant, a child playing tricks. There is no real reason why it should have been Hammett. Or even if it was, why he would follow us. But I can't help feeling uneasy.'

'Your photograph was in the newspapers. I know the inquest was closed to the public, but the press did catch pictures of you, your father and your grandmother as you left the funeral. The case was widely reported. The list of everyone else who attended both the inquests and the funeral was also widely circulated. It could be someone who wishes to try and obtain money from you,' Matt suggested. The offer of such a large reward was a high-risk strategy. It wasn't beyond the bounds of possibility that someone might mistakenly think Kitty was a wealthy woman and wish to target her.

'I intend to speak to Cook later. She is from the village and may well know more about the Hammett family. Plus, I have a Christmas gift for her and for young Gladys,' Kitty said.

'Was Gladys the young maid we met in the summer? That sounds like a good idea. If you find out anything useful, we can pass it on to Inspector Pinch in Exeter.' He couldn't help feeling concerned about the news of a prowler around the church.

It could even be connected with the task the brigadier had given him. He knew however that warning Kitty to be careful risked provoking an argument similar to the one that had caused such a huge rift between them over the summer. Instead he decided to alert Lord Medford, knowing his host would be anxious to ensure both Kitty and his own daughter's safety.

'It may be worth reporting this person in the woods to the local constable. He would wish to know if there was something amiss. As would your uncle's gamekeeper if it transpires that there are poachers,' he suggested.

'Yes, you're right. Better to be safe I suppose, and Uncle will not be amused if his game starts disappearing.' She flashed him a smile and his spirits lifted. 'Now, let's see what we've got in these letters.'

CHAPTER SIX

There were five envelopes in total. All of which bore Exeter postmarks. Kitty held her breath as Matt produced a small folding penknife from his pocket and slit the first one open before passing it across to her.

She scanned the contents and handed it to Matt. 'A dud, as they say in the films. It looks as if this lady has simply read the news reports and rehashed them to try her luck.'

'On to the next one then.' He smiled at her, the dimple flashing in his cheek.

He repeated his actions. 'Any good?' he asked as she read the contents.

'Nothing that we don't already know.' Her spirits fell as she read the letter.

The third envelope merely contained a missive imploring Kitty to find God and save herself along with a religious tract.

'Oh dear.' Kitty discarded the envelope and its contents.

Matt slit open the fourth one and passed it across to Kitty. She took out the sheet of cheap lined writing paper and read.

'Anything useful?' Matt asked noting the furrow appearing across her brow as she scanned the letter.

'I don't know. It's rather strange.' She handed it to him. 'See what you think.'

'Dear sir, I write in hopes as my information may be kept private. I recall the day the lady disappeared very well. I

was fourteen at the time and in my first job, working in one of the shops near the public house. I saw a blonde lady in a smart pink costume. She stood out as we didn't get many quality ladies come our way unless they was lost. She passed by the window and I remember admiring her clothes. She had a little pin that caught the light on her collar, purple and green. I saw her suddenly start up to run but no one come after her, so I don't know why she started to run. I can be contacted at this address.

I hope as this may be useful.

Lilian Thomas (Mrs)'

'There's an address. Do you think it's worth writing back to this woman? Perhaps arranging to see her? It was the mention of my mother's brooch. That hasn't been circulated anywhere so the only way this woman would know about my mother wearing it would be if she had seen her.' Kitty looked hopefully at Matt. The woman must know something.

'She clearly doesn't want anyone to know that she's written to you. She may still be afraid of repercussions. The address is a post office box,' Matt said. He studied the letter.

'It sounds as if she may have more information than is set down here.' Kitty tried not to sound too excited.

'Perhaps. It's certainly something that she mentions the brooch,' Matt agreed.

'We could suggest meeting her in a neutral place. One of the tea rooms, perhaps, near the cathedral, and just see if she does have any more information. Even a small detail may be helpful,' Kitty said.

'I don't see why not. We can choose a safe place. At worst it will cost you an hour of your time and a cup of tea and a penny bun.'

He smiled at her. 'Now let us see what this last one has to offer.'
He slit open the final envelope.

This envelope was dirtier than the others and the writing a
scrawl of black ink for the address. He gave it to Kitty to look at
the contents.

He saw her eyes widen as she read before she dropped the sheet
of paper down. Her hand trembling.

'What is it?' He reached to pick it up from the floor where it
had drifted onto the carpet.

'It's from him. Ezekiel Hammett. Or someone pretending to
be him.' Kitty's gaze locked with his. Fear, mingling with shock,
in her eyes.

Matt scanned the note.

> *'I know where you are. Stop looking for me or it will be the
> worse for you. Dead folk tell no tales.*
>
> *E.H.'*

'This has to go to Inspector Pinch.' Matt looked at Kitty.

She nodded in agreement. 'I agree, and the sooner the better.'

'I'll take it into the police station in Exeter.' Matt collected the
envelope and slid the sheet of paper back inside. He could run in
on the Sunbeam and have a word with the inspector and be back
in time for lunch.

'I'll ask Uncle to speak to the gamekeeper and the local constable,' Kitty said.

*

Matt left her to take the letter to Exeter along with a reply to Mrs
Thomas suggesting a meeting the day after Boxing Day at a tea
room near the cathedral green. If Kitty had had her own car she

could have taken it herself. It was very vexing to have to rely on others all the time. The sooner she put her plan into action to learn to drive, the better.

Robert Potter, the son of her regular taxi driver, had agreed to teach her and was looking out for a suitable vehicle. A little red Tourer was her dream car and she had issued explicit instructions about what she wanted. Her grandmother had not been enthusiastic about the idea, but as Kitty was of age she had been forced to be content with issuing dire warnings and reading Kitty reports of motoring accidents.

Kitty headed for the cloakroom to collect her outdoor things. She would have to venture to her uncle's workshop and disturb him in his work to request his assistance with alerting the local constable and the gamekeeper.

The gardeners had brought the last of the Christmas greenery into the hall to be dispersed about the house. Mrs Jenkinson was already supervising Gladys, one of the lowliest of the housemaids, with its distribution. Kitty noticed there were plenty of red berries on the holly and more than a few sprigs of mistletoe.

The weak morning sun had done little to move the frost from the gardens, especially in the areas shaded by the great trees. The rose gardens, which had been a perfumed mass of flowers in June, were now bare and empty.

Kitty made her way past the small wooden gazebo that afforded a view of the grounds and was somewhat startled to discover she was no longer alone. Count Vanderstrafen was seated inside smoking a cigarette.

'Good morning, Miss Underhay, you are also taking the air?' He smiled at her.

Kitty's pulse settled back to its normal rate. She had been so deep in her own thoughts of finding her uncle that Victor's appearance had surprised her.

'Yes, the house is rather busy, so I thought I'd step outside for a while.' The scent of his cigarette smoke tickled her nose as she edged away, anxious to find her uncle.

'The final Christmas preparations before the party tonight I expect. Your friend, Matt, he is not with you?'

Kitty's cheeks flushed at the slight emphasis the count put on the word friend. 'No, he's gone to Exeter. An errand he needed to run before Christmas.'

'I have embarrassed you, I think. My apologies. I was curious why such a beautiful lady would be walking alone.' Victor extinguished his cigarette.

'Not at all. I like fresh air. It gets a little stuffy when one is inside all the time, don't you find?' Kitty replied.

'Very true. I will not detain you in your exercise. Juliet also has errands to perform in the town and I have promised to take her.' He smiled at her once more and she walked away conscious of his gaze following her as she left the terraced gardens to follow the route to the workshop.

She didn't know why the meeting with the count had unsettled her. He was handsome and charming and had been perfectly courteous. She sighed, it was probably because after being followed to the church she had been unnerved at being taken by surprise. There was also the sense that he disliked Matt so perhaps that too made her slightly uneasy in his company.

She arrived at the door of the workshop at the same time as Mr Harmon, the butler, was making his exit.

'Miss Underhay, may I assist you?' The older man appeared surprised to see her.

'I need to speak to my uncle for a moment. Is he free?' Kitty planted her foot in the doorway preventing the manservant from closing the door.

'Lord Medford dislikes being disturbed whilst he is working.' Mr Harmon frowned and tried to pull the door shut.

'I shall only take a minute of his time,' Kitty insisted.

'What the devil is going on?' Her uncle appeared in the doorway clad in a brown workers coverall.

'Miss Underhay wishes to speak to you, sir. I did tell her you didn't like to be disturbed.' Mr Harmon looked disapprovingly at Kitty.

Lord Medford glanced around as if to check that Kitty was unaccompanied. 'Come in then, m'dear.' He pulled the door open wider and Kitty skipped inside before he closed it on Mr Harmon's startled and unhappy face.

She found herself in a small stone floored lobby. The only furnishings were a set of wooden pigeonholes for post fixed to the wall and a battered wooden desk and chair.

Her uncle produced a key and unlocked a secondary door. 'Come through. I was just about to take my tea.'

Kitty followed her uncle inside his workshop and stepped into what appeared to be a completely different world. A large room, almost like a schoolroom, with a blackboard at one end covered in some kind of formulaic equation. A long wooden bench covered with glass chemistry equipment filled the one side of the room. In the corner a small fireplace had a fire burning cheerily to heat the place and two battered leather armchairs were placed before it. Her uncle's tea tray was perched on a small side table.

'Now then what has sent you here, my dear?' Her uncle waved her to a seat and settled in the chair opposite her. He appeared more like a genial grocer than ever in the brown overall.

She told him of her suspicion of being followed and of the note that Matt had taken into Exeter.

'Hmm, you did the right thing to come and tell me. I'll ask the gamekeeper and the garden staff to keep a sharp eye open. I'll check with the lodgekeeper too, it may well be poachers this close to Christmas. Constable Timms lives a few miles away in the village but he comes around on his bicycle. I'll telephone him and make him aware.' The furrows on his brow deepened as he studied her. 'Make sure you and Lucy and the Vanderstrafen girl have company when you leave the house, especially if you go outside the grounds.'

Kitty wondered about Hattie and Mrs Cornwell but her uncle appeared to read her mind. 'Hattie and Lady Medford are never too far from a fire and I suspect Mrs Cornwell is the same. Not as adventurous as you younger girls.'

Kitty smiled. 'Thank you, Uncle. Shall I tell them there may be a vagrant or a poacher?' She had been thinking about this on her way to the workshop.

'Hmm, probably best. It won't hurt for everyone to be more alert. After what happened here in the summer, I'd rather be safe.'

Kitty rose. 'I'll leave you to your work, Uncle. I fear I've delayed you long enough.'

Her uncle escorted her out of the workshop into the lobby and opened the outer door. 'Not at all, Kitty m'dear.'

He watched her walk away before the door was closed once more.

Kitty walked briskly along the rose terraces towards the house, the heels of her brogues tapping on the stone paving. She glanced at her watch as she neared the front entrance and decided she would go around to the rear of the Hall for a quick word with Cook.

She knew the staff would often take a quick ten-minute break around this time of day so Cook might have a chance to tell her what she knew about the Hammetts. That wretched note was not about to frighten her from trying her best to discover as much as she could about her mother's death. Kitty followed the side of the Hall until she reached the back entrance used by the servants and tradespeople.

As always in a house the size of Enderley there was a great deal of hustle and bustle within. Kitty wiped her feet on the matting at the red quarry tiled entrance and made her way along the short, whitewashed corridor into the scullery.

She spotted Gladys busy at the sink, aiding another young girl of about fourteen with scrubbing pots and pans.

'Oh, Miss Kitty.' Gladys broke off from her chores to bob a quick curtsey, her eyes round at Kitty's sudden appearance in the scullery.

'Hello, Gladys. I'm sorry if I startled you. Do you think Cook could spare me a brief moment? I know she's very busy.'

'Yes, miss, hold on 'ere, miss, and I'll tell 'er.' Gladys scuttled off in the direction of the kitchen. Kitty could smell the delicious scent of roast lamb wafting her way as she waited.

'You'm to go through to Mrs Jenkinson's parlour, miss, and she'll be there dreckly,' Gladys said.

'Thank you, that's very kind of her.' Kitty knew the way to the small sitting room as she had visited Cook during the summer. She had received valuable information back then about her mother's visit to Enderley many years before. Cook had also insisted on reading her tea leaves, something she took great pride in, and Kitty suspected this might well be repeated during this visit.

The heat from the ovens met her as she picked her way around the edge of the busy kitchen to the small parlour reserved for the use of Mrs Jenkinson, the housekeeper, and which she shared with her friend the cook.

Kitty took a seat on one of the clean but old-fashioned armchairs and drew off her gloves to wait for Cook. It wasn't long before the lady appeared, swathed in a white apron, her ruddy face wreathed in a smile as she greeted Kitty.

'My, miss, this is a pleasant surprise. Right glad I am of a five-minute sit down, tea is on the way. My poor knees is killing today. How can I help you, miss?' Cook sank down with a groan on the chair opposite Kitty's.

A young girl, her white cap askew, scuttled in with a tray and placed it down before scuttling off again.

'Cup of tea, Miss Underhay?' Cook placed the strainer over the thick white cups and poured Kitty a cup of inky black liquid before adding a dash of milk.

'Um, thank you. I came to ask if you had any knowledge of a family called Hammett? I understand they used to live hereabouts.' Kitty forced herself to take a sip of the tea in order to be polite.

Cook ladled sugar generously into her cup. 'I were proper sorry to hear about your mother, Miss Underhay. Dreadful.' She tutted and shook her head before taking a sip of her tea. 'I saw in the papers about Ezekiel Hammett and I thought as he was one of they Hammetts from here. I recognised the names. Bad lot they am. Not many of the family left here now the old lady 'as passed over. None here in the village, but they did used to have a farm out Crockernwell way, up on the moors. Not seen any of them show their face in the village for a while now.'

Cook was confirming what the ladies cleaning at the church had said.

'Do you know anything else about them? The police are looking for Ezekiel, as you know. Anything you could remember might help.' Kitty took another sip of tea and suppressed a shudder as a tea leaf landed on her tongue.

'Well, as to Ezekiel, he were the eldest boy, named for his father he were. Then there was a girl, what was her name now? Oh yes, Esther, that was it, Esther. She run off did Esther, when she turned fourteen. Some say as she went bad ways an all. Think as I heard she'd married. Then the mother died, and old man Hammett took Ezekiel to Exeter. That must have been when he took on the pub. He married again, another maid from Crockernwell, and had Denzil. The woman left him and come back to the moors with the boy.

Ezekiel stayed with his father.' Cook sighed and shook her head. 'I always knew they'd come to bad ends.'

Kitty didn't like the sound of this at all. She hadn't realised the strength of the Hammett connection to the area around Enderley Hall. 'I don't suppose that he would try to come back here? Now that he's a wanted man? Is there anyone left here who might shelter him?' She forced herself to finish her tea, leaving the dregs and tea leaves that had escaped the strainer in the bottom of the cup.

Cook's round pleasant features screwed up into a frown. 'I dunno, Miss Kitty. I think he may have kin on Dartmoor. There's none as would have anything to do with him in the village but then there's many of them afraid of him an all.'

Kitty set her empty cup back on its saucer. 'Thank you for the tea. I'm sorry I've taken up your break time.'

Cook beamed. ''Tis no trouble at all, miss, glad of five minutes sit down. Now then, shall we read your cup?'

Before Kitty could respond, the older woman tipped out the liquid dregs into her own cup and inverted Kitty's cup on the saucer. She turned it three times then righted it so she could study the contents.

'Oh dear.' Cook shook her head.

'What is it?' Kitty asked. She didn't really believe in Cook's forecasts but even so it would have been nice to hear something cheery.

'There's a cross there, see? That means as there is danger. And a snake.' Cook pointed a stubby forefinger at a clump of leaves. 'Be careful, someone close to you is playing you false.'

Kitty was uncertain how to respond. 'Thank you. It's good to be warned.' She gathered up her gloves and refastened her coat.

'My pleasure, miss. You take heed, mind.' Cook looked troubled by her reading.

'I will, and thank you again.' Kitty made her way out of the kitchen and back through the scullery. The warning, however nonsensical, had cast a shadow over her day.

The air seemed even colder against her face as she stepped outside leaving the heat of the kitchen behind her. She made her way back around the Hall to the front door, deep in thought.

Matt's motorcycle was not yet back in its place near the tennis courts. She wondered how he was faring with Inspector Pinch. It would be time for lunch soon and her aunt couldn't stand anyone being late for meals. Matt would need to hurry his return if he was to avoid being in Lady Medford's bad books.

Muffy came racing to greet her as she entered the hall, tail wagging as she sniffed hopefully at Kitty's skirt, no doubt scenting the recent visit to the kitchen.

'Kitty darling, wherever have you been?' Lucy followed hot on Muffy's heels.

Kitty removed her outdoor clothing and stowed it all in the cloakroom while her cousin waited for her. 'I went for a walk and then called in to say a quick hello to Cook.' She bent down to fuss Muffy.

'The count said he'd seen you on the rose terrace. It's so cold out there, do come and warm up by the fire. We can get a pre-lunch cocktail.' Lucy tucked her arm into Kitty's and smiled impishly.

'That sounds lovely.' Kitty allowed herself to be led along the hall into the drawing room.

Lucy headed for the small selection of bottles to mix their drinks while Kitty went to stand near the fire.

'Where is everyone?'

Lucy handed her a glass. 'Hattie is still in the music room and Simon is in the library. The count and his sister have just returned from a drive into town and the Cornwells were with Mother and Miss Hart in the orangery. I see Matt's motorcycle is missing?'

'Yes, he had to go to Exeter on a few errands. He should be back soon.'

Everyone except Matt had regrouped in the drawing room when Mr Harmon sounded the gong for lunch. Lucy looked at Kitty and she raised her shoulders in a slight shrug, wondering what could be keeping him.

CHAPTER SEVEN

Matt slipped into the dining room just as everyone was being seated. Lady Medford gave him a hard stare as he took his place at the table next to Kitty and murmured an apology.

'Where have you been?' Kitty asked quietly as she shook out her napkin, placing it on her lap.

'At the police station. I'll tell you all after lunch.' Matt copied Kitty's action and turned his head away from her in order to respond to a question from Hattie who was seated on his other side.

He had indeed spent some time at the police station in Exeter, but he had also followed Count Vanderstrafen and his sister, having spotted the count's distinctive scarlet Austro Daimler Alpine Sedan parked in the city centre.

Matt had left his motorcycle in a side street, posted Kitty's letter and mingled with the crowds of Christmas shoppers to look for either Victor or Juliet. He had soon spotted Juliet exiting one of the high-class jeweller's shops.

He watched her from a distance for a while until he was satisfied that she appeared to simply be completing her shopping, then looked around for her brother. There he was not so fortunate. There was no sign of the count. He wandered down a few of the side streets but to no avail and then, on returning to the main street, he saw the car was gone.

Annoyed at his failure, Matt returned to his motorcycle realising that he was cutting it fine to return to Enderley in time for lunch.

'I do hope you are all ready and prepared to assist in the tree decorating this afternoon?' Lady Medford enquired, looking around the dinner table. 'The servants see to most of the decorations, but the family tree is always finished by ourselves and our guests. Once it's completed, we start to place the gifts for one another underneath it. The stockings will also be hung too on Christmas Eve.'

'It's a tradition that guests make a decoration for the tree to mark their stay and that is used each year afterwards. I've asked Mrs Jenkinson to set out some materials ready while we're eating lunch,' Lucy said.

Matt wasn't certain that making Christmas tree ornaments was in his skill set. He noticed the count and Simon Frobisher also had a slightly alarmed expression.

'I am sure it shall be great fun, and I shall be happy to assist anyone who is not of an artistic bent,' Hattie proclaimed, looking at Simon Frobisher.

'Well, that sounds quite delightful. Such a quaint idea,' Delilah said.

'My honey is so talented in arts and crafts. She can paint, embroider and knit. While me, I'm all fingers and thumbs.' Corny smiled at his wife.

'Then we shall have to hope you do not inadvertently glue yourself to the tree, Mr Cornwell,' Lady Medford declared.

Matt could see Kitty biting down on her lip to stifle a giggle.

After lunch they gathered in a group in the drawing room. A huge evergreen tree was now sited in front of the French windows and there were several boxes of ornaments wrapped in tissue paper. On a low table were pots of glue, pots of glitter, card, colouring pencils, scissors and strands of wool.

'Do make sure you sign your ornament and put on the date,' Lady Medford instructed as she directed her guests to the craft area.

Lucy commandeered Miss Hart and started to hang the ornaments from the boxes.

'Did you complete all of your shopping this morning?' Matt asked Juliet and Victor as he carefully cut out a robin shape from a piece of card. 'I passed your car parked on the high street in Exeter.'

'Yes, thank you. I had some last-minute things to do.' Juliet flushed as she folded her piece of paper into a delicate origami swan.

Victor didn't reply, merely looking at his sister for a second.

'Oh, I do wish I had known you were going into town. I would have adored looking at the Christmas displays and purchasing a few small trinkets.' Hattie sprinkled red glitter liberally over the lopsided decorative flower that Simon Frobisher had drawn.

'If we go again then we will certainly invite you,' Victor said politely.

Matt glanced around for Kitty. She was assisting Lucy while the craft table was full. He wanted to speak to her to tell her about his visit to the police station and to ask if she had seen her uncle.

He excused himself from the group and carried his decoration over to Kitty. 'Another one for your tree.'

She studied it for a moment. 'What is it?'

'A robin, obviously.' He was a little disgruntled at her disparagement of his artistic endeavours.

'Of course, I see it now.' She grinned and hung it on the tree next to a slightly malevolent looking cherub.

'Did you speak to your uncle?' he asked in a low voice as he passed her a bauble.

She nodded. 'Yes, and I found out some more information about Hammett from Cook.' She looked around to ensure they were not overheard and quickly told him all she'd learned.

The others came over to the tree with their completed decorations and he was unable to tell her the results of his visit to the police station. Instead he was press-ganged into taking her place while she went to join the Cornwells at the craft area.

'I didn't know you intended to visit Exeter also?' Juliet smiled at him as she handed him her paper swan to place on the tree.

'I had some errands to do. Post office and bank, you know how it is.' He smiled back at her, conscious of her proximity and the exotic scent of her perfume teasing his senses.

She placed a hand on his arm stroking the sleeve of his jacket. 'Next time you should say. You could have come in with us.'

He swallowed and looked over at Kitty. 'That's very kind of you.' Kitty appeared to be busy creating some kind of sheep out of cotton wool.

'She's very pretty.' Juliet followed his gaze. 'And very… young.'

'Where are you going after you leave Enderley?' Matt ignored her comment and Juliet removed her hand from his sleeve.

Juliet shrugged her slender silk-covered shoulders. 'I would like to go home, to Austria. But Victor, he has business to do so I think we must go to Italy first.'

Matt was conscious that the count was watching his sister closely from the far side of the room where Hattie was busy talking to him. 'It has been unsettled in Austria this year.' He remembered poor Viola Fiser who had been at Enderley in the summer.

A cloud passed over Juliet's beautiful face. 'Yes, one has to hope things will settle down and that order will prevail.'

She moved away and Matt looked back at Kitty who still appeared to be concentrating on her sheep.

*

Kitty stabbed the needle through the ornament she had just constructed in order to secure a thread ready to hang it on the tree. She had seen Juliet whispering to Matt and the way she had placed her hand on his arm.

'Hussy,' she muttered under her breath and smiled at the Cornwells who smiled somewhat doubtfully back at her as if unsure of what they had just heard.

Much to her annoyance she had no further opportunity to speak to Matt before everyone dispersed to dress for the earlier dinner and party to follow. She began to wonder if he was avoiding her. By the time she returned to her bedroom she was feeling quite cross, especially as she saw Juliet Vanderstrafen commanding his attention yet again in the hall as Kitty was ascending the stairs.

Alice was engaged in pressing Kitty's dress ready for the party. Her bright copper curls tucked under her starched cap she hummed happily as she took the creases out of Kitty's dark green organza silk frock.

'I'm nearly done, miss. I thought as you might want this one for tonight as it's got all the beading on the top.' Alice glanced at Kitty and returned her attention to her task.

'For two pins I'd claim a headache and give this wretched party a miss.' Kitty dropped down onto one of the armchairs beside the fire.

Alice stood the iron down on the piece of folded cloth she was using as a stand. 'That don't sound like you, miss.' Her tone held a slight note of reproof. She took Kitty's dress from the large wooden ironing board and slid it carefully onto a padded coat hanger.

'Should you like me to run you a nice bath, miss, with some of those lovely smelly bath salts?' Alice asked as she admired her handiwork with a critical eye. 'Otherwise Miss Vanderstrafen might beat you to the hot water. Her maid says as Miss Juliet is sharing the bathroom across the landing with you.'

'I'm sure Juliet Vanderstrafen is too busy cosying up to Captain Bryant to worry about calling dibs on the hot water.' As soon as the words left her lips Kitty felt more than a little ashamed of her petty remark.

Alice tilted her head to one side and surveyed her with a serious gaze. 'I doubt as Captain Bryant has sought her out now, has he, miss? Miss Vanderstrafen's maid, Maria, she doesn't speak English very plain on account of her being foreign, but she seems to think as her mistress has a secret boyfriend that her brother don't know about.' Alice's brows raised triumphantly at this titbit of information. 'Not as you can trust her word much, if you ask me. Tattletale she is.'

Kitty frowned. 'Hmm, well believe me, she's definitely making a play for Matt and he isn't pushing her away.'

Alice shrugged her thin shoulders and began to gather Kitty's things ready for her bath. 'Perhaps he's being polite or she's trying to throw the count off the scent. I'd best get more towels from the airing cupboard.' Alice whisked out of the room leaving Kitty to mull over this new information.

Once bathed and dressed with Alice styling her hair Kitty started to feel better. It was quite absurd that she was allowing Juliet to irritate her so much.

'There, you look lovely, miss.' Alice stepped back and looked critically at the carefully arranged curls. 'You should wear that nice green band on your head, miss, the one with the sequins and the diamanté clip. It would finish your outfit off lovely it would.'

Kitty gave in and Alice carefully placed the headdress. 'Thank you, Alice. I'm sorry I was such a crosspatch earlier.'

'Cook told me as she had read your future in the leaves,' Alice said.

'Yes, well, I never seem to get a nice happy reading.' The corners of her mouth quirked upwards as she met Alice's gaze in the dressing table mirror.

'She told me as she saw a snake. Someone around you is playing false she said. You was thinking it might be Captain Bryant?' Alice placed the comb and pins she had been using down on the dresser.

Kitty sighed. Alice was sometimes too perceptive. 'Perhaps.'

'That snake could be anyone in this house, miss. According to Maria, Miss Vanderstrafen is playing false with her brother and Gladys took three silver teaspoons out of Miss Merriweather's handbag this morning while she was in the music room.'

'Thank you, Alice.' Kitty smiled and collected the pretty green and gold mesh evening bag that matched her dress. Her spirits were more cheered by Alice's good sense and the party sounded as if it might be interesting. 'Don't wait up for me if you feel tired and it's getting late.'

The girl blushed. 'It's all right, miss. Mrs Jenkinson has invited us all to her parlour for a bite to eat and some card games.'

'How lovely, that'll be fun.' Kitty was pleased the girl would get some entertainment while they were at Enderley.

The rest of the party were gathered in the drawing room when Kitty entered. Lucy spotted her and waved the silver cocktail shaker at her. Kitty smiled and nodded, then looked around for Matt. To her secret relief he was engaged in conversation with her uncle and Mr Cornwell. Juliet Vanderstrafen had been monopolised by Hattie.

'Darling, you've been an absolute age. Miss Hart has been telling me all about her corns for the last ten minutes.' Lucy pressed a glass into her hand.

'Oh dear.' Kitty smiled at her cousin and took a tentative sip of her drink.

'Martini, darling, I'm on my second. I needed another one after the saga of the corns. The gong should go in a minute. Mother has ordered a light dinner as there will be heaps of food later.' Lucy giggled and took a sip from her own glass. 'Chin-chin.'

Matt made his way towards her and Lucy slipped tactfully away. Kitty always thought Matt looked at his best in a tuxedo. The formal attire somehow accentuated his faint devil-may-care appearance.

He bent his head to kiss her cheek. 'You look very lovely this evening.'

Kitty smiled and her pulse speeded up a little. 'Why thank you. You don't look so bad yourself.' She had decided on her way down to dinner that she wouldn't mention Juliet's attentions. It seemed pointless to spoil the evening.

Matt lowered his voice. 'I had hoped to speak some more to you this afternoon.'

The gong sounded from the hallway just as he finished speaking.

'Perhaps there may be an opportunity after dinner,' Kitty replied. She stifled her frustration and allowed herself to be escorted into the dining room.

Dinner was two courses, clear soup and roast pheasant to follow. Dessert was in the form of petit fours taken informally with coffee in the drawing room before the other guests arrived.

Conversation at the table centred around the Cornwells and their travels as they compared notes with Count Vanderstrafen, and, somewhat surprisingly, with Simon Frobisher. Kitty was astonished that they all seemed to have been travelling in similar areas at the same times over the past year or so, and even knew many of the same people. She also noticed that this did not appear to surprise Matt. The conversation continued over coffee.

'Well, the Mayburys' house in Yorkshire was where I first met you, Mr Frobisher, wasn't it?' Hattie trilled. 'Simon was researching some plant or tree or something rare in the grounds and was staying for the weekend. Of course, Tish Maybury – Tish Fuller before she married – and I are old chums.'

Simon Frobisher appeared uncomfortable at this turn in the conversation. 'Um, yes, I believe so.'

'Now that was at the end of September. Where did you say you were staying then?' Hattie asked Mrs Cornwell.

'Oh my, I think we were at a very nice hotel in Harrogate. The Swan? Such a wonderful place, the spas are so good for one's health.' Delilah looked to her husband for confirmation.

'Victor and I also visited Harrogate at that time. We were guests of Lord Norgrave. It is a small world, isn't it?' Juliet did not appear to see the sudden quick look her brother gave her.

Kitty wondered if Alice's gossip about a secret lover might be true, perhaps Juliet had made some assignations in Harrogate.

'Very small indeed,' Matt agreed.

'Norgrave was involved in that caper at the Home Office, wasn't he?' Lord Medford asked. 'Working on part of the data from the formula I came up with in the summer.'

'I seem to recall hearing something about that. It was very fortunate they did not succeed in getting your material, sir,' Matt said.

'Especially after the narrow squeak we had here in June.' Lord Medford scowled at his cup.

They had barely finished coffee when the first of the guests was shown into the drawing room by Mr Harmon making the announcements in his most professional voice.

'Miss Plenderleith and Mrs Baker.'

Miss Plenderleith proved to be an elderly lady with a faraway expression on her face and a faint odour of mothballs about her person. Mrs Baker however was brisk and bosomy in plum velvet.

'So very kind of you to invite us, Lord Medford, Lady Medford,' Miss Plenderleith wittered. Kitty could see why she and Miss Hart had struck up a friendship.

'Yes, thank you, sweet sherry for me.' Mrs Baker waved away Lucy's offer of a cocktail, while Miss Plenderleith looked nervously at the gaily-coloured offering Lucy pressed upon her. Miss Hart greeted her friend, fluttering and twittering at her.

'Reverend Crabtree,' Mr Harmon announced as Hattie put a record on the gramophone.

Reverend Crabtree appeared as oily and odd as when Kitty had first encountered him at the church. She could see her aunt was unimpressed by his attentions, especially as his topic of conversation appeared to be an immediate solicitation for funds for the church roof. He declined Lucy's offer of a cocktail and had some of Lord Medford's Scotch whisky instead.

Everyone appeared to be settling in, enjoying the hospitality and admiring the creative ornaments on the tree, when Mr Harmon reappeared for another announcement.

'Mrs Tabitha Vernon.'

All eyes immediately went to the figure in the doorway. Mrs Vernon was not in the first flush of youth but was what Kitty's grandmother would have described as being well preserved. Mrs Craven would no doubt have made mutterings about mutton dressed as lamb.

She shimmered into the room in a gold sequinned dress, which showed rather a lot of stocking and a touch too much cleavage. Her dyed blonde hair peeked out under a matching glittery cap.

'Darlings, am I late? I'm so sorry.' Mrs Vernon swept into the room and made a beeline for Lady Medford. Mrs Baker scowled and turned her back as Mrs Vernon gave her apologies to her hosts. Kitty noted that she didn't show a shred of contrition and suspected her entrance had been staged for maximum impact. She remembered that Lucy had said she was a retired music hall star.

'Miss Medford, you look divine, darling. Cocktails, how super. Could I possibly have a Negroni, darling, if it's not too much trouble?'

'Wow,' Matt whispered in Kitty's ear.

'I think the fun is about to begin,' Kitty murmured back.

Lucy made introductions to the people Mrs Vernon had not met before. Kitty found that Mrs Vernon appeared to have a sharp eye.

'What a gorgeous frock. That dark green colour suits you very well and a handsome man on your arm too. I'm quite jealous, my dear. Mr Frobisher, I insist you must be my beau for the evening, or I shall be quite desolate and alone.' Mrs Vernon shimmied up to the unwary Simon and pouted before fluttering her eyelashes in the direction of Reverend Crabtree.

'I shall be charmed, of course, dear lady.' Mr Frobisher had no option but to accede despite his unhappy expression.

Mrs Baker looked as if her sherry was disagreeing with her and Miss Plenderleith and Miss Hart seemed to be comparing cooking tips. Uniformed maids and footmen started to circulate with silver platters of bite-sized canapés and the volume of noise in the room increased.

Matt manoeuvred Kitty into a quiet corner. 'I went to the police station in Exeter to give that note to Inspector Pinch.'

'And?' Kitty asked, checking there was no one within earshot.

'He's away ill, influenza according to the desk sergeant. I gave it to him with instructions to contact Inspector Greville.'

'Oh.' Kitty was quite deflated.

'It seems they are terribly short-staffed at the moment. I thought Greville would be the best man to handle it,' Matt said.

'Oh absolutely. You couldn't have done anything else. Let us hope Inspector Pinch makes a speedy recovery.' Kitty swallowed down her disappointment and tried to ignore the ominous feeling in the pit of her stomach.

Matt finished his drink. 'Kitty, about Juliet—'

'Oh, please don't feel you have to explain anything to me,' Kitty cut him off before he could say too much. Much as she would like to know exactly what was going on, at the same time she could see Count Vanderstrafen approaching them.

'Captain Bryant, you are monopolising the prettiest lady in the room and I am in danger of being bored to death by the charming Hattie. Miss Underhay, I throw myself on your mercy to save me.' Victor flashed an unexpectedly charming smile.

Kitty flushed at the unexpected attention. 'You are too kind, Count Vanderstrafen, but I would have thought Mrs Vernon would be by far the most entertaining company in the room.'

'Ah, I fear Mrs Vernon is engaged in entertaining Mr Frobisher and Mrs Cornwell.' Victor glanced at the little group advancing upon Hattie and Juliet.

'May I get you another drink, Kitty?' Matt asked, looking at her glass.

She swallowed the last mouthful and offered him her empty glass. 'Thank you.'

Victor watched Matt walk over to Lucy who was still having fun with the cocktail shaker. 'Captain Bryant, always the gentleman.'

'How long have you and your sister known Matt?' Kitty asked.

Victor smiled. 'We have known each other for at least five or six years. We met first in London at a party at the embassy. His parents have always been most charming and kind to my sister.'

Kitty was somewhat startled at the revelation that the Vanderstrafens were known to Matt's parents. She also disliked the inference that they liked Juliet since she knew perfectly well that Matt's parents were not enamoured of her.

'I hadn't realised you were all such good friends.' Kitty wished Matt would hurry back with her drink.

'We are indeed old acquaintances. I believe you were here in the summer?' Victor asked.

'Yes, it was rather an odd visit. I'm sure you must have read about the murders?' Kitty noticed his gaze resting momentarily on his sister.

'Lord Medford said someone tried to steal his work. He is very well regarded for his brilliant mind. It was quite shocking that someone should try to steal his papers. He has a laboratory here, does he not?'

Kitty smiled as Matt approached bearing drinks. 'Yes, in the grounds, the stone building. He does a lot of his work there.'

Matt rejoined them and handed Kitty a fresh cocktail. Lady Medford crossed the room, regal in dark grey silk. 'Kitty my dear, allow me to introduce you to Mrs Baker. Mrs Baker, my niece, Kitty, and her friend, Captain Bryant.'

Kitty surmised her aunt had taken her fill of Mrs Baker's company and was keen to palm her off onto someone else. The count spied his opportunity to escape.

'Your aunt said you were a private detective, Captain Bryant? The events here during June were most disturbing. And I must confess I read about your mother in the newspaper, Miss Underhay, quite shocking. You were involved in that business at Torquay Pavilion as well I understand. Not that one expects much from those of a theatrical nature.' She sniffed disapprovingly and glared in the direction of Tabitha Vernon.

'Now then, my dear, I'm sure Mrs Vernon has been most generous to the church,' Miss Plenderleith chipped in.

'There is generous and downright ridiculousness,' Mrs Baker declared. 'Take that abomination of a nativity scene. The old one was perfectly good.'

'It had woodworm and a mouse or a rat had eaten a hole in the angel Gabriel,' Mrs Vernon declared crisply, having seemingly heard Mrs Baker's booming complaints.

'There was nothing wrong that a few small repairs could not have put right. Now we have that gaudy thing beside the altar.' Mrs Baker glared at Mrs Vernon.

'Some of us need to move with the times,' Mrs Vernon snapped.

'Ladies, please.' Mr Frobisher was quickly drowned out by Mrs Vernon.

'I've also replaced some of that half-dead greenery you'd placed in the displays. It's much more cheerful and festive now.'

'You had better not have touched my displays.' Mrs Baker drew herself up, her cheeks blooming puce with indignation.

'The vicar thought my additions were more Christmassy.' Mrs Vernon smirked at her rival. 'Did you not, Reverend?'

All eyes turned to Reverend Crabtree.

'Now, Mrs Vernon, Mrs Baker, you ladies have both made such valuable contributions to the church.' He moved closer to the feuding women. 'Mrs Vernon's generosity in providing a new crib is most welcome. Most welcome indeed.'

Mrs Vernon preened, and Mrs Baker muttered something that sounded like 'Poppycock.'

'My dear Mrs Baker, we should be Christian in appreciating the efforts of others. Not everyone can be as upstanding as your good self,' the vicar continued. Kitty saw her aunt rolling her eyes behind Reverend Crabtree's back. Mrs Baker flushed.

'I thought, Vicar, we should perhaps have lights, perhaps around baby Jesus,' Mrs Vernon interspersed before the reverend could continue with his speech.

'Over my dead body. Is there no respect for tradition?' Mrs Baker looked almost apoplectic at the suggestion that there should be additional electrical lights around the crib.

'It might look rather sweet,' Miss Plenderleith ventured from behind Mrs Baker's shoulder.

'I suppose the fairies told you that, did they?' Mrs Baker jerked around angrily. As she did so the contents of her sherry glass spilled out onto both Mrs Vernon and Miss Plenderleith.

Within moments the scene was one of chaos. Lady Medford sent a maid for cloths as Mrs Vernon took to the couch bewailing her distress and at the same time ensuring that everyone knew that she graciously forgave Mrs Baker for the accident.

Miss Plenderleith disappeared from the room, presumably in search of the cloakroom as everyone gathered around Mrs Vernon.

Miss Hart rescued Mrs Baker who appeared mortified and close to tears. Juliet and Lucy were standing next to the Cornwells watching the scene unravel while Lord Medford attempted to restore calm.

'Music,' boomed Hattie and placed another recording on the gramophone.

'Golly,' Kitty murmured to Matt.

'Reverend Crabtree wasn't terribly useful, was he?' Matt said.

The reverend appeared to be having some kind of small altercation with Simon Frobisher in the corner of the room. He looked annoyed and Simon was flushed in the face.

'Poor Mrs Baker,' Kitty said. She wondered what Simon could have said to the reverend to cause them to argue.

Miss Plenderleith came trotting back into the drawing room, the damp patch on her dress evidence of the sponging that had obviously been done to try and remove the sherry. She too looked quite distressed.

'What did Mrs Baker mean about fairies?' Kitty asked Lucy.

'Miss Plenderleith believes in the little people. Pixies and fairies. Her father was a renowned professor of folklore,' Lucy said as Miss Plenderleith joined Reverend Crabtree. The two of them were locked in conversation. Simon Frobisher having moved away to replenish his drink.

Kitty stared at her cousin. 'But that's absurd.'

Lucy rolled her eyes and took a sip from her cocktail. 'I know, she seems so sensible most of the time. Quite an educated lady. She's secretary and treasurer for the parish council and oversees the restore the roof fund, but mention fairies and she's quite mad. She puts out offerings of food and drink at the bottom of her garden every morning and tells them all her news.'

Lady Medford bustled towards them. 'Poor Mrs Baker. I've asked Collins to bring the car around. She feels she would rather go home. Miss Plenderleith too, she's worried about her cat. Lucy dear, can you keep an eye on Mrs Vernon and try to keep the vicar away from your father. He will keep insinuating that we should increase our donation to the church.'

Lucy went to oblige her mother as Miss Hart escorted Mrs Baker and Miss Plenderleith to the cloakroom. Kitty took a seat on the sofa besides Matt and noticed Hattie furtively slipping something shiny into her handbag.

CHAPTER EIGHT

With her rival vanquished Mrs Vernon exerted herself to entertain for the rest of the evening. Kitty found herself quite enjoying the party despite the earlier contretemps. She refused to admit that much of her enjoyment was derived from dancing with Matt at the far end of the drawing room. Lucy partnered Victor, and Juliet danced with Mr Frobisher. Hattie declared that her feet ached and that she was content to manage the music.

Even Lady Medford took a turn with her husband and the Cornwells also joined in. Lord Medford gallantly invited Miss Hart to a dance while Reverend Crabtree sat out and made inroads into Lord Medford's Scotch. Mrs Vernon danced with all the gentlemen in turn and told amusing tales of her days on the London stage. Kitty was relieved that little mention was made of the Davenports who had caused her and Matt so much upset only a month or so earlier.

Even Matt taking a turn to dance with Juliet didn't upset her good mood. Eventually the cars were called, and Reverend Crabtree and Mrs Vernon took their leave in their respective vehicles. Kitty shivered as the cold air from the hall drifted into the drawing room.

'It's quite frosty outside now. Brr.' Lucy shivered as she snuggled up next to Kitty on the sofa.

'Time for bed.' Lady Medford eyed her daughter as Lucy tried and failed to stifle a yawn.

Lord Medford had already said his goodnights and his wife and daughter swiftly followed, along with Miss Hart. Mr Frobisher and

Hattie had departed earlier, as soon as Mrs Vernon and her furs had left the Hall.

'We too shall retire,' Count Vanderstrafen said. 'Come, Juliet.'

'I suppose we should retire too, or Mr Harmon will be scandalised.' The dimple in Matt's cheek flashed as Kitty realised they were now alone in the drawing room.

'Poor Mr Harmon. I've upset him enough for one day by bearding my uncle in his workshop.' Kitty giggled and wondered how much alcohol had been in Lucy's cocktails.

Matt stroked her cheek with a tender forefinger. 'It was fun though, despite Mrs Vernon and Mrs Baker.'

Kitty's gaze locked with his. 'Yes, it was lovely.'

His lips brushed hers and she closed her eyes only to open them just as quickly at the sound of a cough.

'Begging your pardon, sir, miss. I thought the household had retired.' Mr Harmon had begun collecting the glasses and napkins.

'That's quite all right. We were just heading upstairs.' Matt grinned at Kitty.

'Goodnight, sir, miss.' The butler gave them a glacial stare as they left the drawing room.

Kitty did her best to stifle her giggles until they were almost at the landing. 'Poor Mr Harmon.'

'Poor Matt you mean. I didn't get my kiss.'

Kitty glanced up. 'How fortunate, it seems we are stopped under some mistletoe.'

'Very fortunate indeed,' Matt agreed.

Kitty let herself into her room a few minutes later still smiling to herself.

'Have you had a good evening, miss?' Alice was dressed for bed and enveloped in her flannel dressing gown, her hair confined to a long braid.

'Alice, you shouldn't have stayed up,' Kitty protested. 'But, yes, it was a lovely evening.' She slipped off her high-heeled black patent shoes.

'Everyone says it sounded like people was having a good time, at least after that set-to as Mrs Baker and Mrs Vernon had.' Alice busied herself collecting up Kitty's shoes and fetching her thick flannel pyjamas that she'd had warming by the fire.

'Oh dear, yes, that was rather awkward.' Kitty shivered as she changed into her nightwear.

'I heard about it from the under footman. Cook was saying that Miss Plenderleith is a bit of a strange one an all. Says she lives in the cottage nearest the church and swears as she has fairies at the bottom of her garden where it meets the wood. Still plenty of people hereabouts believe in the little people.' Alice clicked her tongue disapprovingly.

Kitty climbed into bed, grateful for the hot water bottles she discovered tucked inside the covers. 'I know there was a fashion for those kinds of beliefs a few years ago but I thought everyone knew that those photographs had been faked and that fairies and their like don't exist.'

Alice finished hanging Kitty's dress. 'I suppose there'll always be some folk who believe in them. There's lots of stories around here, miss, being as we aren't far from the moors. Proper superstitious up there they is.'

Kitty yawned, her eyelids drooping. 'I suppose so. Thank you for the hot water bottles.'

Her bedroom was warm with a fire in the grate when she woke the next morning. Alice was already bustling about the room.

'Morning, Miss Kitty.' She swished the curtains open, filling the room with bright light.

Kitty groaned and closed her eyes. A pulse throbbed in her temple and she suspected the cocktails she'd consumed the previous evening were making themselves felt.

'Cup of tea, toast and an aspirin, miss?' Alice suggested. She whisked out of the room as Kitty squinted at her leather-cased bedside travel clock and sank back under her covers to await her maid's return.

Alice was back a short time later bearing a laden tray. Kitty propped herself up on her pillows as Alice set the tray on her knees.

'There, that will have you feeling right as ninepence,' Alice declared.

'Thank you, Alice. I hope you brought an extra cup for yourself?' Kitty said as she swallowed the aspirin the girl had thoughtfully provided.

Alice disappeared into the small room containing her cot and came back bearing a thick plain white china cup. Kitty grinned and poured a cup for her friend from the small silver pot on her tray.

'The frost is proper thick this morning, miss. Mr Golightly isn't happy. He reckons as there might have been a vagrant or poacher around last night. There's footprints around the house and in the gardens. Him and the gamekeeper is out looking about.' Alice took a sip of tea clearly relishing the offer of a drink and the opportunity to impart news.

From her vantage point on the bed Kitty could see out over the grounds. Everything was indeed frozen and sparkling white. Hence the bright light when Alice had opened the curtains. Although the sun was out it appeared to be making little impact on the frost.

'Are any of the party up for breakfast yet?' Kitty asked as she tucked into the slice of crisp buttery toast that Alice had provided to accompany her tea.

'None of the ladies is up. I think the count and Mr Cornwell might be having breakfast and his lordship has probably already gone to his workshop,' Alice said as she peered out of the window. 'Oh, now there is Captain Bryant and he has a constable with him.'

Kitty set her tray aside and scrambled out of bed, pulling on her dressing gown as she headed to Alice's side.

'The constable must have come from the village as he has his bicycle.' Kitty stood back a little from the windowpane not wishing to be seen being nosey.

'They'm having a fair old chinwag,' Alice observed.

Kitty wondered if the policeman had been summoned in response to the mystery footprints. Alice was correct, however, the two men were engaged in conversation for quite some time. Finally, the conversation finished and the constable continued to wheel his bicycle around the side of the house towards the servants' entrance.

Matt glanced up to Kitty's window and she saw him smile. He knew her curiosity well and had no doubt guessed she would have been watching. She moved closer to the window and raised her hand so he would know for certain that she was there. Matt nodded and pointed, indicating to her to come downstairs.

'Something is afoot, Alice.' Kitty turned away ready to head to the bathroom in order to wash and dress for the day. Her maid was already at her wardrobe selecting clothes.

'Here you go, miss. I thought as you would want to be down as quick as possible.' Alice grinned at her as she passed her things across.

Kitty was dressed in her tweed suit and pale blue sweater in quick order. A quick flick of her comb through her hair and a dab of her favourite rose perfume and she was on her way down the main staircase to find Matt.

'What is it? Have they caught Hammett? I saw the constable arrive,' Kitty asked as soon as she spotted Matt outside the door to her uncle's study.

'Golightly reported seeing footprints around the house and in the grounds. The constable was on his way here already, however, for a different reason. It seems Miss Plenderleith has been found dead this morning. I have just taken the constable's message to your uncle.' Matt looked as shocked by the unexpected news as Kitty felt.

'Dead?' She couldn't believe it.

Matt sighed. 'She was discovered outside her back door this morning by the milkman. The constable was sent to inform your uncle by Inspector Greville. He thought the house should know as Miss Plenderleith was a neighbour and the constable had informed him that he had been tasked with looking out for untoward events.'

Kitty frowned. 'What happened? She seemed perfectly all right when she left last night. She was more concerned about returning home to her cat than the small spill on her dress.'

'The constable thought at first it might have been an accident. She was in her day clothes and he thought perhaps she had slipped on the ice and banged her head.' Matt looked uneasy.

'You do not believe it to be an accident?' Kitty asked.

'The back door to the house was open and it looks as if someone had been there. Her papers and those records for the church were in disarray. There were footprints in the frost around the house.' Matt glanced around the hall to ensure that they could not be overheard.

'Can they tell anything from the prints?' Kitty asked.

'The constable didn't say much, just passed on his message and pedalled back to his post at the cottage. It's the white one near the church.'

'But it could have been an accident?' Kitty persisted. The whole scenario did not sit well with her. Especially with her suspicion that Ezekiel Hammett was somewhere in the vicinity of the Hall.

'Hard to say, depends if anything has been taken I suppose. The footprints may have been made by the milkman. It seems that Inspector Greville has been called in again as Pinch is indisposed. Greville at least is discreet and is aware of the nuances of the case.'

Kitty looked at Matt. She wondered what he meant by nuances. 'Do you think Miss Plenderleith was murdered?' It didn't sound like an accident, not if the cottage had possibly been ransacked. She wondered why Matt was trying to play it down. Perhaps he was concerned that it could be Hammett's doing after all.

'I think it likely. Greville is on his way to Miss Plenderleith's cottage. The chief constable has agreed to his deployment according to the constable. I think it might be best to allow everyone to believe poor Miss Plenderleith's death is an unfortunate accident for now.'

Kitty nodded. She could see the sense in the rationale. She would very much like to go and take a look around Miss Plenderleith's cottage for herself.

'Have you breakfasted?' Matt asked as they neared the dining room.

'Just a slice of toast. Have you?' She guessed he must have been awake fairly early.

Matt peeped around the dining room door. 'No one here yet.'

Kitty grinned, an idea popping into her head. 'We could just collect some toast and bacon and nip over to Miss Plenderleith's cottage. It would be nice to see Inspector Greville again.'

He looked at her. 'When you say nip?'

'No one is around.'

'No.' Matt met her gaze.

'It will only take a moment, you said the constable told you the cottage wasn't far from the church.' She smiled beguilingly at him and placed a quick kiss on his cheek.

Matt sighed and they hurried into the empty room and wrapped some toast and bacon in a linen napkin before scurrying along the hall to the cloakroom.

'Come on.' Kitty pulled at Matt's hand to tug him outside once they had donned their outdoor coats.

'Your aunt will not be happy if she discovers us,' Matt warned as he took the tarpaulin cover off the Sunbeam.

Once he was astride, Kitty hitched up her skirt and slid onto the seat behind him. 'We're only going down the drive. Hurry.' She held on tight as he gunned the engine and they set off down the long, gravelled driveway to the main gate.

The cold air was exhilarating as it rushed past her cheeks and she hoped she had secured her plain felt cloche hat securely enough to her head. She didn't fancy having to chase it halfway round her uncle's grounds.

A couple of minutes later they were puttering past the church towards a small white rendered cottage with a thatched roof set a few feet back from the edge of the road. All around the small house was woodland. Inspector Greville's plain black police car and another familiar car were drawn up outside next to the constable's bicycle.

'It seems Doctor Carter is here.' Matt part-turned his head and raised his voice so she could hear him over the noise of the motorbike engine.

He stopped the bike behind Doctor Carter's car and switched off the motor. Kitty quickly hopped off before anyone could see how she had arrived. Matt retrieved the parcel of toast and bacon from the pannier at the rear of the bike and Kitty lifted the latch on the small red painted front gate of the cottage.

She and Matt made their way carefully along the narrow crazy-paved path turning off at the side of the house to go around to the back. The frost had finally begun to melt and whatever footprints had been there earlier were now simply big dark splodges of bare earth. No discernible clues remained that she could see.

The constable stopped them as they rounded the corner, stepping forward to block their way. Despite his obvious recollection of speaking to Matt earlier his eyes narrowed in suspicion under the brim of his helmet when he saw the linen parcel.

'No one's allowed back here, sir, miss.'

'Inspector Greville and Doctor Carter will vouch for us. Besides we are carrying breakfast,' Kitty said as she attempted to peer around him.

As she spoke the rounded cherubic form of Doctor Carter emerged from the cottage. 'Miss Underhay and Captain Bryant.' He waved happily at them and the constable was forced to step aside, allowing them through.

'Kitty thought you and the inspector might appreciate some toast and bacon.' Matt smiled at the genial doctor as they approached.

'Marvellous, just the ticket. Do mind Miss Plenderleith. They are coming to collect her in a moment or two.' Doctor Carter led them neatly around the prone form of the late Miss Plenderleith and into the cottage. Kitty suppressed a shudder, relieved they had covered the poor lady with a blanket.

They entered into a small neat kitchen with a red quarry tiled floor. A couple of earthenware dishes were placed on the floor next to the cooker and Kitty wondered what would become of Miss Plenderleith's beloved cat.

'Greville my boy, found visitors bearing what smells like bacon.' Doctor Carter opened the door at the rear of the kitchen and shouted into the hallway.

Kitty and Matt followed him as he led them into what was obviously the front room of the cottage. The tall moustached figure of Inspector Greville stood at the small lattice-leaded window studying some documents. All around him was chaos. Papers were strewn higgledy-piggledy over the parquet floor, across the old-fashioned floral sofa and spilled out of the open polished oak bureau.

The china shepherd and shepherdess on the mantelpiece seemed to disapprove of the unaccustomed untidiness in the confined space of the sitting room. The fire was out, and a chill pervaded the air. A few Christmas cards hung sadly from a string amid some paper chains.

'Miss Underhay and Captain Bryant, good morning.' The inspector appeared unsurprised to see them.

'Kitty thought you might appreciate a little breakfast,' Matt said.

'Capital.' Doctor Carter took the bundle from Matt and helped himself to toast and bacon, forming a sandwich before offering some to the inspector.

'What happened to Miss Plenderleith?' Kitty asked. She tried to suppress a shiver. The air in the sitting room felt colder than the air outside.

Doctor Carter chewed and swallowed. 'In layman's terms I'd say, given the position of the contusion on her head, she was coshed by something heavy and left where she fell. Probably by one of the logs from the firewood store at the side of the cottage.'

'I take it robbery was the motive?' Matt looked at the disarray surrounding them.

'It's difficult to say exactly what's been taken. It looks as if someone has rooted through the accounts for the church roof fund and the milkman said Miss Plenderleith usually kept a locked box containing the money in her bureau here. That's missing. Miss Plenderleith's purse is also empty.' The inspector nodded towards a discarded brown leather handbag with a matching purse lying open beside it.

'Poor Miss Plenderleith. I suppose she must have gone to the back door perhaps thinking to let her cat in or out and then been attacked.' Kitty shuddered.

'Or she opened the door to someone she knew,' Matt suggested.

Inspector Greville finished the last bite of his unexpected breakfast and looked regretfully at the empty napkin before brushing toast crumbs from his moustache with his handkerchief. 'The constable informed me that there has been a spate of petty thefts recently in the village. The loss of a large meat pie taken from a windowsill where it had been cooling. A couple of chickens and eggs. A few shillings taken from purses inside houses.'

'A vagrant, or a man on the run?' Kitty's veins felt filled with ice. She knew she was jumping to conclusions that Hammett was involved but it all fitted. This was exactly the kind of crime an unscrupulous man on the run might commit. Especially a man who had killed before.

Inspector Greville peered through the window. 'I think they are come for Miss Plenderleith.'

Doctor Carter tipped his hat to Kitty and said his farewells as he went out through the kitchen to supervise the unfortunate woman's removal by the undertakers.

'Was anything taken from the upstairs? Jewellery?' Kitty asked. She didn't recall Miss Plenderleith wearing any jewellery at the party other than a few coloured beads.

'Everything appears to be in order. As you can see, even the small ornaments are undisturbed. No, it looks as if whoever did this just wanted money.' Inspector Greville frowned as he looked around at the scattered papers.

Kitty wondered why the sheets of paper had been torn and scattered from the accounts for the parish council and the church roof fund. Surely the money would have been easy to see in the tin. Why cause all this devastation and leave everything else untouched?

CHAPTER NINE

Matt and Kitty left the inspector to finish his search of Miss Plenderleith's cottage and walked back outside. The body of Miss Plenderleith had gone, as had Doctor Carter. Only the constable remained on duty to prevent unwanted sightseers.

'What do you think?' Kitty asked as soon as they were out of earshot.

'I think Inspector Greville is right to keep an open mind. It could simply have been a vagrant opportunistically taking advantage of an elderly woman alone in an isolated cottage.' Matt saw Kitty's lips purse and knew she didn't agree with this theory.

'I don't understand why the accounts for the church fund and the parish records were damaged though. I would be interested to discover if any pages are missing. Did you notice that Miss Plenderleith's other papers were undisturbed?' Kitty's brow creased.

'It did seem peculiar. We had better return to the Hall before we are missed. Tonight is the carol concert at the church and I expect there will be plenty of talk about this flying about the congregation.' Matt tugged on his thick leather gauntlets and waited for Kitty to hop up behind him.

She gave a last glance at the cottage, hitched her skirt above her knees and climbed onto the motorbike. 'Don't go too fast. I thought I might lose my hat on the way here.'

'Hold tight.' He grinned to himself as he started the engine and drove back along the lane and into the entrance to Enderley Hall at a more sedate pace.

His hope that they would make it back undiscovered were dashed when he saw Hattie outside the front door of the house accompanied by Miss Hart. He pulled the motorbike around to his parking space and turned off the engine ready for Kitty to hop off.

'I'm afraid we've been spotted.' He nodded towards the approaching figures of the two ladies.

Kitty straightened her skirt and hat and tried to appear nonchalant as Hattie bustled up to her. 'My dear Kitty, how terribly avant-garde! Captain Bryant, a motorcycle, so very thrilling.'

Matt focused on placing the tarpaulin back over his beloved Sunbeam. The garage was full housing the count's car and Lord Medford's Bentley, so he was quite content to keep his motorcycle outside.

'But, my dear, you must be absolutely frozen riding in a skirt,' Hattie continued, her eyes wide with admiration.

Miss Hart clearly did not approve. Her pinched mouth and stony gaze made it clear to Matt that Kitty did not rate highly on that lady's approval list.

'Matt very kindly just took me down the drive and back. I wanted to know what it was like to ride a motorcycle,' Kitty demurred.

Matt thought it was a good thing that Miss Hart had not been present the last time Kitty had hitched a ride as his pillion passenger.

'I wouldn't have thought riding a motorcycle to be an activity of which your aunt would approve,' Miss Hart declared with a sniff.

Matt saw Kitty's jaw tighten and her chin tilt up at this statement.

'Lady Medford is much more progressive than you might think, Miss Hart.' Matt smiled at the lady and hoped he had managed to avert whatever Kitty's response might have been.

'I think it's simply marvellous the things girls do these days,' Hattie declared. 'Why, I myself would have loved to have led a more adventurous life, but alas, dear Mother could not be left. I do envy your freedom, Kitty my dear.'

Miss Hart looked even more disapproving. 'Even so I consider such hijinks a little disrespectful considering we have just been informed of poor Miss Plenderleith's unfortunate accident.'

'Yes indeed, poor woman. A fall we heard,' Matt said.

'She was such a wonderful person. So educated and refined. One can hardly believe it has happened, the path must have been very icy for such an accident to occur. After all, she barely had anything to drink at the party.' Miss Hart appeared deeply distressed at the loss of her friend and Matt remembered seeing the two ladies deep in conversation last night.

'She seemed very pleasant,' Kitty said, her tone casual.

'Oh yes, we had such a nice conversation yesterday evening. She had such interesting beliefs you know. Her late father was a very respected man,' Miss Hart mused. 'Although that accident with Mrs Baker's drink did seem to upset her. She was quite out of sorts afterwards when she returned from the cloakroom.'

Matt thought back to the incident. Miss Plenderleith had rushed out, presumably to sponge her dress while the maid had attended to Mrs Vernon. Miss Plenderleith had seemed distressed on her return, now he came to think of it. She had spoken to Reverend Crabtree and had then decided to return to her cottage. It seemed a slight overreaction to a simple accident.

'I think the altercation upset her,' Kitty said.

'Yes, it was all terribly dramatic, wasn't it?' Hattie sounded quite thrilled, confirming Matt's initial impression of her that she was someone who enjoyed drama.

Miss Hart looked disparagingly at the happily oblivious Hattie. 'We must get on and find Mr Golightly if Lady Medford is to have more holly with berries for the entrance hall.'

The women moved off towards the gardener's hut and Matt followed Kitty inside the house.

'Brr, I am quite chilly now.' Kitty shivered as she began to unbutton her coat.

She tidied her hair from where the wind and her hat had fluffed out her blonde curls. 'Alice will be most annoyed with me. She always feels it reflects badly upon her if I'm seen to be untidy.'

Matt laughed. 'Poor Alice. You must disappoint her on a regular basis.'

Kitty gave his arm a playful swipe and they emerged laughing into the hall only to come face to face with Juliet.

'You have heard about Miss Plenderleith?' Juliet asked abruptly. Her face was pale, and her careful use of cosmetics had failed to completely hide the dark shadows under her eyes.

'Yes, Hattie and Miss Hart met us outside,' Kitty said. Matt noticed her voice had acquired a cool note.

'Matt, I wonder if I might speak with you alone for a moment. You would please excuse us, Kitty?' Juliet asked.

Matt wondered what she wanted. He knew Kitty would not be amused by her request, but he sensed this could be important.

Kitty stiffened. 'Certainly. I'm going to the drawing room to thaw out.' She walked away, the heels of her brogues clicking on the tiles underlining her displeasure.

*

Lucy was in the drawing room with her mother. Muffy, the dog, was lying on the sofa next to her cousin having her belly rubbed.

'Kitty darling, I thought you might be Hattie and Miss Hart,' Lucy said.

'Matt and I met them outside. I think they were going to look for Mr Golightly, something about more holly.' Kitty perched on the other side of Muffy.

Lucy and Lady Medford exchanged slightly guilty looks.

'I must confess I sent them both off on an errand. Hattie was insisting I get the piano in the music room retuned and having heard her practising her scales I rather think it may be Hattie who has the tuning problem. As for Miss Hart, well, I fear I may have made an error of judgement in employing the woman.' Lady Medford appeared uncomfortable but clearly felt she could trust Kitty with this information.

Kitty could well understand her aunt's desire for some respite from both Hattie and Miss Hart.

'You will have heard of course of Miss Plenderleith's unfortunate accident? Miss Hart has been most affected,' her aunt continued. 'I understand Inspector Greville has been called in once more as the local man is unwell.'

'Yes, Matt and I saw Doctor Carter and the inspector earlier this morning.' Kitty gave her aunt and cousin an edited version of the meeting.

Lucy looked up, a surprised expression on her pretty face. 'Really? Oh dear, I hope it was an accident and nothing more sinister?'

Kitty avoided her cousin's gaze. 'I expect they have to check these things if there were no witnesses. The coroner will be bound to ask questions.'

To her relief both her aunt and Lucy appeared to accept her answer.

Delilah Cornwell opened the door and entered the room. 'I just heard about Miss Plenderleith. How very shocking.' She took a seat on the vacant chair opposite and crossed her elegantly stockinged legs. 'It's so cold out today. I expect we shall have to wrap up well for the carols tonight at the church. It's a good thing I got Corny to pack my furs.' Mrs Cornwell appeared very pleased with her forethought as she smoothed her navy worsted skirt with a well-manicured hand.

'Most fortunate,' agreed Lady Medford. Delilah appeared oblivious to the note of irony in Lady Medford's reply.

Matt failed to reappear until the gong sounded for lunch. Kitty wondered if he had been closeted with Juliet for all of that time. She wondered if he would tell her what Juliet had wanted. It seemed to her that Matt was keeping some kind of secret from her and she was determined to winkle it out. The count it seemed had been playing billiards with Mr Cornwell while Mr Frobisher had been tucked away as usual in the library.

'I hope everything was all right with Juliet?' Kitty murmured to Matt as he took his place next to her at the dinner table.

Juliet was seated beside her brother at the other end of the table. Matt glanced in her direction before replying. 'Yes, I think so. She is having a difficult time at the moment. You may have noticed Victor is quite protective of her.'

'Does he need to be?' Kitty asked with a touch of asperity.

Matt didn't reply. He merely lifted an eyebrow and concentrated on his soup, irritating Kitty immensely.

Discussion during lunch was mainly centred around the unfortunate Miss Plenderleith's demise and arrangements for attending the carol concert which was to occur after an early dinner.

'I believe snow has been forecast. We may even have a white Christmas as we are closer to the moors here.' Simon Frobisher pushed his spectacles back onto the bridge of his nose with a nervous gesture.

'How perfectly darling, though of course snow will be romantic to look at through a window but not so pleasant to venture out in,' Mrs Cornwell said. 'I expect you are very used to snow, Count Vanderstrafen?'

'Of course. It is a way of life in the mountains of my country,' the count responded courteously.

'The Alps, of course. It must look so majestic. Is your home in the mountains?' Hattie asked.

'Our family home is in the mountains, although of course we travel extensively so have spent little time there recently,' Juliet answered in a cool tone.

Hattie waved her hand about, almost spearing Simon Frobisher's ear with her fork. 'How I long to travel. Of course when dear Mama was alive I didn't feel I could leave her and I fear the time has passed now when I could venture abroad.'

'If ever you are in Austria you must of course come to visit us,' the count offered.

'Or us too. Virginia is such a darling place and we would make you most welcome,' Mrs Cornwell chirped up.

Kitty suspected that neither offer would ever be taken up given that those making the offers were well aware of Hattie's straightened financial circumstances.

Hattie professed her effusive thanks to both parties and conversation continued around places everyone had visited. Kitty only listened with half an ear, conscious that she had little to contribute on the subject. She had never travelled far from Torbay, with occasional excursions to London or to visit her great-aunt Livvy in Scotland. Even Miss Hart appeared to have been abroad in her youth to Nice and Cannes.

She still felt slightly disgruntled and out of sorts as lunch concluded and everyone drifted back to their various employments. Her annoyance increased further when she realised that Matt had somehow slipped away once more and she had no idea where he had gone.

She longed to know what was happening with the investigation at Miss Plenderleith's cottage. It would take her mind off whatever Matt was up to if nothing else. Instead she was inveigled into spending her afternoon assisting Lucy with her jigsaw puzzle.

It seemed however that Simon Frobisher's prediction of snow was correct and by the time the curtains were drawn when Kitty went upstairs to dress for dinner a thin layer of snow was already covering the ground.

'I've set out your velvet dress for dinner, miss, and I thought perhaps as you would want your thicker jumper for afterwards to change ready for the carol service. 'Tis much colder here than we're used to.' Alice as usual had been keeping herself busy.

Lucy had said that many of the servants were going to the carol service as Lord Medford had arranged for transport via the estate's horse-drawn carts. Alice was looking forward to the outing.

'Did you find out much, miss, about Miss Plenderleith? Gladys saw you on the back of Captain Bryant's motorcycle this morning heading down the drive.'

Kitty groaned. 'I expect I am the talk of the servants' hall now. Keep it to yourself Alice but Inspector Greville and Doctor Carter believe Miss Plenderleith's death was no accident. Her papers have been ransacked and money is missing from her cottage.'

Alice's eyes rounded at this news. 'Oh my goodness, you don't think as it could have been that person you thought was following you and Miss Lucy the other afternoon?'

'I don't know, Alice. I expect the inspector will sort it all out. Just be careful this evening and stay with the other staff at the church,' Kitty said. She took a seat on the armchair beside the fire and took off her shoes.

Alice immediately pounced ready to clean them ahead of the outing to the church after dinner. 'Mr Golightly said as there has been things taken from the village and some of the outlying farms. Food and money and things.'

'That's what the constable said. It all points to a vagrant living rough in the countryside.' Kitty wished she could shake off her concern that Ezekiel Hammett was behind the thefts and Miss Plenderleith's death.

'This house seems proper unlucky.' Alice gave a shudder. 'Funny as nobody has reported a tramp. You'd have thought if someone was hard up they would have seen them. They usually go about looking for work or a place to sleep.'

Once again Kitty thought that her friend had hit the nail squarely on the head.

She had little opportunity to talk to Matt and discover where he had been all afternoon as dinner was taken up with talk of the carol concert and she soon found herself in her uncle's Bentley along with her uncle, aunt, cousin, Miss Hart and Hattie for the short journey to the church.

Matt was with Mr Frobisher, Juliet, and the Cornwells in the count's gleaming scarlet car. The cart containing the house staff that were attending clopped along behind them. Kitty was relieved to see that they were all securely bundled up under blankets and Alice's slight form was sandwiched between the sturdier figures of Cook and Gladys.

The church's stained-glass windows glowed in the darkness as they approached, spilling jewel-like colours out over the snow. All around them large white flakes tumbled softly to the ground, like duck down in the silent landscape.

The small black cassocked figure of Reverend Crabtree stood at the open wooden door of the church waiting for their arrival. A few other horse-drawn carts and a couple of delivery vans belonging to the butcher, the grocer and the baker were parked in the lane beyond the church wall.

Kitty couldn't help glancing around her as her uncle assisted her from the car. Memories of her previous visit and Miss Plenderleith's demise played on her mind. She shivered, glad of her thick red jumper and warm coat over her all-purpose tweed suit. Lucy tucked her arm through hers.

'Be careful, Kitty, it's rather slippery underfoot.'

The count's car slid into place behind her uncle's Bentley and Kitty was irked to witness Matt assisting Juliet from the rear seat. She wondered how he had coped with the dark confined space. The group made their way along the path to the entrance and Reverend Crabtree, who greeted them with his by now familiar obsequious smirk.

The vicar shook hands with them all as they entered. He murmured what she assumed were a few words of welcome to some of their party, her aunt and uncle, Count Vanderstrafen, and the Cornwells. She noticed that Simon Frobisher avoided greeting the reverend, slipping in with Hattie in a decided snub to the vicar.

The interior of the church was lit mainly by candlelight with just the one electric light on in the entrance porch. The choir stalls were filled with children from the village, their breath hanging in plumes in the chilly air of the church as they shuffled and giggled together under the watchful eye of an elderly lady. A scholarly looking gentleman was playing the small organ and music rippled around the church mingling with the chatter of the congregation.

The front pews had been left empty ready for the party from the Hall and they took their places, Lord and Lady Medford nodding and smiling to people they knew. Kitty was sandwiched between her cousin and Hattie. Matt, she noticed was between Juliet and Miss Hart. Mrs Baker and Mrs Vernon were on opposite sides of the aisle. Mrs Baker wore black with a fox stole around her shoulders. Mrs Vernon, like Mrs Cornwell, was swathed in fur.

The nativity scene looked attractive and Kitty noted that sprays of red and gold had been added to the greenery adorning the windowsills and displays. On the other side of the church she saw Inspector Greville had taken a seat and she wondered where he was staying. In the summer he had stayed at the Railway Engine public house in Newton St Cyres, the local village.

Once everyone was inside, the doors to the church were closed and Reverend Crabtree made his way to the front to address the congregation.

'Lord and Lady Medford, friends and neighbours, thank you for attending this evening. Our joy at the celebration of our Lord's birth is of course tinged with sadness this evening with news of the untimely death of our dear friend, Miss Marguerite Plenderleith. I hope you will all join me as we take a moment to pray for her.'

Everyone obediently closed their eyes. Kitty sneaked a peep before closing her own to see Inspector Greville taking the opportunity to look around at the people within the church. Did he hope to see someone in particular attending, she wondered. Was that the reason why he had come?

The prayer said, the elderly lady who had been supervising the children gave a bible reading before the carols began. Kitty shared a hymn book with Lucy and tried not to wince at Hattie's loud and wavering off-key notes.

Mercifully the service was not overly lengthy and before too long everyone was spilling back outside into the crisp wintery air. The snow had continued to fall, and the cars now bore a thin white covering. The horses snickered, stamping their hooves, their harnesses jingling with their impatience to be off. Inspector Greville's black police car was parked behind the count's red one.

'Inspector, I wasn't expecting to see you here this evening.' Kitty fell into step beside Inspector Greville as they exited the church.

'I thought it would be a pleasant diversion.' The inspector smiled at her.

'Of course, are you staying locally?' she asked.

'Your uncle and aunt have very kindly offered me accommodation.' His moustache twitched. 'In fact, if I can offer any of the party room in my car?'

Matt appeared at Kitty's elbow. 'Kitty and I will be happy to take you up on your offer, sir.'

She didn't protest as Matt expertly cut her away from her cousin's party and installed her next to him on the rear seat of the inspector's car. The thick blue travel rug she discovered provided her with welcome warmth across her knees.

'Any further news on the investigation, sir?' Matt asked as the inspector started the engine and executed a neat turn to head towards Enderley. The car headlamps showed that the tyre and cart tracks from their earlier journey to the church had almost been completely obliterated by the falling snow.

'It looks as if key pages from the accounts for both the church roof fund and the parish funds are missing along with the money. Reverend Crabtree is proving somewhat evasive in his answers, so we are uncertain how much money has actually been taken,' the inspector replied.

'That seems a little odd. Has anyone reported seeing a vagrant in the vicinity recently?' Kitty asked, enjoying the sensation of being snuggled up next to Matt. She could almost forgive him for his attentions to Juliet.

'No, just the reports we've received about the spate of petty thefts. We're being hampered at present by the weather and the lack of manpower.' The inspector pulled the car to a stop alongside Matt's tarpaulin covered motorcycle.

'Does that not seem strange to you, sir, that no one has reported seeing a stranger in the vicinity?' Kitty voiced the same question that Alice had put in her head.

The inspector turned off the engine, preparing to get out of the car. 'At this time of year there are less people abroad. Everyone has their thoughts fixed on Christmas. The cattle and other livestock are closer to the farmsteads, if not inside, so a man might travel relatively unnoticed.'

His response didn't give Kitty any reassurance. 'What do you make of the missing pages from the accounts?' That at least was unlikely to be Hammett's work.

Matt coughed. 'Perhaps we may be looking at something else with that, especially if the vicar is being somewhat vague about the finances.'

Kitty accepted his arm to help her from the car. If there was something wrong with the accounts, then that could bring Miss Plenderleith's murder much closer to home.

'Who else is involved with the financial affairs for the parish council and the church roof?' Kitty asked as they waited for the inspector to lock his car.

Snow was falling rapidly now, blurring out the ugly dark shape of the Hall.

'Reverend Crabtree, as one would expect. Miss Plenderleith checked the books and was responsible for banking the money from the collection plates and the fundraising. Mrs Vernon and Mrs Baker were part of the parish committee along with Mr Isiah Golightly, the verger. He is the brother of Lady Medford's gardener. Reverend Crabtree said Miss Plenderleith had intended to take the money to the bank in Exeter the day she was killed.' The inspector dropped his car key into his coat pocket.

CHAPTER TEN

Kitty held tight to Matt's arm as they walked the short, slippery distance to join the rest of the party who had all hurried inside the brightly lit hallway. Mr Harmon and Mrs Jenkinson had remained behind to tend to the house and to prepare a steaming aromatic silver bowl of hot punch accompanied by mince pies and slivers of rich fruit cake ready for their return.

The butler and the housekeeper assisted the party with their coats as people stamped the snow from their shoes onto the entrance mat. Mrs Cornwell made a great deal of fuss about the care of her furs as she handed her coat to Mrs Jenkinson.

Inspector Greville's arrival had not gone unnoticed. The policeman waited quietly at the back of the group. Once the party had finished divesting themselves of their outerwear Lord Medford made the introductions.

Kitty observed the reactions around her. The Cornwells and Simon Frobisher exhibited polite curiosity. Miss Hart seemed appalled that there was a policeman in the house while Hattie became quite animated. Juliet Vanderstrafen appeared paler than usual while her brother barely blinked.

'Come through, refreshments are prepared.' Lady Medford ushered her guests into the drawing room.

One of the uniformed maids stood by, ready to ladle out the punch which scented the air with a heady aroma of cinnamon, wine and apple. Mrs Cornwell made a beeline for the fire and stood warming her hands while her husband collected two glasses of punch. Hattie headed for the gramophone and put on some festive music.

Kitty took a seat on the sofa next to Lucy while Matt fetched punch for them both.

'Inspector Greville, this weather is quite a contrast to the summer and your last visit here, isn't it?' Lucy said as she cradled the mulled drink in her hands.

The inspector nodded, his mouth full of mince pie. He chewed and swallowed.

'Indeed, Miss Medford. I'm very grateful to your parents for the offer of accommodation.'

'Will you be staying for long, Inspector? It is Christmas Eve tomorrow after all.' Miss Hart looked down her long, thin nose at the policeman, her tone implying that it would be better if he were gone before Christmas.

'That all depends, Miss Hart. If this weather continues, I may not be able to leave.'

'Oh dear, I hope you will be able to spend Christmas with your family.' Kitty knew the inspector had several young children who would no doubt be looking forward to spending time with their father.

'My good lady wife understands the difficulties of my job, and Mrs Greville's mother is spending Christmas with us, which will no doubt assist with the children.' Inspector Greville's moustache took on a depressed air as he contemplated the possibility of spending Christmas away from his family.

'I am surprised, Inspector. I would not have thought an accident such as the one which killed poor Miss Plenderleith would have occupied so much police time?' Victor Vanderstrafen enquired.

Kitty held her breath as she waited to hear how much the inspector was prepared to reveal.

'Unfortunately, the circumstances surrounding Miss Plenderleith's death are proving more complicated. There is evidence of a theft of a considerable sum of money from her cottage.'

'You mean she may have been robbed, and… murdered?' Corny Cornwell asked.

Kitty couldn't be certain, but she thought she heard Simon Frobisher give an audible gasp.

'Precisely.' Inspector Greville looked around at the assembled group and popped a bite of Christmas cake into his mouth.

'If robbery was the motive then surely it must be someone who would know she had money in her home?' Lucy looked at the inspector, a puzzled frown on her face.

'Not necessarily, Miss Medford. It could of course be a vagrant or an opportunist theft. Miss Plenderleith lived alone in an isolated spot,' Inspector Greville replied.

'What was that? Miss Plenderleith murdered you say? How terribly thrilling!' Hattie bounced across the room, her eyes sparkling with excitement.

'My dear Hattie!' Lord Medford admonished.

'It is quite awful, of course,' Hattie mumbled.

Mrs Cornwell clutched at her pearls. 'Oh my, well if there is a murderer on the loose, my dear inspector, then I'm glad we have a police officer in the house. Don't you think so, Corny?'

'Absolutely, sweetie pie,' Mr Cornwell reassured his wife. 'I'm sure the inspector here has everything in hand, isn't that right, Officer?'

'We are pursuing several lines of enquiry,' Inspector Greville answered suavely. 'You may rest assured, Mrs Cornwell, that you are perfectly safe.'

Lord Medford concurred with the inspector. 'Absolutely, my dear Mrs Cornwell.'

Miss Hart had taken a seat on a low stool next to Kitty. Her hand shook as she pressed a lace-edged handkerchief to her lips.

'Miss Hart, are you feeling unwell?' Kitty asked, alarmed at the elderly woman's pallor.

'You must excuse me, Miss Underhay. I am finding this whole experience most distressing. Miss Plenderleith was such a nice, genteel lady and had become a dear friend. To think that she may have been deliberately harmed, well, I confess I am not used to such things. Dear me, no.'

'Do take a sip of punch,' Kitty suggested, offering the woman a cup of the mulled spirit.

'She and I had such a pleasant conversation yesterday evening. We had so much in common, you see. Such an educated lady, she had travelled a great deal with her father in her youth, she spoke seven different languages, I believe. Naturally she was distressed by the accident to her dress, and she was concerned about her cat. Oh dear, her cat. Has anyone thought about the poor thing?' Miss Hart looked at the inspector.

'The cat has been taken care of, Miss Hart. Miss Plenderleith's milkman has given it a home. His daughter is very fond of cats,' Inspector Greville reassured her.

This appeared to mollify the lady somewhat. 'Thank you, Inspector.'

'Poor Miss Plenderleith, such a shame she was so upset over the accident with Mrs Baker's drink,' Lucy mused.

Miss Hart sniffed and dabbed delicately at the end of her nose with her handkerchief. 'I think it might have been more than that, Miss Medford. I don't know, but when she returned from sponging the sherry from her dress she went straight to Reverend Crabtree and appeared quite, well, out of sorts. They seemed to have quite an intense conversation. I presume about Mrs Baker and Mrs Vernon. I'd expected her to return to our conversation but then she said she had to go. I do hope it wasn't something I'd said or done. Oh dear, to think I shall never speak to her again.'

'I'm sure you have said or done nothing with which you could reproach yourself, dear lady,' the count said gallantly.

Whether it was the effects of the punch or the count's reassurance, Miss Hart began to perk up and allowed Hattie to persuade her to join in with a game of cards along with the Cornwells. Lucy moved to sit with her mother closer to the fire and the punch bowl.

Juliet Vanderstrafen took Miss Hart's place on the stool. Kitty was more than a little irked by this move as she would have liked to talk to Matt and gather his impressions. The count had joined Lord Medford and Inspector Greville and the three of them seemed deep in conversation.

'I wouldn't be surprised if it was Reverend Crabtree who upset Miss Plenderleith,' Simon Frobisher said suddenly.

Kitty hadn't noticed him taking a seat nearby. 'Well, the vicar doesn't seem to have made himself terribly popular locally.'

Simon Frobisher snorted. 'He's a dreadful man, quite dreadful. If you only knew the half of it, Miss Underhay. If you knew what I knew of his true character.' He shook his head and mumbled something else before going off to replenish his drink.

Matt exchanged a glance with Kitty.

'Do you think he's had a little too much of the mulled wine? Uncle has put quite a lot of brandy in the bowl,' Kitty murmured.

Simon returned to his seat.

'What do you know of the vicar, Mr Frobisher? I noticed that you did not shake his hand at the church tonight?' Juliet fixed her steady blue gaze on Simon.

It was exactly the question Kitty had intended to ask. She waited for his reply.

'I know things about Reverend Crabtree. This posting to St Mary's is his last chance.' Simon gulped at his drink.

'Really?' Matt said. 'How do you know?'

Simon Frobisher looked at Matt with bloodshot eyes. 'I know. I have personal history with the man. I'm sorry to say I am related to him, although he refuses to recognise the connection.'

Kitty sat up straight at this unexpected piece of information. 'You are related to Reverend Crabtree?'

'My mother was his sister. She married against the wishes of the family and they cut her off. She died a few years ago and I wrote to my uncle advising him when she became ill. It was her dearest wish that she should be able to reconcile with her only brother before it was too late. Her parents had died several years before. The reverend ignored my letter, and later the invitation to her funeral.' Simon blinked owlishly behind his glasses.

Kitty's heart squeezed in sympathy. She could see that he was deeply affected by his uncle's actions.

'And you had not heard from him or seen him until you came here?' she asked.

Simon gave a harsh laugh. 'I did not hear from him personally, but he did contact my mother's solicitor to see if she had left him anything in her will and to enquire after a necklace that had been in her possession. Apparently, it had belonged to their grandmother and he wanted it returned to him.'

Kitty gasped. 'How awful, not at all the behaviour you would expect from a man of the cloth.'

Simon's lips twisted in a mirthless smile. 'My mother was buried wearing that necklace. It had been a personal gift to her from her grandmother when she was twenty-one and was her one link with the past. She never took it off.'

'This is a terrible story, Mr Frobisher. I take it he still does not wish to acknowledge you?' Juliet's eyes were wide.

He shook his head. 'No, not at all. He pretended he had no idea who I was when I introduced myself yesterday evening at the party.'

Kitty was determined to try to find out why Simon had said this might be Reverend Crabtree's last chance. 'You said this posting to St Mary's was the reverend's last chance?'

Simon took another gulp from his glass. 'Financial skullduggery, complaints from other members of the clergy and lay staff. A scandal involving a married lady. Rumours of blackmail. Take your pick.'

'You seem to have taken quite an interest in your uncle's past?' Matt remarked mildly.

'I had to track him down when mother was ill. He'd moved around quite a lot and everywhere I tried I heard these different stories and none of them were good. The Bishop of Exeter is a good friend of a friend of mine and when he knew I was searching for Reverend Crabtree he shared his information with me.' Simon rubbed a hand over his face, pushing his spectacles up to scrub at his eyes.

Kitty's ears had pricked up at the mention of financial irregularities. With the money missing from Miss Plenderleith's cottage and the accounts being destroyed, could Reverend Crabtree be Miss Plenderleith's killer?

She glanced at Matt and could tell from his expression that he too was thinking hard about what they had seen at the cottage.

'It may be worth you sharing all of this with Inspector Greville,' Matt remarked, his tone still casual.

Kitty had already decided that if Simon didn't tell him then either she or Matt certainly would.

Simon Frobisher sighed and finished his drink in one last gulp. 'Yes, you're right. I doubt it is of any relevance to Miss Plenderleith's demise, but my uncle has some undesirable acquaintances. They could have followed him here I suppose.' He rose and ambled across the room to where the inspector was conversing with Lord Medford and the count.

Juliet shivered. 'I think it may be more relevant than he thinks, yes?' She looked at Matt and Kitty.

'Do you think Reverend Crabtree might be capable of murder?' Kitty asked, curious to know how Juliet may have picked up on the significance of Simon's words.

Juliet shrugged her slender shoulders. 'The policeman said there was money missing and the reverend seems fond of money. He must have known it was in the house of Miss Plenderleith. Sometimes the most unexpected people can be capable of murder, do you not agree, Matt?'

Kitty's jaw tightened as Matt replied. 'On the surface they may seem unlikely, but the clues are always there I suppose if one cares to look for them.'

Juliet was silent for a moment. 'And do you think murder can ever be justified, Miss Underhay?' She looked directly at Kitty, the pupils in her eyes wide and black as if she had somehow seen all the horrors of the world.

'The planned destruction of one person by another? That is how I have heard others define murder. No, I don't know if you can.' Kitty shifted uncomfortably on her seat. Something about Juliet's expression and the strangeness of the question caused a chill to run along her spine.

'Not even if it is to save other innocent people?' Juliet persisted.

'The death of one to save the many? I fear, Miss Vanderstrafen, that is a question more fitted for a philosopher than a humble hotelier.' Kitty forced a smile.

She noticed that Inspector Greville and Simon Frobisher were no longer in the drawing room. Instead the count appeared to be conversing amiably with her uncle. Lady Medford was busy with her embroidery while Lucy leafed through a fashion magazine. The card game was proceeding amicably. Everything appeared normal and Christmassy with the brightly decorated tree and the mantelpiece now covered in cards. Yet, there was something not quite right.

Kitty shivered.

'Are you feeling the cold, old thing?' Matt asked, concern on his face as he moved closer to her.

'A little, I think I'm tired. It's been a long day.' Kitty checked the time with the clock on the mantelpiece and saw it was close to midnight. 'Almost Christmas Eve.'

'Ah, Christmas Eve, the time the little children look for Father Christmas or as we say, the *Christkind*.' Juliet shifted on her stool. 'I think I shall call it a night.' She looked across at her brother and the count's gaze met his sister's. 'You will excuse me.' Juliet stood and walked towards the door, her brother, clearly having said his adieus to Lord Medford, followed her from the room.

'Miss Vanderstrafen is quite an extraordinary person, isn't she?' Kitty said.

Matt placed his arm around her shoulders. 'Yes, she has not had an easy life despite her family's wealth and status.'

'Is that why he is so protective of her?' Kitty asked, wondering if Matt knew of the alleged secret lover.

'Partly.' Matt smiled at her. 'Warmer now?'

Kitty returned his smile. 'Yes, a little. Although I think I should follow Juliet's example and retire to bed. I believe we have another busy day tomorrow.'

'Will you be hanging up your stocking for Father Christmas?' Matt asked, his grin widening and causing the dimple to quirk in his cheek.

'Of course, I have been a good girl this year. You, on the other hand, will have to hope that Father Christmas does not leave a lump of coal in your sock,' Kitty replied demurely.

Matt laughed out loud, causing Lucy to glance their way with a smile on her lips.

'I am going to bed. Alice will be waiting for me, no doubt.' Kitty stood and said goodnight to the rest of the group. Matt followed her example and accompanied her into the hall.

'Kitty, please don't allow Juliet to upset you. There are things that I'm not at liberty to tell you at present, instead I have to ask you to trust me.'

His gaze locked with hers and her pulse speeded. She knew that what she had sensed was correct, there was something dark and dangerous going on at the Hall. Something other than poor Miss Plenderleith's murder.

'Very well, but you know that I shall find it out.' She smiled to show she was teasing.

He lowered his head, his lips brushing hers. 'Come, it's freezing in here.'

He said goodnight at her bedroom door with another kiss. Alice opened her door for her, and Kitty watched Matt stroll away along the landing before slipping inside her room.

*

Matt made his way along the landing towards his own room deep in thought. His original task from the brigadier had seemingly been made much more complex with Miss Plenderleith's death.

Was her death simply a robbery gone wrong? Or was it more complicated? Could it be connected with the task he had been given? Had Miss Plenderleith seen or heard something she shouldn't have done while she had been cleaning her dress? Lord Medford's words about the deaths of the brigadier's operatives were tumbling about in his mind.

His feet carried him past the turn to his room and on to the long gallery with its vast leaded windows offering an icy panorama of the grounds. The rose terrace was now covered in a blanket of snow and the lawns offered a smooth and uninterrupted vista of white towards the distant inky waters of the lake.

He took out his cigarette case and lit up, inhaling the first burst of nicotine to try and clarify his thoughts. Frobisher's revelations had pitched Reverend Crabtree into the frame for stealing the money but was the man capable of murder too?

Then there was Juliet.

A faint creak from near the top of the stairs told him that he was no longer alone. He took another pull from his cigarette, alert to the possibility of danger.

'Quite some picture, ain't it?' Corny Cornwell emerged from the shadows to stand at his side. 'Mind if I join you for a minute. Little woman is gone to bed and I was still feeling a mite restless.'

Matt nodded his assent, curious about the other man's motives for seeking him out.

Corny took out his own monogrammed silver case and lit up. They stood side by side for a moment taking in the wintery vista before them.

'I don't suppose that policeman will be going very far tomorrow with all this snow.' Corny glanced at Matt.

'Not unless they manage to clear the main roads,' Matt replied, looking out at the whirling snowflakes that continued to tumble from the sky. A stray flake carried by a gust of wind hit the glass before them with an icy splat.

'From what Frobisher said downstairs I guess the inspector will be paying the vicar a visit tomorrow, snow or no snow,' Corny mused. 'Lord Medford said the vicarage wasn't too far away from Miss Plenderleith's cottage.'

'So I believe.' Matt stubbed out his cigarette in a large onyx ashtray that stood conveniently nearby on a small black lacquered oriental style table.

'Delilah said she saw you and the girl on your motorcycle this morning heading down the driveway. I take it you know this Greville fellow from what he was saying downstairs?'

Matt wondered if this was what Cornwell was fishing for, to discover if he and Kitty had inside knowledge about the murder. 'We've worked together in the past.' He kept his tone casual.

'Lord Medford is an interesting chap. Amazing inventions and knowledge.' Corny blew out a narrow stream of smoke. 'Incredible the things he's developed in that little workshop of his down there.' His gaze was focused on the band of trees where the formal gardens ended, and the lawn gave way to informal woodland and grass. Lord Medford's workshop lay just beyond there, further along the path from the small stone gardener's hut.

'I believe so, Mr Cornwell. Kitty is very proud of her uncle. I understand you are in a similar line of business?'

'Oh, I'm just a humble salesman, nothing like Lord Medford.'

'Your employment seems to take you around the world. I doubt you occupy as humble a position as you say.' Matt glanced at Corny.

'Well, I've made some very good trade deals for my company.' Corny extinguished his own cigarette.

Matt nodded at the well-built American. 'I think I'd better turn in, it's getting late. Good night, sir.'

He left Mr Cornwell still standing and contemplating the snowy vista. It had been a curious conversation, as if the man were sounding him out in some way. Or attempting to ascertain information about Lord Medford's work. The man had also been evasive over his own employment.

Matt let himself into his room and switched on the small green shaded lamp on his bedside table before crossing to his fireplace to stir a little more life into the embers still glowing in the hearth.

He pulled his tie undone and removed his cufflinks, dropping them onto the small gilt tray on the top of the dressing table. As he did so, something caught his eye. The top drawer of the dresser was not quite closed, the edge running slightly out of line with the drawers below.

Matt frowned and opened the offending drawer. On the surface the contents appeared undisturbed. Except he knew they had been. He slid the drawer shut and quickly checked the others. Someone had been in his room and had searched through his things. They looked neat and tidy, the way he had left them, but there were subtle changes; a handkerchief with a monogram facing a different way, a tie slightly askew.

He knew this wasn't the work of the servants. Someone had been deliberately looking for something. He sat on the edge of the bed. Looking for what exactly? Did someone suspect that he was at Enderley Hall as a spy? Vanderstrafen? Cornwell? Or even Frobisher?

He turned to the small rosewood bedside cabinet and carefully took out the top drawer. To all intents and purposes the drawer was empty and unused. Matt travelled light. He had little option, with his Sunbeam.

The weight of the drawer however told him all was well. He turned it over and checked beneath it. The bottom of the drawer was raised leaving a space on the underside, something he had discovered on his arrival when he had been searching his room for a suitable hiding space.

Still firmly taped in place at the very back of the underside was the small but deadly handgun he had collected from the hidden floor safe in his office after his telephone call with the brigadier had concluded. Better to be safe than sorry. If the intruder had been looking for a weapon it seemed he or she hadn't found it. Unless the drawer was removed and inverted the gun was well hidden, and an apparently empty drawer was of no interest to anyone.

Matt replaced the drawer and changed for bed. He would need to remain on his mettle. The brigadier and Lord Medford had been right to be concerned. Things could become very dangerous at Enderley. Thank goodness Kitty was blissfully ignorant of the whole thing.

CHAPTER ELEVEN

The snow had almost stopped in the morning when Alice opened Kitty's bedroom curtains to reveal a pale blue sky with just the odd snowflake drifting down from nowhere. The fall in the night however had been extensive. Kitty estimated it had to be at least five or six inches deep and where the wind had blown it, drifts lay along some of the walls and hedges.

'His lordship has got the gardeners and such clearing a path down the driveway. Mr Golightly is grumbling about his lumbago already. I don't know if it'll be clear enough for the motors to use. Might be the horse and carriage tonight to get to the service if a thaw doesn't start,' Alice observed as she placed the morning tray of tea on Kitty's knees.

In the distance, Kitty heard the sounds of scraping and shovels mixed in with masculine voices. She poured a cup of tea and took a sip, savouring the warmth of the fluid.

'Lucy said that the presents were to be placed under the Christmas trees this morning. Would you take the ones I have for Cook and Gladys to the servants' hall later for me? I have a large jar of sweets for the others to share too,' Kitty asked.

'Of course, miss.'

Kitty hoped Alice would like the present she had selected for her, a fine pair of navy kid gloves with a fur trim, as worn by Hollywood's leading ladies. Or so the sales material in Miss Veronique's exclusive shop in Paignton had promised.

She had deliberated long and hard about what she should buy for Matt. In the end she had seen a small picture, a watercolour of Dartmouth Castle that she had thought might enliven the bare walls of his office. With this in mind she had chosen a nice modern frame and had wrapped it ready for Christmas morning.

Alice frowned as she went to the chest of drawers to take out Kitty's clothes so she could dress. 'Do you know, miss, I always lock your door when I goes downstairs but I could swear as someone has been a messing with your things.'

'What do you mean?' Kitty asked.

'Well, they aren't how I put them. I'm very particular about how I folds things and I put a bit of lavender or rose in between your things to keep them nice.' Alice appeared perplexed.

Kitty frowned. She hadn't been in the drawers; she'd had no reason to disturb Alice's meticulous arrangements. She knew her maid was telling the truth as the girl took great pride in her promotion to lady's maid on Kitty's trips.

'How very odd. If you find a teaspoon in there, then I suppose Hattie must be our first suspect.' She tried to make light of the matter, but it was most peculiar and a little disturbing. 'Is there anything missing?'

Alice shook her head, causing a small auburn curl to escape from under her cap. 'Not as I can see, miss.'

'Hmm, carry on keeping the door locked and if you notice anything else that seems odd tell me immediately,' Kitty instructed.

'Of course, miss,' Alice agreed, clearly not very happy with the idea that someone may have been interfering in Kitty's things.

'Have your things been disturbed too?' Kitty asked.

Alice disappeared into the tiny room where she had a small truckle bed and washstand. Her things were in a chest at the side of her bed.

'I can't be certain, miss, but I think they have. I'd left a marker in my magazine…' she held up a copy of *Film Pictorial* with Greta Garbo on the cover '… and the marker is on the wrong page.' Alice's cheeks were pink with indignation.

'Someone was searching for something then. I wonder what? Say nothing to anyone and keep your ears open. See if anyone else mentions their things being disturbed,' Kitty cautioned.

Kitty was still puzzling over Alice's unexpected discovery as she made her way down the main stairs for breakfast. Matt caught her up as she was almost in the hall, falling into step beside her. Kitty glanced around to ensure no one else was around. 'Someone has been searching my room. Mine and Alice's things have been disturbed.' She spoke quickly in a low voice as they halted near the telephone table.

'You're quite certain?' Matt asked.

'Yes. You know how meticulous Alice is.'

'My room has been searched too. There are only small things out of place, but someone has definitely been through my belongings. Was anything taken?' Matt asked.

Kitty shook her head. 'Nothing, it's most peculiar. I've asked Alice to say nothing but to listen out in case anyone else remarks on anything.'

The baize-covered door leading to the staff area at the end of the hall opened and Mr Harmon appeared with fresh coffee pots for the dining room. Matt linked his arm with Kitty's and they strolled casually on.

'Good thinking. Say nothing to anyone,' Matt murmured in Kitty's ear as they reached the dining room door.

Kitty helped herself to a generous portion of eggs and bacon before taking her seat at the table. The snow outside the window made the room bright with the silverware sparkling on the white cloths.

Matt had not seemed unduly surprised by her revelation. It was almost as if he had half expected her to say something. What was going on at Enderley that she wasn't being told? Was it tied up with Juliet? He took his place beside her and she was about to ask him, but the door opened and Muffy trotted in followed by Lucy.

'Heavens, have you seen the snow? I don't know if it will clear enough for us to get to church tonight.' Lucy waited until Mr Harmon had turned his back and promptly fed Muffy a sausage. She filled her plate with eggs and came to join them.

'I fear Inspector Greville may not be able to get home for Christmas,' Kitty remarked.

'He was out and about quite early this morning. I met him in the hall when it was still dark. I'd gone to persuade Muffy that she needed to go outside and the inspector had borrowed some galoshes from the cloakroom and was about to set off across the park,' Lucy said, tucking into her eggs.

'I wonder where he was going?' Kitty mused.

'Probably to arrest Reverend Crabtree,' Lucy suggested, her eyes sparkling with mischief.

The telephone rang in the hall and Mr Harmon departed to answer it. He returned a moment later.

'A telephone call for you, Miss Lucy.'

Lucy jumped up and hastily wiped the corners of her mouth with her napkin. 'I expect that will be Rupert.' She disappeared into the hall.

Mr Harmon collected the empty plates and left just as Victor arrived.

'Snow for Christmas, it is very festive.' He smiled at Kitty and nodded at Matt as he piled up his plate with sausage, eggs and bacon.

'I expect you are used to much more snow than this in your country?' Kitty poured herself another cup of coffee and added cream.

'Indeed, this is as nothing compared to the snow in the mountains at home,' the count agreed and sat opposite Kitty.

'Victor is an expert skier,' Matt said.

'I've never been skiing, it looks frightfully difficult.' Kitty helped herself to another piece of toast from the silver toast rack and began to apply butter.

'In Austria we learn as soon as we can walk. It helps to keep one fit.' Victor's piercing blue eyes surveyed her shrewdly. 'You must visit, Miss Underhay, and I shall have pleasure in teaching you.'

Kitty chewed and swallowed her bite of toast. 'That's terribly kind of you. I would love to travel. Listening to everyone talking the other evening I realised that I must try and visit more places.'

'I would be delighted to advise you at any time if you desire any recommendations, although I am sure Captain Bryant here would also be able to assist you.' Victor smiled at her. 'I believe you have visited many countries, is that not so?'

'I think we are both well travelled.' Matt's tone was neutral, and Kitty again sensed that strange undercurrent running between the two men, as if they shared some private code.

Lucy returned to the dining room; her cheeks flushed delicately pink. 'Oh bother, my eggs have gone cold.'

'Is Rupert well?' Kitty asked.

Lucy's colour deepened. 'Perfectly, thank you. He asked me to wish you all a merry Christmas on his and Daisy's behalf.'

Kitty grinned but didn't tease her cousin any further. She was more convinced than ever now that an engagement announcement would soon be forthcoming.

After breakfast both Matt and the count declared their intention of seeing how the drive clearing was going and assessing if there was any chance of a thaw. Kitty volunteered to help her cousin place all the gifts beneath the tree in the drawing room.

Lady Medford liked the parcels to be sorted into piles for each guest to make the distribution easier on Christmas morning. Everyone had brought their gifts and placed them untidily under the tree, so it would take some time to decipher the labels and sort them out.

*

Matt wrapped up warmly in his leather greatcoat and cloth flat cap and went to assess the progress of the men clearing the drive nearest to the house and in front of the garages. He intended to lend his services for an hour. Count Vanderstrafen accompanied him.

The men had made good progress and there were a few signs of a thaw commencing thanks to the weak wintery sun. He watched the inspector making his weary way back up the drive towards the house as he assisted Mr Golightly.

He wondered how the inspector had faired with Reverend Crabtree. He had no doubt that Kitty would do her best to try and winkle information from him.

'This cold is quite the contrast from the heat and dust of Egypt, is it not, Captain Bryant?' The count paused for a moment, leaning on his spade as he too watched Inspector Greville's progress.

'And yet there are some things still in common,' Matt said.

'An unexpected death?' Victor suggested. His lips twisted as he spoke. 'You surely do not think I am responsible for the death of Miss Plenderleith?'

'Not at all.' Matt's jaw tightened. Unlike Alexandria when he had been certain that Victor had definitely had a hand in the events there.

'I am relieved to hear it,' Victor said. 'I would not wish to have ill feeling between us. My sister still has nightmares about what happened in Egypt.'

Matt could understand that. Juliet had been the one who had found the body. It had been horrific; the official verdict at the time had been suicide, a self-inflicted gunshot wound to the head. The local inquest had cited financial worries. Yet there had been no note and Matt had known Charles Whitworth well enough to be certain that he would have left a note. He also knew that Charles had loved Juliet.

'I'm sorry to hear that. It was a terrible thing.' Matt had been elsewhere when it had happened. Business on behalf of the embassy had seen him gone from the city for the day. When he had returned in the evening it had been too late. His friend was dead.

He knew Victor had not approved of Charles' relationship with Juliet. He disliked anyone who became too close to his sister. Victor had hidden his dislike well enough, but Matt had noticed it, even if Charles had not. Despite that though he could, very possibly, have reluctantly accepted the suicide verdict, but for two things.

One, he knew Charles to be the most happy-go-lucky carefree man he had ever known, despite his lack of money. The second was Victor himself. On the surface he had been tender towards his sister and seemingly upset at Charles' death. Then he had let the mask slip.

Victor had thought no one was observing him when he had been reading the order of service for Charles' funeral. Matt had thought at first that he had imagined the expression on Victor's face. It had been so fleeting, but it had been there. Triumph.

Inspector Greville raised his hand in greeting as he neared the front door of the Hall before entering.

'Do you think the vicar is involved in Miss Plenderleith's death?' Victor asked.

Matt shrugged. 'Mr Frobisher clearly thought he might be.'

They resumed their work in silence, only stopping half an hour or so later when the area was clear.

'Reckon as how the sun will do the rest for a few hours now.' Mr Golightly straightened up and surveyed their handiwork. 'Iffn lane in't too shady reckon us can get to church tonight.'

'Will Reverend Crabtree be able to get there? Or the villagers?' Matt asked.

'Horse and carts will get through. Don't suppose the reverend will be using that bicycle contraption of his though. Him'll have to get a lift.' Golightly rubbed at the base of his back. 'Come on then, lads, reckon Cook will have kettle on,' the gardener called to the rest of his staff and the men walked off towards the servants' entrance. 'Thank you for your help, sirs.' He doffed his cap at Matt and the count.

'I think we are dismissed,' Victor observed as Golightly left to follow the other men.

Matt leaned his shovel against the wall next to Victor's. 'I think so. A cup of tea doesn't sound like a bad idea though.'

'I shall go and check on Juliet. You will excuse me.' He nodded to Matt, and without waiting for a reply strode off towards the front entrance.

Matt paused for a moment, taking time to stretch and rotate his shoulder, which had begun to ache now the shovelling had ceased. Had Victor known Juliet's secret in Alexandria? Had that been why Charles had died?

Kitty and Lucy had just finished sorting the Christmas presents under the tree and had rung the bell for tea when Inspector Greville arrived. He looked tired and cold as he went to stand by the fire, holding out his hands to feel the heat from the flames. His fingers were blue, and a hoary red flush brightened his complexion.

'Inspector, you look frozen,' Lucy said.

'We've just sent for tea. Where have you been? Have you been outside all this time?' Kitty asked. She was concerned for the inspector's welfare, as he appeared to be quite exhausted.

He sank down onto the armchair closest to the fire as the maid wheeled in a trolley laden with tea things, biscuits and mince pies.

Kitty poured the inspector a cup of tea while Lucy added a generous splash of her father's malt whisky and filled a plate for him.

'Thank you, Miss Underhay, Miss Medford, most kind.'

Kitty and Lucy poured tea for themselves, then sitting back down they waited for the inspector to answer their questions.

Inspector Greville sipped his tea and heaved a sigh of relief. 'This is most welcome. I went out to walk to the vicarage to speak to Reverend Crabtree. I tried telephoning but the snow has taken out his telephone wire.'

'Goodness, that's quite a walk in this weather. How was the lane?' Lucy asked, her eyes wide with astonishment that he had attempted such an endeavour.

Inspector Greville took another sip from his cup. 'Getting to the gatehouse was not too bad as the wind had blown the snow onto the field. However, the lane had several drifts once I had passed the church and Miss Plenderleith's cottage. The road to the vicarage was pretty bad. It was up over my knees in places.'

'Did you manage to speak to Reverend Crabtree?' Kitty asked as she added another couple of mince pies to the inspector's plate.

Under the comforting influence of a good fire and Lord Medford's whisky the inspector was slightly more forthcoming than he might normally be.

'A very cagey character, Miss Underhay. He admitted there had been questions about his financial propriety at his previous parish. Hence Miss Plenderleith overseeing the accounts and taking the money to the bank.'

'Then he must be a likely candidate for ensuring that any sheets showing financial issues were removed along with the money?' Kitty queried.

'Very likely, but he has an alibi for Miss Plenderleith's murder. The milkman who found her took his cart to the vicarage to telephone the police. Reverend Crabtree was in his pyjamas boiling an egg when the milkman arrived. I can't see as how it would have given him time to walk to Miss Plenderleith's, knock her over the head and get back into his nightwear in time to be cooking his breakfast.' The inspector surveyed the contents of his teacup with a gloomy air. 'No motor car.'

'I see. Then it seems it may have been an intruder after all?' Lucy said. 'The papers being disturbed at the cottage is a red herring.'

Inspector Greville's moustache took on an even more depressed air as he considered Lucy's question. 'I don't know, Miss Medford, but I don't like it.'

CHAPTER TWELVE

Everyone made a special effort with their dress for dinner as befitted the occasion. Kitty wore a red satin and chiffon dress with a low back, which Alice assured her looked very festive when teamed with a silver headband, shawl and shoes. She had to admit it was pleasant to dress up even if they would have to change again later in order to attend the midnight service.

Lord Medford had been out earlier in the evening accompanied by Mr Golightly and the drive and lane were declared passable. Cook had surpassed herself with mock turtle soup followed by a haunch of beef with an assortment of side dishes. Dessert was a rich plum crumble with custard, all accompanied by a selection of wine from Lord Medford's cellar.

Kitty felt quite uncomfortably full as she accompanied the other ladies into the drawing room. The talk at the table had been kept firmly on Christmas and the weather, which had done much to lighten the atmosphere. With the fire burning in the grate and the cards and tree, it actually felt quite Christmassy.

Matt had gone with the rest of the men to the library for port and brandy. He had been quiet throughout the afternoon, reading the previous day's copy of the newspaper. Kitty had spent her time with Lucy building a giant jigsaw puzzle of a snowy village scene.

Inspector Greville had been busy using the telephone in Lord Medford's study. Kitty presumed he had been reporting the results of his interview with the reverend to the chief constable and verifying Simon Frobisher's claims about the vicar with the bishop's office.

Delilah Cornwell as usual was seated near to the fire. She was wearing another trouser suit, an evening one in black and silver that she had apparently acquired in Paris. From Lady Medford's expression Kitty could see that it didn't matter where Delilah had acquired her outfit. Her aunt did not approve of it.

'I do declare I really cannot face changing and going out in the cold to sit in that freezing church again tonight. I shall catch pneumonia. If you don't mind, Lady Medford, Corny and I will stay quietly here and retire early,' Delilah declared.

'Of course, my dear, whatever you wish. It is not compulsory to attend midnight mass.' Lady Medford's tone implied that if she had her way it certainly would be.

Juliet, who had been seated next to Miss Hart, suddenly spoke out. 'I too will remain at the house if you would be kind enough to excuse me. I think I shall have an early night. I have not felt well today. My head, I get very bad headaches.'

Kitty could see the girl did appear very pale. Her pastel pink gown with its elaborate silver embroidery, while very pretty, seemed to drain her of all her colour.

'Of course, my dear, you must rest. Is there anything we can get for you?' Lady Medford asked.

'No, thank you. Maria, my maid, has my medication. If you will excuse me, I think the sooner I retire the better. I do not wish to be unwell for Christmas Day.' She rose and left the drawing room accompanied by murmurs of sympathy from all the ladies present.

Kitty wondered if the count would still attend without his sister. She presumed he would have to, as his car would probably be required to help transport everyone to the church. Unless he entrusted it to her uncle's chauffeur and her uncle drove the Bentley himself. She wasn't sure if the inspector intended to accompany the household to the church.

The gentlemen rejoined them at that point. Matt coming to sit beside Kitty and Hattie immediately commandeering Mr Frobisher.

'Corny honey, I was just saying to Lady Medford that we would pass on attending church tonight because of the cold,' Delilah called to her husband, interrupting his conversation with Lord Medford and Inspector Greville.

'A wise decision, my love.' He looked around at the others. 'Delilah has a delicate constitution.' Corny smiled dotingly at his wife.

Kitty compressed her lips together to stifle a giggle at her aunt's expression.

Matt bent his head towards Kitty to murmur in her ear. 'Where is Juliet?'

Her good mood instantly evaporated. 'She is unwell. She's gone to bed and won't be attending church.'

Miss Hart, who overheard Kitty's reply, joined the conversation. 'She did appear most unwell. Quite pale, I thought.'

'My dears, it is Christmas Eve, let us have some games,' Hattie called, clapping her plump hands together in glee making her bracelets jangle.

'Lucy, charades or guess who?' Hattie pounced on Lucy, her sudden movements and clanking jewellery startling Muffy into a bark.

With little choice in the matter, everyone ended up succumbing to Hattie's suggestion and a noisy round of parlour games commenced. The count however slipped away halfway through the games, returning just as Lord Medford announced that anyone wishing to attend the service should change and be ready in the hall by eleven thirty.

Alice had Kitty's change of clothes ready and waiting when she reached her room. 'You'll need to wrap up, miss. It's freezing hard now out there and slippy too. There's icicles forming on all the pipes,' Alice said as she carefully placed Kitty's evening gown on its padded hanger.

Kitty shivered as she wriggled into her thickest jumper. 'Brr, no wonder the Cornwells have opted to stay here.'

'Well, they are American, miss,' Alice remarked. 'Maria, Miss Vanderstrafen's maid, said as her mistress had gone to bed claiming as she was unwell. Told Maria to take the evening off and to stop in the servants' hall and enjoy herself.'

'Perhaps she needs to rest,' Kitty suggested, detecting from her maid's tone and expression that there had been something fishy about Juliet's instruction to Maria.

'Maria thinks as Miss Juliet wants to get away from her brother for a bit. She reckons as she plans to sneak downstairs to telephone her lover while everyone is at the church. Mind you, that Maria, she's in Count Vanderstrafen's pay she is. Gives Miss Juliet her medicine in her food sometimes when Miss Juliet don't know about it. I saw her the other day but she don't know as I caught her.' Alice nodded knowingly.

Kitty bent to lace up her brogues. 'That doesn't seem right. Poor Juliet. I take it there is a bit of a party below stairs this evening?'

Alice blushed. 'Mrs Jenkinson is playing the piano and there's to be singing and some games.'

'Well you go and enjoy yourself,' Kitty said.

She left Alice tidying the room and hurried downstairs to put on her hat and coat, winding a thick dark red knitted scarf around her neck. The count had already set off for the church accompanied by Mr Frobisher and Hattie. Lord Medford was driving her aunt, Miss Hart and Lucy. The chauffeur having been given the evening off to enjoy the staff festivities.

Kitty was pretty certain that it was not by accident that Inspector Greville had volunteered to take the police car with herself and Matt as his passengers.

'Have you managed to telephone your family, Inspector?' Kitty asked as she scrambled into the back of the police car. From across the estate grounds she could hear the tolling of the old church bell summoning everyone to the service.

Matt got in beside her and spread a blanket over their knees as Inspector Greville had a couple of attempts to get the engine of the car running.

'Yes, I spoke to Mrs Greville just before dinner. She understands that the process of the law does not stop for Christmas. The children had just had their bath ready for bed. Very excited they were for Father Christmas coming. The eldest is hoping for a train set.'

The inspector pulled out carefully and followed Lord Medford's Bentley down the driveway.

'It's such a shame that you won't be home for Christmas but I can't imagine the roads will be clear by tomorrow,' Kitty said as she gazed out at the drifts at the side of the road where the wind had blown across the exposed field.

The car slid on an icy patch and Kitty clutched at Matt's arm.

The inspector steered the car carefully through the gates of the estate and into the lane. 'No, it looks as if it may take a day or so for everywhere to be passable. It depends on the weather tomorrow if the thaw continues. Mrs Greville has everything in hand at home.'

The headlights picked out the tracks left by the other cars as they made their way at a crawl the short distance to the church. A few carts were stopped outside the walls, breath pluming from the horses' nostrils as they shuffled their hooves on the snowy ground, their harnesses jingling. Kitty hoped the roads would clear enough for her to get to Exeter after Boxing Day to meet the woman who claimed to have information about Ezekiel Hammett.

Light spilled out through the stained-glass windows throwing brightly coloured images onto the hummocked snow covering the graves. The inspector turned the car around and parked next to Lord Medford's motor.

Her uncle was engaged in assisting Miss Hart from the car. Her aunt and cousin had already started arm in arm through the lychgate along the short path to the church door. Kitty presumed that Victor and his passengers had already entered the church.

She slipped her arm through Matt's and they followed at the rear of the procession. Reverend Crabtree was not at the door to welcome them this evening. Instead the verger, who Kitty assumed must be Mr Golightly's brother, showed them to their pew and wished them a merry Christmas.

The congregation was considerably smaller than for the carol service, which was unsurprising given the state of the roads and the absence of Lord Medford's staff. Kitty wondered how Reverend Crabtree could stand at the pulpit and preach given Mr Frobisher's revelations about his conduct.

However, she banished the thoughts from her mind and focused on the pleasure of the ancient story and the singing of the much-beloved hymns. Midnight mass was always a magical time. Mrs Baker and Mrs Vernon were both in attendance and took turns to give readings before returning to their seats to glower at one another across the aisle. The baby Jesus had yet to be placed in the manger and the service was unexpectedly touching.

The service ended and the congregation filed back out into the cold, still night wishing each other merry Christmas as they left. Kitty noticed that Mrs Baker shunned Reverend Crabtree's attempt to say farewell and bustled away with the group that had presumably given her a ride to the church in their cart.

Mrs Vernon however looked rather like the cat who had stolen the cream. Bundled up in her furs with a large diamond brooch sparkling on the side of her matching toque, she smiled graciously at Lady Medford.

'Merry Christmas, such a lovely service. Midnight mass is always so special, and this weather just makes everything quite romantic, doesn't it?'

'Merry Christmas, Mrs Vernon. I'm afraid it also makes one rather cold too.' Lady Medford inclined her head and took her husband's arm to walk back to the car. Lucy followed with Miss Hart clinging tightly to her as they navigated the ice.

Kitty saw Inspector Greville nod gravely at the vicar as he joined Mrs Vernon aboard one of the carts, leaving the verger to see to locking the church. Reverend Crabtree ignored the inspector, focusing his attention on Mrs Vernon instead. The vicar appeared to be giving the lady extra attention, fussing around her with rugs and a cushion. Mrs Vernon, for her part, seemed to be accepting his attentions as her due.

The unexpected display occupied Kitty's mind as she made her way along the path with Matt to the inspector's car. Once more they followed the slow procession of vehicles back along the lane and past the gatehouse onto Enderley's driveway.

The lodgekeeper and his wife bundled up in scarves and coats came out to close the heavy wrought-iron gates behind them. Kitty couldn't help feeling more secure knowing they were closed and locked.

'Reverend Crabtree appeared to be very attentive towards Mrs Vernon,' Kitty mused as the police car inched its way towards the Hall.

'Did he now? I wonder if he wishes to save her soul or her fortune,' Inspector Greville observed.

'I understand Mrs Vernon made a considerable amount of money from her stage days,' Matt said as the car made a slight sideways move on the ice.

'And her marriages. The late Mr Vernon was in sugar.' The inspector righted the car back into the tracks and Kitty released her grip a little on Matt's arm. 'He left her a very wealthy woman and I'm quite sure Reverend Crabtree will be very mindful of that.'

Kitty breathed out now the lights of the Hall were in sight. Inspector Greville pulled to a halt next to the count's gleaming red sports car.

Matt assisted Kitty from her seat, and they made their way inside. From the drawing room they heard the pop of a champagne cork as her uncle started the festive celebrations. Kitty hung her hat, coat and scarf on a spare hook next to Matt's things and paused for a moment before the bronze framed deco style mirror to tidy her hair.

'You do know there is mistletoe above your head?' Matt's breath was warm on her cheek as his gaze met hers in the mirror.

'Really?' Kitty watched as the dimple quirked in his cheek.

She turned around to face him.

'Merry Christmas, old thing.' His lips brushed hers making her pulse quicken at the stolen moment.

'And to you.' The heavy sound of Inspector Greville stamping snow from his boots on the matting in the entrance sent them both smiling out into the hallway.

In the drawing room Lord Medford was pouring champagne into crystal flutes while Lucy offered around a selection of chocolates and marzipan fancies. Once everyone was in and served with drinks, he raised his glass.

'Merry Christmas to all of you. Thank you for sharing this wonderful season with my household and may Father Christmas leave you all you wish for in your stockings.' The group laughed and cheered when he indicated the row of gaily coloured velveteen stockings, each marked with a name that had been put out in their absence.

Kitty noticed that the Cornwells were absent from the celebration, as were the count and his sister. Something she considered ironic as they were the people who had supposedly professed a longing to spend a traditional country house Christmas at Enderley in the first place.

*

Matt also noted Victor's absence. The Cornwells he expected. There was no special reason for them to still be up when the party returned, especially as they had said they intended to have an early night, but he had expected Victor to be present for the champagne toast.

He really wanted to talk with Kitty's uncle and share his thoughts, especially to alert him to the searching of the bedrooms. So far, he had suspicions about most of the guests. Simon Frobisher and his connection with the unsavoury Reverend Crabtree. Was Simon using his uncle's misdeeds to divert attention away from anything he might be doing? The Cornwells, with Corny's rather over-the-top heartiness and the odd interview in the long gallery where he had been slyly hinting about Lord Medford's work. There was something suspicious too about Corny's job.

Then there was the Vanderstrafens. He definitely did not trust Victor, and he wasn't certain how much Juliet was aware of her brother's activities. Or if she might even be involved in them herself in some way. Victor had acted before on behalf of the Austrian Government, in a role not dissimilar to the one Matt had held, but now he wasn't so certain if they were Victor's only paymasters.

He would love to know who had searched the rooms and if every room had been searched or just his and Kitty's. Did someone suspect he was there to spy? And did they believe Kitty was involved in some way because of him? Matt kept a smile on his face as he chinked his glass against hers.

There was nothing that he had seen at the cottage to link Miss Plenderleith's death to anyone at Enderley, but even so, it made him uneasy, especially after Kitty had said she thought she had been watched. He knew she had been concerned that the murder might have been Hammett's doing, but then why destroy pages from the church and parish accounts? No, that had to point to the vicarage in some way, especially given Simon Frobisher's information about the reverend. Assuming, of course, that Frobisher had been telling them the truth about the vicar.

With the champagne finished, everyone began to drift off to their rooms. Matt and Kitty followed behind the others up the stairs from the hall. He saw Kitty to the door of her room and said goodnight before heading back down the stairs once more, safe in the knowledge that Lord Medford had gone to his study and the other guests to their beds.

*

Alice had scarcely closed the door of the bedroom when Kitty had a sudden thought and opened it again intending to call to Matt. To her surprise she saw him glance furtively towards the direction of his room before he started quietly back down the stairs to the hall.

His hands were empty, and she was fairly certain he was not attempting to play Father Christmas by placing more gifts under the tree. No, he was up to something and she was going to find out what.

Impatiently, she pulled off her shoes, discarding them with knotted laces on the floor.

'Miss Kitty?' Alice protested.

Kitty put a finger to her lips to indicate Alice should be silent and slipped out of the bedroom door and onto the landing.

She hurried quietly down the stairs in her lisle stockinged feet anxious not to make a sound. The distant rumble of male voices reached her from one of the rooms leading off the hall. Kitty padded quietly across the tiled floor. Mr Harmon was busy in the drawing room completing the clearing up after the party so she tiptoed past before he could spot her.

The voices were coming from inside her uncle's study. Kitty listened for a moment and decided that it sounded as if her uncle was talking to Matt. She knew she had to move quickly before Mr Harmon came out of the drawing room. It would never do to have him catch her eavesdropping.

At the sound of the trolley jingling with glassware coming out of the drawing room, Kitty ducked inside the open door to the library. She waited with bated breath until Mr Harmon had headed along the hall towards the service corridor before she snuck back out and cautiously placed her ear to the oak panelled door of the study.

Any guilt she may have felt at spying on Matt was swiftly vanquished when she heard her uncle mention her name.

'You have not said a word about any of this to Kitty?' her uncle said.

'No, sir, my instructions on the matter were, as you know, very clear, as were your own. I don't know if the inspector has been briefed at all?' Matt replied.

Lord Medford coughed. 'I don't know. This wretched Christmas malarkey means there is no one manning the telephones at Whitehall. I presume if they had believed Miss Plenderleith's death significant to our affair they might have sent someone from Scotland Yard.'

Kitty held her breath as there was a moment's silence. Her heart was beating furiously, and she was aware that Mr Harmon might return at any moment. What were they talking about? Where did Whitehall fit into all of this? And why wasn't she to know anything?

'Let us get Christmas over and then it may become clearer,' her uncle continued.

'Very well, sir. The weather is not helping the matter either at the moment,' Matt said.

Kitty was poised ready to flee should she detect any sign of movement within the room.

'Just make sure my daughter and niece are kept out of all this. It's a dangerous affair and I don't like this business with Miss Plenderleith being murdered or the rooms being searched.'

She didn't hear Matt's reply as the faint scrape of his chair on the parquet floor alerted her to his probable departure. Her heart thudded furiously against the wall of her chest as she scuttled away back up the stairs before the study door opened.

She had scarcely made it back upstairs to a wide-eyed Alice before she heard Matt's tread on the stair only a moment behind her.

'Miss Kitty, whatever is going on?' Alice was in her nightgown and flannel dressing gown. Her auburn hair in a long braid swinging over her shoulder as she confronted her mistress.

Kitty noticed that in her brief absence her maid had untangled the laces on her brogues and set them neatly to one side ready for morning.

'Matt was up to something, so I followed him. I had to try and find out what was going on,' Kitty said.

Alice bustled about fetching her nightclothes. 'What? Was you still fretting over him and Miss Vanderstrafen?' Her lips pursed in disapproval.

'No. There is something else going on here at the Hall. This house party with such a disparate collection of guests. Then with Miss Plenderleith being murdered.' Kitty tugged her jumper impatiently over her head shivering as the now chilly air in her room met her bare skin.

'And what did you find out then, miss?' Alice asked as Kitty shimmied into her pyjamas and hurried over to her bed.

'I couldn't hear much. Matt and my uncle were talking in the study and the doors here are terribly thick,' Kitty confessed.

'You was never eavesdropping on Captain Bryant?' Alice tutted as she pulled the covers up over her mistress.

Kitty blushed. 'I know, but I wanted to find out. It's something secret and dangerous, to do with the government.'

Alice turned out the lamp at the side of Kitty's bed leaving the room illuminated only by the faint glow of the coals in the hearth and the small night light next to Alice's own compact cot.

'That makes sense. That's what happens in the films, miss, and the lady doesn't get told anything as it might get them killed. Then they ignores the warnings and lands in trouble. Leave well alone, that's what I say. Best you sleep on it, miss. 'Tis Christmas Day already.' Alice padded away to her own bed and the light was extinguished.

'Night, Alice.' Kitty's own eyes had already closed, lulled by the warm comfort of her bed, and she almost missed Alice's soft voiced reply.

CHAPTER THIRTEEN

It felt as if she had scarcely closed her eyes when Alice woke her with her morning cup of tea. The conversations and events from the previous night were still tumbling about inside her head.

'Merry Christmas, miss.'

'Merry Christmas to you, too.' Kitty yawned and struggled into an upright position in her bed as Alice drew back the curtains revealing a grey damp day. Low cloud swirled in drifts and the snow cover on the ground was melting gradually to reveal the muddy grass beneath.

'Mrs Jenkinson said as everyone is to go to church for the service at ten, miss, and the presents and stockings is to be opened when you get back.' Alice started to efficiently sort Kitty's clothes. 'You have the pretty burgundy velveteen frock, miss, as would be nice for today.' She held it up for Kitty's approval.

'Lovely.' Kitty was still mulling over the snippet of conversation she had overheard between Matt and her uncle.

'Then you'd best shake your feathers, miss, or you'll be going to church on an empty stomach,' Alice reprimanded.

Kitty obediently drank her tea and hopped out of bed.

Once washed and dressed she gave Alice her present. She was rewarded with a squeak of delight and an impromptu hug as Alice undid the wrapping paper. The young maid was flustered and pink with pleasure at her gift.

'Oh, miss, these are lovely. I haven't never had no gloves as nice as these before.'

She darted into her own room and came back with a carefully wrapped gift. ''Tis only something small, nothing near as nice as these, but I saw it and thought as you might care for it.'

Kitty sat on the side of her bed and took the proffered parcel. 'Thank you, Alice, but you really shouldn't spend your money on presents for me.'

She carefully unwrapped the layers of tissue paper to reveal a very fine silver chain with a type of clip fastener.

'The jeweller said as you used it to fasten a brooch or pin to it, miss, as you can wear it as a necklace. I thought as you might like to put that little pin of your mother's on it if you wanted it as a necklace any time.' Alice waited anxiously for Kitty's response.

It took Kitty a moment before she could reply. Her throat was choked with tears at the thought that Alice had put into her present.

'I… oh, Alice, thank you. This is such a wonderful, kind thought. Thank you.' She embraced the maid, knocking the girl's much-prized lace cap skew-whiff as she did so.

When she released her, the girl's face was as red as her hair with pleasure. ''Tis nothing.'

Kitty promptly attached her mother's suffragist pin to the chain and slipped it on under her dress.

'Best hurry down to breakfast, miss, if that inspector has been there before you there'll only be crumbs left,' Alice said.

Kitty gave her friend a last quick hug and hurried downstairs. She was met with a chorus of merry Christmases as she entered the full dining room. She hastily filled her plate with smoked salmon and scrambled egg from the serving dishes before taking her place at the table.

'Happy Christmas, old thing.' Matt smiled at her from across the table and a guilty blush crept into her cheeks, certain he would not be so cordial if he knew she had been spying on him only a few hours earlier.

Delilah Cornwell was wearing another of her trouser suits, this time in a bronze material that shimmered as she moved. Lucy, like Kitty, was wearing a velveteen day dress but in a silver grey with silver embroidery.

Lady Medford was resplendent in plum velvet, while Miss Hart was dressed in a sort of cabbage colour. Hattie was in an unfortunate scarlet dress that seemed singularly unsuitable both for her figure and for the occasion.

Certainly, every time she moved her arms around to make a point, Mr Frobisher appeared embarrassed by his view of her cleavage. The Vanderstrafens were the last of the group to arrive for breakfast. Juliet was in a pale blue knitted suit and the count, in a stylishly tailored suit, smiled genially as he greeted everyone.

Inspector Greville had a well-stacked plate before him and was busy tucking in, much to Kitty's private amusement. She and Alice were well aware of the officer's fondness for food. She wondered if he would leave to visit his family later during the day if the roads cleared sufficiently.

The mood amongst the guests was good and it seemed the shadow cast by Miss Plenderleith's murder was already lifting. Kitty once more found herself with Matt in the inspector's car to go to the church.

As they were driving towards the gatehouse Kitty could see just how well the thaw had started to expose the ground. Only where the drifts had been especially deep were there still significant deposits of snow.

Matt and Inspector Greville chatted together about the upcoming festive sporting fixtures while Kitty tried not to fall asleep. She noticed the inspector did not appear to be too distraught at not being at home for Christmas morning. His unhappiness no doubt alleviated somewhat by his substantial breakfast. The lane too had cleared in those patches where the overhanging branches were thinnest. Water dripped down and the ruts in the road were muddy.

Mrs Vernon was at the door with the verger to wish everyone a merry Christmas as they made their way up the path to the church. She was wearing her furs once more and diamonds sparkled at her lapel and on her hat. She appeared very pleased with herself as they approached.

Mrs Baker had arrived at the same time as the party from Enderley in a small chauffeur-driven motor car. Kitty assumed the road from the village to the church must now be passable. Mrs Baker looked dressed more for a funeral than a joyous festive occasion with her black coat and hat. She nodded and wished Kitty and Matt season's greetings. They walked along at the tail end of their group, so Mrs Baker failed to see her rival until she was at the church door.

For a split second Kitty thought she was about to refuse to go in. She halted on the path, causing Inspector Greville to bump into Kitty.

'You can keep your merry Christmas, you trollop.' The words were hissed in a low tone but were vehement enough to cause Hattie and Simon Frobisher to turn around in the vestibule to witness the stand-off. 'How you have the brass nerve to stand there calling yourself a Christian I do not know. You're an affront to every respectable body here.' Mrs Baker glared at Mrs Vernon.

Her rival seemed unperturbed by the insult. 'Is that the best you've got? Well, it's up to you. You can come in or stay away, I'm sure my conscience is clear, unlike some persons present.'

'Now then, ladies. Mrs Vernon, p'raps 'ee should be taking your seat. You too, Mrs Baker.' The verger frowned at Mrs Vernon.

Mrs Baker lifted her chin and swept past Mrs Vernon as if she were a bad smell, bustling past Hattie and Simon in her haste to get inside and take her place.

'Well, whatever was all that about?' Hattie murmured as they entered the church.

Simon Frobisher looked at the cassocked figure of his uncle standing at the pulpit. 'Whatever it is, I am prepared to wager that he is at the back of it.'

Kitty exchanged a glance with Matt, and they took their place in the Medford family pews at the front of the church. She wondered what Mrs Vernon had meant by her parting comment to Mrs Baker. There was a buzz of excitement amongst the congregation as they no doubt anticipated a generous Christmas dinner later in the day.

The children were dressed in their best with freshly scrubbed faces and sparkling eyes as they swapped tales of what Father Christmas had left for them. The women were distant and slightly harried, no doubt thinking of the meat they had roasting in their ovens at home. While the men appeared self-satisfied as they contemplated a festive ale at the local hostelry before returning to their respective cottages to carve the meat.

Reverend Crabtree too appeared quite gleeful. Pleased with himself, Kitty decided. During the service he would dart self-satisfied smirks in the direction of Inspector Greville. Mrs Vernon was positively preening herself from her place opposite Mrs Baker. She noticed too that the reverend's gaze would flicker occasionally towards the section where his nephew was seated alongside Hattie and the count and his sister.

The service was short and joyous, even if Kitty felt there was a strange atmosphere within the church. She decided that the source had to be because of the ill feeling and jealousy between Mrs Baker and Mrs Vernon. The baby Jesus had been placed in the manger unscathed by the glare of Mrs Baker whenever she looked at it.

Reverend Crabtree stood at the church door as they made their exits. Kitty watched as he smarmed over her aunt and uncle, shaking their hands, and thanking them for their attendance and generous donations.

She noticed that he did not afford Miss Hart or Hattie, who had less to give, the same amount of attention. Simon Frobisher made a point of ignoring him while the Cornwells, with their wealthy appearance, were also smarmed over.

Count Vanderstrafen and his sister escaped the reverend as swiftly as possible and Kitty and Matt followed their example. Inspector Greville however paused for a few words. Words that temporarily removed the smirk from the vicar's face and left him glowering angrily after them as they picked their way down the path to the waiting cars.

'Beastly man,' Kitty muttered as they halted by the black police car.

'Not someone you would want as a man of the cloth,' Inspector Greville agreed as Matt assisted her into the car.

'What exactly did you say to him, sir?' Matt asked as he took his place next to Kitty.

Inspector Greville turned his head to look at them and smiled. 'Given some of the things I have learned recently about that gentleman I reminded him that I was still investigating not only Miss Plenderleith's murder but also the stolen money and alleged irregularities in the accounts. I've also uncovered a few other things. Blackmail, as Mr Frobisher intimated. It seems Mrs Baker may be his latest target, something about her marriages that the reverend had discovered. I informed him that I had spoken to the bishop's office. Perhaps setting him on his mettle may help the investigation along a little. I have requested that he call at Enderley tomorrow around teatime.'

Kitty settled back in her seat. The mist from earlier continued to swirl about the car and Inspector Greville was compelled to use the car's headlamps to light the way.

When they arrived back at Enderley they discovered Hattie was in a state of great excitement. 'Do hurry through to the drawing room. It's time for stockings.' She clasped her hands together with glee making her bracelets jangle.

Mrs Jenkinson had arranged for coffee and tea to be served in the drawing room on their arrival. Kitty was quite pleased to see the trolley waiting for them with a smartly uniformed young maid ready to pour.

'Hattie, do calm yourself, my dear,' Lady Medford ordered as she accepted a delicate china cup and saucer from the maid. She took her usual position beside the fireplace as the rest of the group were served.

Kitty took a seat on the sofa next to Lucy. Juliet promptly took the other space. As if sensing Kitty's irritation, Matt sat on the arm beside Kitty and they waited for Lady Medford to direct the proceedings.

'Miss Hart, please can you distribute the stockings.'

'I'll help.' Hattie abandoned her tea and rushed over to the pile of brightly coloured velveteen stockings, which were now knobbly and bulging with hidden delights. She swiftly usurped Miss Hart, leaving that lady floundering in her wake. Everyone received the stocking marked with their name.

Hattie dived straight in, exclaiming loudly with great delight as each treasure was unearthed. 'An orange, some nuts, a pretty handkerchief, how lovely, sweets. Look a new penny.'

Everyone's stocking appeared to contain more or less the same items.

'My, this is such a lovely tradition.' Delilah looked at her husband.

'Just wonderful, honey,' Corny dutifully agreed.

'Hattie gets excited every year,' Lucy murmured to Kitty as Hattie pored over her treasures. Then in a louder voice, 'Mother, shall I give out the parcels?'

'Yes, thank you, Lucy dear.' She frowned at Miss Hart who dithered uselessly beside the Christmas tree. 'Miss Hart, do sit down or collect the empty cups or something.'

Miss Hart flushed and subsided onto one of the armchairs, her stocking next to her. Kitty noticed Juliet frown slightly as she examined the contents of her stocking and heard the faint crinkle of paper as the girl swiftly palmed something that could have been a note concealed with her gifts.

No one else appeared to have noticed. Lucy was up distributing packages, Matt was talking to Inspector Greville and Victor was in conversation with Lord Medford. Kitty wondered who the note could be from. Someone in the house clearly, and Juliet obviously didn't want anyone to see it.

For a brief second, she considered whether the note could have been from Matt but, based on the conversation she'd overheard in the study, it seemed unlikely. An assignation message perhaps, or a smuggled love note from Juliet's alleged secret lover?

She was compelled to put the matter to one side as everyone was busy opening their pile of presents and she was forced to give her full attention to unwrapping her own gifts. She found herself in possession of some rather nice stockings, scarves and handkerchiefs. A brooch from Lucy and a very generous cheque from her aunt and uncle.

She waited for Matt to unwrap the picture she had bought for his office and was relieved to see him smile as he opened her present. Delilah received a very ornate diamond and emerald ring from her husband, which drew cries of admiration from Hattie.

Lady Medford received gardening gloves and secateurs from Lord Medford. A gift that Kitty knew would give her as much pleasure if not more than Delilah found in her diamonds. Juliet too had a jeweller's box from her brother, containing some pretty sapphire and diamond earrings. She presented him with a new leather wallet.

Kitty had opened all her presents before realising that she had not opened one from Matt. She looked at him questioningly.

'I couldn't decide what to give you to open, so I was late wrapping your present.' He smiled and felt inside the breast pocket of his jacket.

He pulled out a long slim parcel wrapped in scarlet paper. She opened it carefully to reveal a pair of crimson kid driving gloves and a small dark blue leatherette jeweller's box. Her heart thumped at the sight of the box wondering what its contents might be.

Lucy leaned over to see what she had received. 'What gorgeous driving gloves. Open the box, Kitty.'

Kitty laughed at her cousin's enthusiasm. She took a breath and lifted the lid. Inside, nestled on the navy velvet was a silver key ring with a small initial K and a key. She looked at Matt.

'Robert Potter has found you a car, a Morris Tourer. It's waiting for you back at Dartmouth.'

Kitty stared at him. 'What… I'm so confused.'

Lucy laughed. 'Darling, this is a key to your car. Robert Potter has found the one you wanted, and Matt has bought it for you.'

Kitty frowned at her cousin. 'Were you in on this?'

Lucy nodded, her eyes sparkling with merriment. 'We planned it all when I stayed with you in November.'

'Merry Christmas.' Matt kissed her flushed cheek as she struggled to hold back tears of joy.

'But I only got you a picture.'

Matt chuckled. 'A beautiful picture that's perfect for my office.'

'Thank you.' Kitty stared at the key, still slightly overwhelmed by the generosity of Matt's gift.

'A very serious present,' Juliet commented, calling a flush to Kitty's cheeks.

'I shall of course expect you to chauffeur me around when the weather is too inclement for the Sunbeam.' The dimple flashed in Matt's cheek as he ignored Juliet's remark.

'I knew there had to be some kind of catch.' Kitty smiled back and closed the lid of the box. A car of her own, power to go where she wanted whenever she wanted. It was a serious gift.

Christmas dinner proved to be a lavish five-course feast including turkey with bread sauce, plum pudding with brandy butter. Lady Medford had ordered dinner to be served in place of lunch so that they might listen to King George's Christmas message on the radio during the afternoon.

A cold buffet was then provided for the afternoon and evening, giving the staff time to enjoy their own festivities.

Later, when the broadcast was finished, Kitty wrapped up warmly and joined Matt, Lucy, Simon Frobisher and Juliet Vanderstrafen on a walk along the terraces in an attempt to walk off the huge quantity of food they had consumed. The snow had mostly cleared leaving the paving wet and a little muddy. There was still a great deal of mist over the grounds and Kitty was unsurprised by the decision of the rest of the party to remain indoors.

Lucy was kept busy throwing a ball for Muffy to retrieve and Simon appeared to be discussing plants with Juliet. Kitty enjoyed the luxury of strolling arm in arm with Matt despite the damp air.

'You shouldn't have bought me a car you know. It really was extraordinarily generous of you.' She peeped up at him.

'It's not a brand new one, a few months old, but it is red and the kind you wanted. You deserve it after all the scrapes we've been in this year.' His eyes were shadowed by the brim of his hat. 'I wanted you to have something special.'

'Thank you.' She looked ahead to where Juliet and Simon had their heads close together as they examined the bare stem of some kind of plant. 'They make an odd pairing, don't you think?'

Matt shrugged. 'I'm only surprised that Victor is not out here keeping watch.'

'I believe he is enjoying my uncle's hospitality and talking about chemicals and formulas. Mr Cornwell is with them,' Kitty said.

She continued to watch Simon and Juliet. There was a pink tinge in the girl's cheeks, and she had a look about her that struck a chord with Kitty. She noticed Simon's attentions towards her and decided that maybe she had discovered a clue to both the identity of the sender of the note, and Juliet's mystery admirer.

*

Matt was pleased that Kitty had liked his gift. He had wondered if she would object that it was too much. The cost hadn't been something he had worried about, he was more concerned that he had given her something she truly wanted.

He too watched Juliet and Simon Frobisher together. Victor would not be pleased if he thought his sister might be becoming attached to a humble botanist. Matt thought it was nice though to see Juliet relaxing and with a little more life about her. The Juliet he had seen so far at Enderley was a far cry from the vivacious, dazzling creature he had known first in London and later in Alexandria.

'I'm going in. I need to dry Muffy's fur and paws or Mrs Jenkinson will complain. Hattie is planning more party games,' Lucy called to them from the far end of the terrace.

Juliet and Simon had vanished. He presumed they had already turned back towards the house as it was growing dark.

'We should go back inside. I'm not sure if you're prepared for Hattie's entertainments however.' He glanced at Kitty.

'She is terribly excited about the whole thing, isn't she? I do hope she won't sing or recite any of her poems though.' Kitty smiled up at him and his heart skipped a beat. The sooner he could complete the brigadier's mission the better it would be. He hated having to keep Kitty in the dark about his instructions from Whitehall. At the same time, he wanted to keep her out of danger.

They turned at the end of the rose garden terrace to take the short flight of stone steps up to the path that would lead them around to the front of the house. A prickling sensation of being observed swept over him. The same feeling he used to get during a military operation and one that had saved his life more than once.

Matt looked around discreetly trying to see what, if anything, may have triggered the sensation. The twilight shadows and swirling mists made it difficult to be certain, but he thought he detected something, or someone over by the tennis courts. A servant, perhaps, or a member of the household.

'Come, it's getting dark.' He squeezed Kitty's gloved hand where it rested in his.

He gave a final quick glance over his shoulder as he led Kitty away from the area nearer to the courts and towards the front of the house where the lights either side of the front door spilled out a welcoming glow in the dusk.

There was definitely someone there, behind them watching them leave. A flare of a match and a glimpse of dark clothing was all he had. He shivered as they hurried into the hall and the safety and comfort of the house. As soon as he was certain Kitty was safely inside the drawing room he slipped back outside. Whoever had been there had gone, only a cigarette end, still warm, lay on the gravel where the watcher had been.

Christmas night passed with Hattie orchestrating games of charades, music and the pulling of crackers. Miss Hart became quite squiffy after a glass too many of Lord Medford's port and Juliet was persuaded to sing for the group. He noticed that with their return to the house, she and Simon Frobisher were politely distant once more.

All evening Matt felt tense, the earlier festive pleasure of the day had dissipated since he had seen the unknown figure watching them. Inspector Greville announced his intention of returning home the next day for a few hours to see his family before meeting the vicar at teatime. Matt wondered if, with the inspector absent, the hidden agent in their midst might make a move. Once Boxing Day was over then perhaps the inspector would be able to make more progress on catching Miss Plenderleith's killer.

A clay pigeon shoot had been arranged for the next morning to entertain any of the guests who were minded to participate. He knew both Victor and Juliet were excellent shots and his host was also a keen sportsman. Corny also professed himself interested and they cajoled Simon Frobisher to join them.

'Captain Bryant, will you be joining us?' Lady Medford asked.

'Certainly, if Kitty does not object?' He knew Kitty wasn't fond of shooting.

'I have a new book to read and will be perfectly content beside the fire.' Kitty smiled at him.

'Splendid,' Lady Medford declared. 'So, Hattie, Miss Hart, Mrs Cornwell and Kitty are to remain here and the rest of us will join the shoot.'

'I've asked my gamekeeper to set up for ten o'clock tomorrow in the eastern pasture near the woods. The mist is set to clear I believe.' Lord Medford beamed at them all and prepared to light his cigar.

Matt was glad that Kitty would have company at the Hall. With the strange figure lurking about he would have felt uneasy at her staying in the house alone. He knew many of the servants had been given a day off to see their families so there would be less staff in attendance.

'Excellent, my dear.' Lady Medford frowned at the smoke emanating from her husband's cigar. 'I do enjoy a shoot.'

'Mother is a first-rate shot and is horribly competitive,' Lucy declared.

'Nonsense.' Lady Medford blushed. 'It's true though, I learned to shoot when I was young. Your father was always an excellent shot, too, Kitty my dear.'

Kitty looked faintly surprised, since her aunt rarely said anything positive about her father.

'I must ask him about it in one of my letters.' She smiled at her aunt and Matt could see that she was genuinely fond of her father's family.

In the short time she had come to know them they had seemingly taken to her and she to them. Kitty and Lucy were as close as sisters.

'Time for a little music, and perhaps a spot of dancing,' Hattie declared, dropping the needle down on the gramophone record. She clapped her hands in glee as the soft sounds of a waltz commenced to play. Lord Medford extinguished his cigar and held out his hand to his wife.

'Hortense my dear.'

Lady Medford blushed an even deeper pink and took her husband's hand as a wider space was made for dancing. Victor gallantly offered his hand to Hattie, and Simon to Juliet.

'Kitty?' Matt asked.

There was little space but holding Kitty's slender form in his arms while swaying to the music was the closest thing to heaven that he knew. Over the years since he had lost his wife and child, he had come to dread Christmas.

He had hoped that spending this Christmas with Kitty at Enderley where there would be company would assuage those feelings and lay them to rest. Instead the weight of the brigadier's mission and Miss Plenderleith's unfortunate death had served to underline his thoughts.

Matt closed his eyes shutting out the darker thoughts bubbling at the fringe of his imagination. For now, he was with Kitty, enjoying her company and the dance.

CHAPTER FOURTEEN

Kitty awoke the next morning with a dry mouth and a fuzzy head.

'Alice, you are an absolute treasure.' She accepted the delicate china cup of tea from her maid and gulped a reviving sip. 'I rather think I may have had a little too much of my uncle's champagne last night.'

'If you did you wasn't on your own, miss. I heard that Miss Merriweather a singing her head off coming up the stairs last night. She in't no Billie Holiday. Some of them notes could fair fetch the wax out your earholes.' Alice shook her head and swished open the curtains to reveal a dull, grey morning.

'It looks as if it's a dry morning for the shoot.' Kitty looked out at the wind blowing the trees on the edge of the estate as she sipped her tea.

'The gamekeeper has already started preparing the guns and the inspector went off early back to Torquay. The roads are mostly clear now except for some high on the moors so Gladys said. Cook and Gladys said to thank you for their presents, miss. They was very pleased as you'd remembered them with a gift.' Alice bustled about the room, tidying and folding as she moved.

'Did you have a nice day yesterday?' Kitty had been concerned that Alice may have been missing her family.

'It was smashing, miss. We had a lovely dinner, his lordship sent some champagne for us and all just to toast the king when we heard him on Mrs Jenkinson's radio. I never had champagne before.' Alice sighed happily.

Kitty relaxed against her pillows and finished her tea. 'That was lovely. I'm looking forward to a nice quiet morning while the others are off shooting.' She glanced at her bedside table where the latest Dorothy L. Sayers book sat waiting for her to start reading.

A nice peaceful morning sounded like just the ticket after the social events of the last few days and Kitty was relishing the opportunity to simply sit quietly with her book and the box of delicious looking Austrian chocolates that the Vanderstrafens had gifted her for Christmas and maybe discover a little more about the guests who were not attending the shoot.

She was pleased to discover that most of the house party had already breakfasted when she ventured downstairs, with her book in her hand.

'Good morning, Kitty.' Victor was seated at the dining table with a cup of coffee before him.

'Good morning, are you looking forward to the shooting?' Kitty placed her book on the table and went to help herself to poached eggs and bacon.

She returned with a loaded plate to see Victor looking at her book. 'Yes, I think it will be very good. I like to be outside. You are fond of murder books?'

Kitty laughed as she sat down. 'Of the books, yes, of real-life murders, no. I hope the inspector catches Miss Plenderleith's killer soon.'

Victor's expression sobered. 'Indeed. Though I think the inspector has gone home to visit his family for a little while. It is difficult at this time of year to investigate when everyone is not in their place of work.'

Kitty selected a slice of toast from the silver rack and began applying butter. 'Very true. I hope the police will catch the man suspected of killing my mother too. He has connections to this area. Who knows, he may even be the man responsible for Miss Plenderleith's murder. He is known to be violent and desperate.'

Victor nodded. 'Yes, I have heard of what happened to your mother. Miss Hart was telling my sister and I about it. It must be very distressing. You have offered a reward she said?'

Kitty swallowed her bite of egg and toast before replying. 'Yes, we have a lead to follow up tomorrow in Exeter. I do hope we don't get more snow later or it could make getting into town very difficult.'

'If I can assist you with transport at any time, you must tell me.' The count finished the remains of his coffee and smiled at her.

'Thank you, that's most kind.' Kitty was pleasantly surprised by the offer.

'It would be my pleasure.' Victor took his leave and left Kitty to enjoy having the dining room to herself for a moment to eat her breakfast.

She had just poured herself a fresh cup of tea and selected some more toast when Miss Hart fluttered in. 'Good morning, Miss Underhay.'

Kitty greeted her and continued to spread strawberry jam on her toast as Miss Hart hovered indecisively next to the covered dishes on the sideboard. The elderly lady finally chose an egg and came to take her place at the table.

'I'm surprised you are not intending to watch the shooting, Miss Underhay,' Miss Hart remarked as she selected the smallest triangle of toast available in the rack.

'I'm looking forward to reading my book. I rather think field sports tend to be more fun for the participants rather than the onlookers,' Kitty said as she savoured her toast.

Miss Hart gave her a thin smile. 'Still, I suppose that you have little experience in such events, as a working person.'

Kitty licked a stray speck of jam from her finger. She wasn't sure exactly what Miss Hart was implying. 'It's true that running a busy establishment like the Dolphin leaves me with little leisure time, but I am quite familiar with field events. I just don't care for them.'

Miss Hart sniffed and nibbled at the edge of her toast. 'Miss Medford, of course, has had the benefit of an excellent education and exposure to the best society.'

Kitty narrowed her eyes. 'Yes, my cousin is very fortunate.'

'I myself have always been accustomed to moving in the upper echelons of society. I must admit I have felt a little disappointed, since agreeing to assist Lady Medford, at the level of person invited to this house, and indeed at the persons invited here now.' Miss Hart glanced around the dining room with a disparaging air.

'I'm sorry to hear that, Miss Hart.' Kitty forced herself to remain polite even though she was very tempted to put this woman firmly in her place.

'The count and his sister are of course aristocracy, but really, that American woman. Trousers, no sense of decorum. Then Miss Plenderleith confided in me that Mrs Baker is not the person I had taken her for.' Miss Hart took a sip of her tea.

'Really, Mrs Baker seems most respectable and well thought of.' Kitty was intrigued. Perhaps this could be what Mrs Vernon had been implying at the church.

Miss Hart snorted. 'Some question about the legality of her marriage to Mr Baker. Oh all very hush-hush, but Reverend Crabtree is aware I believe. I think I may have made a mistake accepting the position here. And with poor Miss Plenderleith's death, on the doorstep almost, it is quite shocking.'

'Well, I'm sure the murderer will be caught soon, and you can always seek another position. I'm sure my aunt will be able to find another companion more suited to her needs.' Kitty dabbed at the corners of her mouth with her napkin anxious to escape and enjoy her book.

Miss Hart appeared affronted as Kitty placed her napkin down and collected her book ready to find a quiet spot where she could read without being disturbed.

'My services are always highly sought after, Miss Underhay, I am very well connected.'

'Then I'm sure you will be able to find another position more conducive to your requirements, Miss Hart. If you'll excuse me.' Kitty swept out of the room leaving Miss Hart gaping indignantly after her.

She spotted Hattie heading towards the music room and loitered near the large grandfather clock hoping she wouldn't be seen.

'I think it's safe to come out now,' Matt's deep voice rumbled in her ear. He was dressed for shooting in a Harris Tweed suit.

She had been so focused on avoiding Hattie that she hadn't realised that Matt was behind her. 'Where did you come from? You made me jump.'

Matt laughed. 'Your uncle asked me to check something with Mr Harmon so I came along the staff corridor and saw you hiding.'

'I was not hiding. I was merely ensuring that I wasn't seen.' Kitty bit back a smile.

'I think everyone will be gathering soon ready to walk out to the field for the shoot. Are you sure you won't come?' Matt asked, his eyes twinkling.

'No, thank you. I have a pleasant morning planned in the company of my book.' She waved the paperback at him. This latest confirmation about Mrs Baker had also given her something to think about.

The sound of paws bounding down the stairs announced Muffy and Lucy's arrival in the hall. She was swiftly joined by the Vanderstrafens and Simon Frobisher.

'It seems you were right. Have a lovely morning. I'm going to sit in the library, I think. There should be a nice fire in there.' Kitty smiled up at Matt and dropped a quick discreet kiss on his cheek. 'I'll see you all later for lunch.'

She walked away quickly into the library before she could be seen by the others and persuaded into attending the shooting competition. The fire had indeed been made up and the room was a comfortable temperature.

Kitty tucked herself up on one of the large dark green leather studded armchairs near the fireplace and opened her book. Outside in the hallway she heard the hustle and bustle of the rest of the guests being marshalled by her aunt and uncle, punctuated by Muffy's excited barks.

Once the house became quiet again Kitty lost herself in her book, enjoying the pleasure of being alone for once. She only stirred an hour or so later realising her legs were stiff and she was in need of a cup of tea. She also realised that she had left her box of chocolates with a few of her other gifts under the Christmas tree in the drawing room.

She decided to stretch her legs and go to the drawing room to collect her chocolates. She could hear Hattie in the music room playing the piano and practising her scales. The door to the drawing room was ajar and Kitty slipped quietly inside hoping Miss Hart was not there. She didn't wish to encounter that lady again so soon after their clash at breakfast.

At first Kitty thought she was in luck and the room was empty. It wasn't until she was further into the room that she realised she was mistaken, and Delilah Cornwell was on her hands and knees under the Christmas tree.

Kitty paused for a moment. Delilah had obviously not heard her enter the room. To Kitty's surprise Delilah appeared to be busy going through the remaining gifts that people had not yet removed and taken to their rooms.

Kitty coughed artificially and watched as Delilah shot up from where she had been crouched over the small pile of gifts that belonged to Lucy.

'Oh my, Miss Underhay, you gave me quite the fright.' Delilah spread her hand dramatically across her heart.

'Can I help you, Mrs Cornwell? Have you misplaced something?' Kitty asked.

Spots of high colour had appeared on Delilah's cheeks. 'I seem to have lost one of my earrings last night while I was dancing and wondered if it could have been kicked under the tree.'

Kitty recalled that Delilah had been wearing some quite lovely emerald and diamond earrings in the Egyptian style. She certainly hadn't noticed her missing one of them and it seemed unlikely that the missing earring would land inside the remaining gifts.

'Oh dear, shall I help you look?' Kitty made the offer feeling quite certain that Delilah's earring was highly unlikely to be beneath the tree. It occurred to Kitty that perhaps Delilah had been behind the search of her room. But for what purpose?

'Well, I've had a good look, but I can't seem to see it. I dare say it will turn up. I'll ask Mrs Jenkinson to keep an eye out for it.' Delilah drifted away from the Christmas tree to take a seat on the sofa.

'I came to collect my chocolates and to ring for some tea.' Kitty picked up the pretty little box. 'Would you care for a cup?' She crossed to the side of the fireplace and tugged on the embroidered bell pull to summon one of the staff.

'Well, I dare say a cup of tea would be quite nice,' Delilah agreed.

Kitty gave her request to the maid who answered the bell and took a seat opposite Delilah.

'Hattie is in the music room I believe, although I don't know where Miss Hart has gone, unless my aunt has given her some tasks to keep her busy in her absence,' Kitty remarked as she opened her chocolates and studied the contents.

'Yes, I've heard Miss Merriweather practising.' Delilah winced slightly. 'Miss Hart was here when I first came in, but I think she's gone to the orangery.'

The maid entered the room carefully pushing a small trolley set with tea things.

'Thank you, we can see to ourselves.' Kitty smiled at the girl, aware that she probably had a large list of tasks from Mrs Jenkinson.

'Very good, miss.' The girl left the trolley next to Kitty and Kitty set out the delicate floral china cups and saucers for herself and Delilah.

'I must say I'm quite glad not to be outside on a freezing cold field,' Kitty remarked conversationally as she handed Delilah a cup of tea.

'I quite agree. I cannot abide the cold.' Delilah helped herself to sugar and stirred her drink.

Kitty took a sip of her tea then set the cup down to allow it to cool a little. 'You must be relieved when your husband's work takes him to warmer climates.' She smiled at Delilah. She seemed to recall from the conversation at dinner the other evening that the Cornwells had travelled extensively.

'My word, yes, although some places can get a little too warm. When we were in Egypt a couple of years ago, I swear I thought I was going to melt.'

Kitty selected one of her chocolates and popped it in her mouth, offering the box to Delilah who promptly refused.

'Matt was in Alexandria a couple of years ago, as were the Vanderstrafens. It's a small world, isn't it?' Kitty said after she had swallowed her sweet.

Mrs Cornwell gave a tight smile that didn't reach her eyes. 'I'm sure it is. Corny's work takes him all over the place meeting with manufacturers and securing contracts. Although don't ask me what it's all about as I'm sure I don't really understand the technicalities of all that engineering stuff. Corny always says to me, Lila, don't you worry your pretty little head about my work.'

Kitty picked up her tea and tried another sip. 'You must have visited some very interesting places?'

Delilah preened. 'Oh my, yes indeed. We've been all over. Corny always says he could write one of those travel guides.'

'And how are you enjoying a traditional English Christmas?' Kitty asked.

'Well, apart from poor Miss Plenderleith getting herself murdered, it's been mighty interesting. Lord and Lady Medford are just wonderful hosts. So very generous.' Delilah eyed her over her teacup. 'This must make a change for you too? From working at your hotel?' She opened her small handbag to retrieve her handkerchief, closing it swiftly when she realised that Kitty might be able to see the contents. Although Delilah was fast Kitty was prepared to bet her last shilling that she had glimpsed a small silver gun inside Delilah's handbag.

'Yes, it is rather. I'm very fortunate that Grams was able to spare me for a little while,' Kitty agreed, keeping her voice level, determined not to allow Delilah to detect that she had spotted anything untoward.

'Miss Hart was telling me that you've had your own share of quite disagreeable experiences this last year. What with being caught up in so many murders and your mother and all.' Delilah's voice was silky smooth.

'It has certainly been quite an eventful year,' Kitty replied. She sensed that Delilah intended to probe her, but she wasn't sure why. Or why Delilah would have a gun in her possession. 'I'm hoping to uncover some new information about my mother's death.'

Delilah's immaculately pencilled eyebrow lifted slightly. 'But, honey, it's been such a long time. Is there anything to be gained, now you've finally found her and laid her to rest?'

Kitty struggled to keep her temper in check. 'If anyone is still alive today who had a hand in my mother's death then I want to see them brought to justice. At the very least I need to know who killed her and how she came to be interred in the cellar of a public house.'

'Oh my, you poor thing. Of course, you must want answers.' Delilah hastily back-pedalled, her expression taking on a look of concern.

Kitty swallowed the last of her tea. 'At least the roads have cleared. Matt and I have an appointment tomorrow in Exeter with someone who may have some information for us.' She closed the lid on her box of chocolates. Her appetite for them had faded completely.

'Then I hope you manage to get the answers you're seeking,' Delilah said.

*

Outside in the east pasture the morning mist had faded away and the day was dull and dry. Pockets of snow lay here and there on the rough grass where the winter sun had failed to reach. Lady Medford had settled herself on her shooting stick and was talking amiably with Lucy and Juliet.

Lord Medford was giving Simon Frobisher instructions on how to use his gun. The gamekeeper was readying the clay pigeons ready for the start of the contest. Victor and Corny were selecting a gun and debating the merits of the various makes.

'Are we ready?' Lady Medford called.

'Almost, m'dear.' Lord Medford looked towards his gamekeeper and his assistant, who both nodded their heads to their master's unspoken question.

It had been agreed that the ladies were to shoot first. After drawing straws, Lucy went first and scored creditably. The young lad acting as assistant to the keeper chalked up her score on a small blackboard. Juliet went next. Victor stood next to Matt as his sister took her turn.

'I have not seen Juliet shoot for two years. I did not think at first that she would wish to participate,' Victor said, his gaze fixed on his sister's pale face.

'She was always an excellent shot,' Matt replied, hardly knowing what response to give. Juliet and Victor's relationship was a complex one.

It took Juliet a couple of cartridges to get her eye in, but Lucy was still in front when Lady Medford took her turn. It was very quickly apparent that Lady Medford was indeed both very competitive and an excellent shot.

'Well done, m'dear,' Lord Medford called as his wife resumed her perch on her shooting stick.

'Lady Medford is a first class shot.' Victor sounded impressed.

'Time to draw straws, gentlemen. We musn't allow ourselves to be outdone by the ladies.' Lord Medford approached to draw straws for the shooting order for the men.

Victor went first, his skills matched those of Lady Medford garnering him a grudging 'well done', from that lady.

He returned his gun to the gamekeeper and nodded at Matt. 'We could make this more fun. A little wager between us, perhaps? You were a good shot yourself once I seem to recall.'

'I haven't fired a shot in over twelve months,' Matt murmured as Corny stepped up to take his turn.

The corners of Victor's mouth twisted upwards. 'Five pounds and I'll give you two clays.'

Matt shrugged. 'Very well, if it amuses you.' The wager was relatively small by Victor's usual standards and he suspected this was more about the man's ego than the five pounds.

He noticed Simon Frobisher looking increasingly more nervous as it came closer to his turn. Every shot seemed to send a tremor through the man's tall, lean frame as the cartridges shattered the clay discs. He was surprised the man had agreed to attend the shoot if it had this effect upon him and he wondered if Simon too bore scars from the war.

'Corny is doing well,' Matt remarked conversationally to Simon. 'Your turn next.'

'Yes. I've never shot before.' Simon frowned as he watched Corny in action.

'Clay shoots are pretty straightforward,' Matt assured him.

'You did not shoot during the war?' Victor overheard the conversation; his tone held a faint note of derision.

'I was an ambulance driver,' Simon said stiffly. 'I have a weak heart.'

Victor moved away, evidently unimpressed by Simon's reason for not participating in the fighting. Matt guessed the man must have seen some pretty horrific sights as a driver. The sound of gunfire would no doubt trigger some of those memories, even when it was something as harmless as a clay pigeon shoot.

Corny finished his round with a creditable score and earned a round of applause from the rest of the group. Lord Medford stepped up to assist Simon with his gun, adjusting his position.

Victor watched with open derision on his face as Simon fired and missed every clay. Matt glanced at Juliet, curious to know what her reaction might be, but she appeared deep in conversation with Lucy.

Simon returned his gun to the gamekeeper with obvious relief and Matt wondered afresh why he'd agreed to attend this morning.

Lord Medford clapped him on the back. 'Better luck next time, old bean.'

Simon managed a weak smile and mumbled something in reply. Lord Medford took his turn, his shooting as good as his daughter's. It was clear that Lady Medford was the star shot in their household.

Matt was the final competitor of the morning. Victor smirked at him as he shouldered his gun. He sucked in a deep breath. It had been quite some time since he had fired a gun. He did however want to wipe the smile from Victor's face.

'Pull.' Matt tracked the clay and fired. The gun roared near his ear and the clay shattered. He released the breath he had been holding.

'Lucky shot,' Victor commented as the gamekeeper reloaded the trap and the assistant handed him fresh cartridges.

Matt's jaw squared and he raised his gun once more. 'Pull.'

Victor's expression changed as Matt held his nerve to hit target after target until the final clay was done.

'Well done. It seems you did not require an advantage after all.' Victor pulled out his wallet then hesitated.

Lord Medford looked enquiringly at the count.

'What do you say to double or nothing? Best of three clays each?' Victor suggested to Matt.

'A sporting wager to finish the morning, eh? Capital.' Lord Medford nodded his approval and the gamekeeper scurried to prepare the clays for the two of them.

Juliet frowned. 'Victor, really, I do not think this is a good idea.'

Victor scowled and ignored his sister.

Matt gritted his teeth. Victor had left him with no choice but to accept. He'd had no desire to participate in whatever mind game the count wished to play, but with the rest of the party looking on he had no other option.

They tossed a coin to decide who should shoot first. Victor won and opted to shoot. Matt stood back as Victor smirked and picked up his gun.

Juliet came closer to stand beside Matt. 'I am so sorry. I do not know what to say when he is in one of these moods,' she whispered.

Victor hit his first clay and waited while Matt took his gun from Lord Medford. He sucked in a breath to steady himself before he took aim. The clay shattered. One each.

The pattern was repeated on the second clay.

'Last one, Bryant.' Victor strode confidently to the mark.

The gun fired but this time the shot clipped the edge of the clay rather than shattering it cleanly.

'Oh bad show, old boy,' Lord Medford remarked as Victor returned his gun.

Bolstered by the count's ill luck Matt steadied himself and took aim. The clay shattered and Matt breathed a sigh of relief. His shoulder ached along his scar from the tension and extra exertion.

'Bravo!' Lady Medford rose from her shooting stick. 'Excellent shooting, Captain Bryant. Such a shame Kitty was not here to see it.'

He wondered if Kitty was enjoying her peace and quiet back at the Hall. He accepted the silver flask and miniature cup Lord Medford proffered and took a slug of the Scotch it contained. The fiery liquid making him cough even as it warmed his stomach.

Victor produced his wallet once more and paid his debt. 'Good shooting, Bryant. You have improved I think.'

Matt merely nodded and accepted the money wondering if he had imagined the small telltale bulge under the count's shooting jacket in the place where a small handgun might be kept. Victor had always used to carry a gun when he was abroad but why would he have it now?

'Well done, everyone.' Lord Medford looked at his watch. 'Perfect timing to head back for a spot of lunch.'

The group left the gamekeeper and his young helper to clear away and started the trek back across the field towards the sheep path that would lead them back into the main part of the grounds of Lord Medford's estate.

Simon Frobisher appeared to have recovered some of his colour and equanimity and was walking between Lucy and Juliet. Victor and Corny were walking together and Lady Medford had hold of her husband's arm.

Matt was content to loiter at the back of the group minding his own business. So far he felt he had seen little that would reward the brigadier's confidence in asking him to observe the group. There just remained the overall impression that something was off somehow, and the possibility that Victor was armed for some reason.

Yet Miss Plenderleith was dead and his and Kitty's rooms had definitely been searched by someone. Then there had been the ominous and threatening note that Kitty had received in the letters he had brought from his office. They had approached the field stile they needed to climb in order to enter the more manicured grounds of Enderley's estate. Matt had fallen a little behind the group.

Lucy and Juliet hopped over assisted by Victor and Simon. Corny and Lord Medford aided Lady Medford. Matt was about to clamber over the stile when he caught a flash of light in the trees and bushes near the boundary wall of the estate.

As he climbed over, he kept his gaze on the spot where he had seen the gleam of light. At first he thought he had imagined it, but he caught it again as he entered the field. There was someone down there amongst the trees. Someone using field glasses who had their party under observation.

A poacher perhaps? Unlikely at this time of day unless they thought the house party would be occupied at the Hall. A local man would know Lord Medford's traditions, however, so it seemed to him to be more reasonable that this was someone who was looking for their group.

He continued to follow the rest of the guests along the path, and when he looked back towards the trees the watcher seemed to have gone. He pondered a possible police presence or even someone dispatched by the brigadier. Both were possible. The brigadier could very well have made arrangements that had not been disclosed to either Lord Medford or himself.

Lady Medford had arranged for a late luncheon to accommodate the shooting party. Matt found Kitty in the drawing room with Hattie and Delilah.

'How was your morning?' Kitty asked as he entered the room.

'Very good. And yours?' He took a seat beside her.

She waved her book at him. 'I got to chapter five and only ate one chocolate. There, are you proud of me?'

He laughed. 'Then I expect you are longing for lunch.'

'Roast beef today,' Hattie said.

'Sounds delightful,' Matt responded politely.

The room filled with the rest of the party and the gong sounded from the hall to summon them into the dining room.

Kitty caught Matt's sleeve as they went to file out into the hall. 'I need to speak to you,' she whispered.

He nodded an acknowledgement as they took their places at the table. He wondered what she had discovered in his absence and what she would make of Victor's wager at the shoot. He had no intention of mentioning that he thought Victor was carrying a gun, however.

CHAPTER FIFTEEN

Lunch was delicious and very welcome. Tomato soup and roast sirloin of beef followed by fruit compote. Conversation at the table was centred around the morning's activities and plans for the evening.

As soon as was decently possible, Kitty and Matt slipped away from the others.

'Billiard room,' Kitty whispered.

Once they were inside, Matt closed the door. Kitty had avoided it so far during this visit to Enderley. Memories from her previous stay were still fresh from when she and Lucy had been attacked in that very room.

She quickly told Matt what Miss Hart had said about Mrs Baker and about Delilah's behaviour. 'Do you think she may have been behind the search of our rooms?'

She could see Matt considering her question. 'I'm not sure why she would do so, unless perhaps she is some kind of petty thief.'

'Nothing was taken, though.' Kitty frowned. She wished Matt would spill the beans and tell her what he was really up to at Enderley. She was willing to wager that Delilah's odd behaviour was somehow connected with it all. 'She also has a gun in her handbag.'

Matt's brows raised. 'Many Americans do carry guns.'

Kitty was not convinced but let the comment slide. Perhaps this was all to do with the conversation she had overheard between Matt and her uncle.

'There was something strange at the shoot this morning.' Matt told her about his suspicions that someone had been watching the group.

'Do you think Inspector Greville may have asked the local police constable to maintain his observations? My uncle had mentioned to him about the person hanging around the church before Christmas.' Kitty thought this could well be a possibility.

Especially since Miss Plenderleith's murder.

'Inspector Greville is expected back in time for tea this evening. We can ask him then,' Matt suggested.

'Tomorrow we shall need to organise a car to take us into Exeter. My uncle has offered the use of his Bentley and chauffeur.' Kitty crossed her slender lisle stocking clad legs.

'That's very good of him. I take it he would rather you not ride pillion again on my motorcycle?' Matt grinned at her.

Colour pinked her cheeks. 'I do hope word of that doesn't reach Grams' ears.'

'Or Mrs Craven's.' Matt's smile grew wider at the idea of Mrs Craven discovering that Kitty had been aboard his Sunbeam.

'I suspect she would be as disapproving as Miss Hart is about Mrs Cornwell's trousers. Although I have to say I think they look rather fetching and very comfortable.' Kitty sniffed.

They passed their time peacefully bickering and discussing their fellow guests until Kitty sat up suddenly. 'Matt, shush, can you hear that?'

Matt stilled and joined her in listening. Somewhere in the distance a bell clanged.

'That's the church bell, I'm sure of it. But there are no services due today, and especially not at this time. It's already growing dark.' Kitty jumped to her feet.

They dashed into the hall where they were met by Mr Harmon looking unusually flustered.

'Sir, miss, the church bell appears to be sounding.'

'Please don't worry, Mr Harmon. Captain Bryant and I shall investigate. Perhaps you could inform my uncle discreetly of what has happened?' Kitty said.

The rest of the party appeared to be oblivious to the faint sound as Kitty heard the sounds of music and hum of general chatter coming from the drawing room.

'Come on.' Kitty tugged Matt towards the cloakroom, and they hurried into their coats. 'It seems I must shock the populace once more.'

Matt groaned as he threw the tarpaulin back from his motorcycle. Outside in the gloomy cold air the mournful note of the bell sounded even louder. In the distance the sinking sun had already begun to paint the sky with shades of orange and pink.

Matt climbed onto the Sunbeam and fired up the engine as Kitty swiftly hitched up her skirt and hopped onto the pillion behind him.

'Hurry, Matt, there is something wrong at the church, I know it.'

She held on tightly and pressed her head against his back as they roared off down the drive. Kitty decided that if this were to become a habit she might need to invest in trousers like Delilah's. Skirts were horribly impractical for riding pillion.

Matt pulled to a halt in front of the lychgate. The lights were on inside the church and the main door stood slightly ajar. A couple of black-framed bicycles stood against the church wall. Kitty had dismounted from the Sunbeam before Matt had time to stop the engine. The remorseless clang of the bell sounded again.

'Kitty, wait,' Matt called as she went to hurry along the path to the church. 'We don't know who is in there or what this is about.'

He caught her up and went in front of her as they made their way inside. The interior of the church was ice cold and deserted. The nativity stood unaltered, but Kitty could see that the embroidered cloth that had adorned the altar was gone, as were the tall silver candlesticks that had been present the day before during the service.

'Hello, who's in here?' Matt's voice echoed off the ancient stone-work as the bell clanged once more making Kitty's eardrums ring.

'Bell tower.' Matt led the way to the small arch topped door that led to the vestry and the tower. Kitty followed in his wake, her heart thumping.

'Hello!' Matt called again as they entered the tiny vestry.

'Who's that?' a gruff male voice responded, startling Kitty.

'Captain Bryant and Miss Underhay, from the Hall,' Matt answered.

The door leading to the bell tower opened slightly and Kitty peered around Matt to see Mr Golightly, the verger. His complexion was waxy under the harsh green-shaded electric light of the vestry.

'Best as you stay there, miss. Sir, come through here, I needs your help urgent like.' The verger swallowed and looked at Matt.

'Stay here for a moment, Kitty, while I see what's amiss. I expect your uncle to be here shortly,' Matt murmured and went through the door into the tower. The door closed firmly behind him much to Kitty's chagrin.

She heard bumping and scraping noises inside the bell tower and male voices in muted conversation. The door opened once more, and Matt looked out.

'What is it? What's happened?' Kitty asked.

'Reverend Crabtree is dead. Mr Golightly found him when he came to check on the church.' Matt's face was sombre.

Kitty gasped. She hadn't expected this. 'How?'

Matt emerged into the vestry. 'Mr Golightly discovered him hanging from a rope thrown over one of the beams. He had been there for some time it seems and was beyond help.'

'He has taken his own life?' Kitty asked, still trying to understand what Matt was telling her.

The verger appeared in the doorway. 'Happen as that's what someone would like us to believe,' he replied darkly.

Kitty looked at Matt.

'I have advised Mr Golightly that the bell tower be locked until the police can come. Inspector Greville is due back at the Hall at any moment. I think Dr Carter is best placed to form a hypothesis of what has happened to the vicar.' Matt glanced at the verger.

Kitty itched to enter the bell tower and take a look for herself.

'Mr Golightly, this must have affected you greatly.' The man was trembling and his forehead was clammy with sweat. She was concerned for the elderly man's health.

'Indeed, miss. I admit I was not fond of Reverend Crabtree. Not many folk were, but for this to happen, in the sanctity of the church.' The man shook his head.

'Go outside for a moment and take some air. I'll lock the door and see no one enters.' Matt held out his hand and the verger thrust a large iron ring containing a set of keys at him before he stumbled past Kitty into the church.

As soon as he was gone Matt opened the bell tower door. 'Be careful to touch nothing. I should like your opinion before the police arrive.'

Her pulse quickened as she entered the bell tower. It was a small square space with a narrow stone flight of stairs leading to the upper floor where the one great bell hung from a thick oak beam. A thick rope hung down from the bell, which Kitty surmised was the one used by the verger to summon help to the church. Above her head was another set of beams running crosswise, and around one of them she noticed the cut end of a piece of rope, thinner than the one used to sound the bell.

The body of Reverend Crabtree lay to the side, his face thankfully turned towards the wall. Kitty could see the rest of the rope still tight about the vicar's neck just above his white clerical collar. A small brown wooden stool stood neatly beside the wall.

'The rope used to hang him is the secondary rope which usually secures the bell to stop it swinging about if it gets very windy. The top of the tower is open to the elements at the sides,' Matt explained.

'Why does Mr Golightly think that there is something wrong?' Kitty asked.

'There is a large lump on the back of the reverend's head suggesting he was hit by something before being strung up. The stool was also in the position it is in now. If he had hung himself, he would have kicked it away. I would have expected to see it in a different place.' Matt looked around the space.

'I see. I wonder if Mr Golightly knows about the candlesticks?' Kitty mused.

'Candlesticks?' Matt frowned at her.

'The altar cloth is missing along with the silver candlesticks that were there for yesterday's service. They may have been put away of course but I have a feeling they have been taken. Strange though, the vicar's watch is still on his wrist.' Kitty shivered.

'And his wallet is still in his pocket.' Matt checked quickly. 'Come, let's lock this door and go and find the verger.' Matt's mouth was compressed in a grim line.

Kitty waited in the vestry while he secured the door. Outside the church they heard the sound of a motor car coming to a halt.

'I expect your uncle may have arrived. Let us hope the inspector is with him.'

*

Matt was relieved to see that the familiar black shape of Inspector Greville's police vehicle was halted next to the Sunbeam. Sure enough, Lord Medford had accompanied the inspector and they were both now in urgent conversation with the verger.

Kitty nudged his elbow. 'Let's go and see what Mr Golightly has to say about the candlesticks.'

She held his arm as they walked along the path to the gate. Inspector Greville nodded and tipped his hat to Kitty as they approached.

'Kitty, Captain Bryant, Mr Golightly was just telling us what's happened.' Lord Medford appeared perturbed and Matt knew he was thinking of the information they had received from Whitehall. Was this latest death something to do with the alleged agent amongst the house party?

'Mr Golightly, I noticed that the silver candlesticks are gone from the altar along with the linen altar cloth. Have they been locked away?' Kitty asked.

The verger's face paled and he began to visibly tremble. 'I never noticed, miss. My mind was that took up worrying about the dratted roof with the snow melt that I was a gazing up until I went through to the bell tower.' He paused and gulped. 'Then, when I saw the vicar a dangling there, I could see as there were nothing I could do for him and I couldn't get him down on my own. I thought as if I rang the bell as someone would hear it and come. I never looked upon the altar.'

Matt exchanged a glance with the inspector. 'So, the candlesticks may have been stolen? You feel it unlikely that Reverend Crabtree would have removed them?'

The verger shook his head. 'The vicar didn't bother about such things. He only came to the church when there was a service due or iff'n I called on him to come see something as wanted mending.'

Matt held out the bunch of keys. 'I locked the tower, sir. Everything is as Mr Golightly discovered it, except of course we took Reverend Crabtree down.'

Inspector Greville took the keys. 'Mr Golightly, may I trouble you to accompany me?'

The verger walked back towards the church at the inspector's side.

'This is a pretty kettle of fish and no mistake. Kitty m'dear, forgive me but this is no place for you. Perhaps you would care to take a seat in the inspector's motor until he returns. It's growing very dark and cold now,' Lord Medford suggested.

At first Matt thought Kitty was about to refuse her uncle's suggestion but then she nodded and smiled demurely at him. 'Of course, Uncle.' Her ready acquiescence took Matt by surprise.

Once she was safely stowed on the back seat of the inspector's car, Lord Medford walked a little further away.

'Golightly said he didn't think it was suicide and now Kitty says the candlesticks are missing.' Lord Medford pulled out his cigarette case and proffered it towards Matt.

Matt accepted a cigarette and the two men shared a light from his lordship's silver monogrammed lighter. The sight of the vicar dangling like a broken puppet from the end of the rope had shaken him more than he'd expected.

'I expect Greville will want Doctor Carter to confirm it, but it looks to me, sir, as if the vicar was knocked out before whoever killed him strung him up. The missing candlesticks may provide a motive, but we cannot rule out that this may be somehow connected with this agent.' Matt blew out a thin stream of blue grey smoke and glanced towards the car where Kitty sat watching them. 'There also remains the possibility, sir, that this is connected with Ezekiel Hammett.'

Lord Medford frowned. 'The fella that murdered his brother? The one Kitty is trying to find?'

'Yes, sir. Kitty, as you know, is convinced that he may be in the area. She has received a threatening letter.'

All around them now was dark, somewhere in the wood an owl hooted. The tips of their cigarettes glowed red in the night.

'Hmpph, I suppose she could be right. I expect the inspector will take that into consideration.' Lord Medford finished his cigarette.

Matt followed suit as Inspector Greville and the verger reappeared from inside the church.

'I need to telephone Doctor Carter and inform the local constabulary. May I use your telephone, sir?' the inspector asked Lord Medford.

'Of course.'

'Captain Bryant, I wonder if you would mind remaining here with the verger until I return?' The inspector glanced at Mr Golightly who still appeared shaken by the unpleasant events of the afternoon.

'Certainly, sir.' Matt wanted to poke a little more around the church just to see if there was anything that might provide some kind of clue.

He knew Kitty would be pretty annoyed at being sidelined so he would have to try and provide her with as much information as possible on his return to the Hall.

He watched the inspector drive away with Kitty and her uncle and went to join Mr Golightly inside the church.

*

The short drive back to Enderley was silent. Neither the inspector nor her uncle appeared inclined to talk. Kitty's head was busy with questions, but she knew that she was unlikely to get answers right at that moment in time.

She was, however, determined to get as much information as possible from Matt when he returned to the Hall. Before Inspector Greville went to her uncle's study to make his calls, she quickly told him what she had learned about Mrs Baker.

'Thank you, Miss Underhay. This ties in with the information Mr Frobisher has given me previously about his uncle and the rumours of blackmail in his former parish. I shall have to speak to Mrs Baker too.'

Kitty removed her outdoor clothing and tidied herself in the cloakroom before returning to the drawing room to warm up before the fire.

Her aunt was seated beside the fire with Miss Hart. Hattie was completing a jigsaw puzzle and Count Vanderstrafen was reading a book when she entered the room.

'My dear Kitty, wherever have you been? Harmon came in with such a tale,' her aunt exclaimed.

Kitty was unsure how much detail the inspector would wish her to share, but news of the vicar's demise was bound to spread quite quickly.

'Matt and I went to the church to find out why the bell was ringing.' Kitty came to stand closer to the fire. The air outside had chilled her.

'Your uncle has gone there too with the inspector. Harmon seemed quite perturbed about it all.' Lady Medford looked at Kitty's legs and Kitty realised that she had acquired a few splashes of mud on her stockings thanks to her ride on Matt's motorcycle.

'Yes, they are in the study. I believe the inspector has to place some telephone calls,' Kitty edged.

Lady Medford raised an eyebrow. 'I see. Did you establish a reason for the bell being sounded?'

'Regretfully, yes, Reverend Crabtree is dead.' Kitty felt she had to tell her aunt the truth.

Miss Hart gasped and pressed her handkerchief to her mouth. 'Oh dear, what kind of place is this? At Christmas too.'

'The vicar is dead?' Count Vanderstrafen set aside his book.

'What happened? Did you see him? Who was ringing the bell?' Hattie asked, her eyes gleaming with excitement.

Kitty was saved from answering when her uncle entered the room.

'My dear, is this true? Kitty says that Reverend Crabtree is dead?' Her aunt looked expectantly at her husband.

Lord Medford placed a hand on his wife's shoulder. 'I'm afraid so, m'dear. Golightly's brother, the verger, found him at the church.'

'Well, what happened? An accident, a heart attack? What is it?' Lady Medford demanded.

'It appears that the church has been robbed. Some valuable silver candlesticks taken from the altar. The vicar it seems has been murdered.' Lord Medford glanced at Kitty as he spoke. She was relieved he didn't provide any details of how Reverend Crabtree had been killed.

'Another murder! One is not safe in one's bed. I'm sorry, Lady Medford, but when I accepted this position I really did not expect to be thrust into a hotbed of crime,' Miss Hart wailed.

'Oh, do be quiet, Miss Hart. I cannot bear histrionics from either my staff or my family.' Lady Medford glared at her hapless companion who subsided into a sulky silence at the force of the reproof.

'Inspector Greville is breaking the news to Mr Frobisher. He is, after all, the vicar's nephew, even if they were not on good terms,' Lord Medford said.

'Of course, I had forgotten that,' Count Vanderstrafen mused.

Kitty too had temporarily forgotten Simon Frobisher's familial connection with the late Reverend Crabtree. She wondered how Simon would feel. He hadn't seemed to like or approve of his uncle but nonetheless he was family.

The clock on the mantelpiece chimed the hour.

'I expect we shall discover more when the inspector has made his enquiries. In the meantime, I shall go and dress for dinner.' Lady Medford rose. 'Come, Miss Hart.'

'Two murders,' Hattie said gleefully and followed Lady Medford and Miss Hart out of the room.

'You are inclined to think these deaths are linked, sir?' Victor asked, looking at Lord Medford.

'Well, money was taken from Miss Plenderleith's and now these candlesticks are gone.' Lord Medford rubbed his chin thoughtfully. 'What say you, Kitty?'

Kitty was pleasantly surprised to be consulted. 'Robbery could be the motive for both, I agree, sir, but why hang Reverend Crabtree? Why not simply finish him off with a bash over the head? Does it not seem a little odd?'

'The vicar was hanged?' Victor asked. 'Most puzzling. It was not a suicide? He was, I think, suspected of robbing Miss Plenderleith, was he not?'

'Hmm, I expect we shall learn more when Doctor Carter has paid a visit,' Lord Medford mused.

'Matt may be able to tell us something when he returns also,' Kitty said.

'Captain Bryant is still at the church?' Victor enquired in a silky tone. 'Is he part of the investigative team?'

Kitty found the question slightly irritating. 'No, not at all. It was simply that the poor verger was most distressed by the discovery and the inspector asked Matt if he would stay with him until the constable and Doctor Carter arrived to take over.' She smiled at her uncle. 'You must excuse me, I must go and change for dinner.'

'Of course, m'dear, run along.' Her uncle smiled back at her.

Kitty nodded to the count and escaped upstairs.

CHAPTER SIXTEEN

Alice had already heard about the vicar's death.

'Mr Harmon heard it from the inspector and Gladys overheard him telling Mrs Jenkinson. Then our Mr Golightly wanted to go and see his brother. They share a cottage together as they've never married and he was proper worried about him,' Alice explained as she bustled about the bedroom, tutting at the mud stains on Kitty's stockings and her skirt.

'The church candlesticks are missing so I think the inspector believes that the vicar may have been killed by the thief.' Kitty tugged off her stockings and handed them to Alice.

'Two murders and it being Christmas and all.' Alice shivered and pulled a face. 'And to kill a vicar in his own church. Shocking that is.' She gathered up a pile of towels. 'Your bath is run ready, miss. I started it thinking as you would be up. It just needs the bath salts and a dash more hot in it.'

'Thank you, Alice.' Trust her maid to have thought of everything. She took the towels and her robe and crossed the landing to immerse herself in the deliciously warm, rose-scented water.

It was lovely to lose herself for a short while and relax without fretting about Ezekiel Hammett or Matt or who might have murdered the vicar and Miss Plenderleith. Something was bothering her about both deaths, but she couldn't quite work out what it was.

Alice had selected a black silk crepe dress with silver embroidery for her to wear to dinner.

'I thought it best, miss, in the circumstances. With Mr Frobisher being related and all.'

'Yes, it will be interesting to see how he has taken the news of his uncle's death.' Kitty shimmied into her dress.

Alice set to fastening the tiny buttons at the back with her deft, nimble fingers. 'I don't reckon as the vicar will be much mourned, miss. Gladys says as how he was known to be a bit smarmy like with the ladies. Not at all like a vicar, and there's tales abroad of him not knowing the difference between mine and thine as me dad says.'

'It must have been difficult for Mr Golightly's brother, the verger, having to work with such a man.' Kitty sat down obediently so Alice could brush and dress her hair.

'He weren't happy. Gladys says as he wrote to the bishop himself and your aunt wrote as well.' Alice brushed Kitty's short blonde hair with short strokes before swapping to a pin tail comb to tease some curls back in. 'Mr Golightly told Mr Harmon as he reckoned as the vicar had been for the high jump in the new year.'

Kitty winced as Alice enthusiastically secured her narrow silver headband to her hair with a bobby pin. 'I wonder if Matt has discovered anything more from Doctor Carter.'

Alice fastened a silver chain around her neck. 'I expect as Captain Bryant will have been having a good look about, miss.' Her gaze met with Kitty's in the dressing table mirror. 'That's what they would do in the films.'

*

Doctor Carter was his usual cheerful self as he entered the church carrying his battered leather medical bag. 'Here we are again then, better let the dog see the rabbit.' He clapped Matt on the arm and wished the verger a good evening as Matt took him into the bell tower.

He made a speedy but efficient examination of the late vicar. 'Definitely a large contusion on the back of his head caused shortly before death. Unlikely to have occurred accidentally.' He looked at the rope around Reverend Crabtree's neck. 'I take it the man was attached to that beam up there?' He indicated the frayed end of rope still attached to the rafter where Matt had cut the vicar down with his penknife.

'Yes, sir. The verger discovered him when he came to check the roof.'

'He must have been killed much earlier in the day I should say. Probably early this morning judging by the state of his skin and the rigidity.' The doctor scrambled to his feet. 'Odd time of day for him to have been here I'd have thought. There's no service or anything was there?'

'No, sir, and the verger said the vicar never came to the church unless he sent for him or for a service. Perhaps he came to meet someone,' Matt confirmed.

Inspector Greville arrived with the local constable just as he spoke.

'Good evening, Doctor. I take it your findings agree with our suspicions?'

Doctor Carter's cheerful face beamed at them. 'Absolutely. I'm all done here. My estimate is that your man was killed early this morning. I think I've just heard my men arrive to take him to the mortuary, is that all right with you, Inspector?'

'I don't think we'll find much else out here. I'm going to go to the vicarage to see if there's anything there.' Inspector Greville shook hands with the doctor and wished him a good evening.

'Would you care for some company at the vicarage, sir?' Matt asked.

The inspector nodded. 'If you're up for it, Captain Bryant. It may make us rather late for dinner.'

Matt grinned. 'I'm sure Lady Medford will understand under the circumstances.'

The two men walked back into the church leaving the constable to deal with the mortuary attendants. The verger was only too glad to be dismissed with the promise that the constable would secure the church and return the keys to him when they were done.

'Begging your pardon, sir, but what shall I do with the vicar's bicycle?' the verger asked as he collected his own cycle from by the church gate.

'The vicar had assured me that he didn't own a bicycle when I questioned him after Miss Plenderleith's death. He insisted that it had been stolen a few days earlier. Lock it in the church for now,' the inspector instructed. 'We can deal with that later.'

Matt followed the inspector's police car on his motorcycle. The wind had started to rise and the light from the police car and motorcycle headlamps threw strange and eerie shadows across the road.

The vicarage was in darkness. A square red-brick building with a tiled roof, it had a straggly, unkempt front garden surrounded by a beech hedge. The brown leaves rustled and rattled in the breeze as they unlatched the wooden sunray patterned garden gate to walk down the path.

'The verger said there was a spare key under the doormat.' The inspector grunted as he bent to lift the mat sending a small woodlouse skittering over the toe of his shoe as he retrieved the key.

The inspector unlocked the front door and reached inside to turn on the light. Matt followed the inspector inside the surprisingly spacious hall. A small pile of post lay opened on an old-fashioned oak table beside the black telephone.

Inspector Greville started leafing through them, his eyebrows raising when he read the uppermost one on the pile.

'It seems Reverend Crabtree was indeed in trouble with the bishop. This is a letter inviting him to a meeting in the new year to discuss various concerns that have come to light. Hmm.'

He picked up the telephone receiver and listened. 'And it seems the problem with the line has been resolved.'

Matt walked to the end of the hall and turned on the kitchen light. He heard the inspector placing a call to Enderley informing their hosts that they would be late for dinner. From the appearance of the kitchen it seemed as if the vicar had been having breakfast when he had suddenly decided to leave and go to the church. A half-eaten slice of toast still lay on the plate next to a cold half-drunk cup of tea.

A peep into the dining room and lounge revealed nothing out of place, a small Christmas tree was on the table in the window and a handful of cards stood on the mantelpiece. There were no photographs or personal items on display other than the Christmas cards. The inspector led the way up the polished oak staircase. Two of the bedrooms were bare and empty, the iron bed frames stripped bare. It seemed the vicar was not anticipating receiving any guests over Christmas.

Inspector Greville turned the round brass doorknob to open the door to the vicar's bedroom. It was the only door upstairs that was closed.

'It appears Reverend Crabtree was planning a trip,' Matt remarked. The bed was made but the wardrobe doors were ajar revealing empty hangers. A cursory examination of the chest of drawers revealed that it too, had been emptied. Two large brown suitcases stood at the end of the bed and a small brown leather bag lay open on top of the bed covers.

Inspector Greville was busy looking through the contents of the open bag. 'The reverend appears to have quite a sum of money stashed in here.'

Matt's eye widened as the inspector pulled out a bundle of white banknotes. 'An awful lot for a man of the cloth. No sign of the candlesticks though. I take it, Kitty told you the story she heard regarding Mrs Baker and the possibility that the vicar may have been blackmailing her?'

'Yes, I intend to verify that with Mrs Baker tomorrow. Mr Frobisher has provided me with information that he had discovered about his uncle blackmailing another person in one of his previous parishes. Nothing could be proved however as the alleged victim took his own life.'

Matt noticed a few fragments of paper in the grate amongst the ashes. He crouched down to try and extract them.

'I rather think, sir, that I have discovered what became of those missing pages from the accounts.' Matt showed the inspector the fragment of paper. A few figures and lines clearly showed it was from a balance sheet of some kind.

'Indeed.' Greville produced an envelope from his pocket and carefully tucked the discovery inside.

Their conversation was interrupted by the shrill trilling of the telephone in the hall. Matt headed downstairs, closely followed by the inspector, to answer the call.

'Mervyn darling, at last, I was beginning to become concerned.'

Matt recognised the breathy tones of Mrs Vernon. 'Good evening, Mrs Vernon, this is Captain Bryant—'

He didn't get an opportunity to say anything more before Mrs Vernon cut in. 'Captain Bryant? But why are you answering the vicarage telephone? I have been connected properly, haven't I?'

Matt handed the receiver to Inspector Greville. 'Mrs Vernon,' he murmured.

'Mrs Vernon, this is Inspector Greville. I'm afraid Reverend Crabtree is unable to come to the telephone.' He looked at Matt as he spoke, and both men waited for Mrs Vernon's response.

'Inspector Greville, I don't understand. Is something wrong? Is Mervyn in any kind of trouble? I was expecting him this evening for supper after he had seen you at the Hall.' The shrill anxious notes of Mrs Vernon's reply reached Matt and his brows raised.

'I take it that you and Reverend Crabtree have a close friendship, Mrs Vernon?' Matt knew the inspector was phrasing the question delicately in an attempt to gain as much information as possible before breaking the news of the vicar's demise.

'Well, of course. It's not public just yet but, well, Mervyn and I are engaged to be married. May I speak with him, Inspector? Is he there? If there is a misunderstanding, then I'm sure it can be worked out.' Mrs Vernon sounded anxious and Matt wondered how much she knew about her alleged fiancé.

'I'm very sorry to have to tell you this, Mrs Vernon, but unfortunately Reverend Crabtree was found dead just a few hours ago.' The inspector winced as he spoke, and Matt sympathised. It was not a pleasant job to have to break such shocking and terrible news on a telephone call.

There was a moment's silence and Matt wondered if the woman on the other end of the line had fainted.

'Mrs Vernon, are you still there? Are you all right?' the inspector asked.

'Yes, I'm sorry, for a moment I thought you said Mervyn was dead.'

'The verger found him at the church this afternoon. Sadly he was beyond aid. I wonder, Mrs Vernon, do you know if he might have been intending to meet someone at the church this morning?' the inspector asked.

Mrs Vernon's voice sounded tearful and shocked. 'No, Mervyn was coming to my home for supper. I can't believe it. I've just finished packing my trunk. We were leaving tomorrow to get married in London and to start a new life together. We were going to France on the boat train and then heading south.' Her voice broke with a sob. 'This is awful, what happened to him? Was it his heart?'

'I'm afraid it seems he was murdered. Do you know of anyone who the vicar may have upset or quarrelled with recently?'

Matt listened carefully for Mrs Vernon's response.

She gave a bitter laugh. 'Mervyn was a greatly misunderstood man, Inspector. His nephew, Simon Frobisher, held a grudge against him I believe. Of course things were awkward as well between Mervyn and Mr Golightly, the verger. He wrote to the bishop, the nerve of the man. Mervyn also argued with Count Vanderstrafen and with Mr Cornwell at the drinks party at the Hall. All over that dreadful incident with Mrs Baker and Miss Plenderleith getting upset. He was terribly hurt that he might be suspected of injuring Miss Plenderleith.' Mrs Vernon's tone took on an accusatory note at this point.

'I see, thank you, Mrs Vernon. Just one more question if you wouldn't mind. Reverend Crabtree was in possession of a large sum of money at the time of his death. Do you have any idea where it may have come from?' the inspector asked.

'I don't think I like what you are implying, Inspector. Naturally Mervyn had money, we were about to be married and were intending to travel.' The call ended abruptly.

Inspector Greville appeared thoughtful as he replaced the receiver in its cradle. 'Well, well, I suppose I shall have to check the vicar's bank accounts tomorrow. Funny thing though, but if the motive for murdering the vicar was robbery it seems strange that they only took the candlesticks.'

'Kitty noticed the vicar had quite a good quality watch on his wrist and his wallet was still in his pocket when I checked,' Matt said.

'Did she now?' The inspector's lips quirked. 'I might have known Miss Underhay would spot that.'

'Perhaps they were in a hurry, sir,' Matt suggested.

'Perhaps, but they took time to string the poor soul up and the church is remote so it's unlikely they would have been disturbed.' Inspector Greville shook his head. 'Odd, very odd indeed.'

The inspector collected the bundle of notes from the vicar's bedroom before they left the house, locking the front door behind them.

'I'll ask Lord Medford to keep the money in his safe for now and I'll hang on to the vicarage key. I don't fancy putting it back under the mat. I rather think this may be the money taken from Miss Plenderleith's.' The inspector prepared to climb back into the police car. 'Let's hope her ladyship has asked for a plate to be kept for us.'

Matt bit back a smile as he clambered back onto the Sunbeam. Only Inspector Greville could think of his stomach in the midst of a murder investigation.

*

The main topic of conversation over dinner, naturally enough, was the murder of Reverend Crabtree. Although, with the exception of Hattie who appeared incapable of tact, everyone was suitably polite in front of Simon Frobisher.

Simon appeared to be completely numbed by the news that his uncle had been murdered. Kitty decided her best option was to remain silent and to keep her ears open. She had no wish to be quizzed by the others about why she had accompanied Matt to the church and what she had seen while she was there.

Matt and Inspector Greville had not yet returned by the time the ladies adjourned into the drawing room for coffee. Kitty wished she knew what was happening. Had the inspector an idea of who the murderer might be?

'Now that Simon is out of the way, tell us all what you saw at the church, Kitty.' Hattie squashed herself on the sofa in between Kitty and Lucy.

'I didn't really see anything.' Kitty accepted a cup of coffee from Miss Hart.

'I think it is most distasteful. The vicar is dead, and we could all be murdered in our beds.' Miss Hart glared at Hattie.

'Oh pish, was there blood?' Hattie persisted.

'Hattie!' Lucy protested.

Hattie shrugged her plump organza covered shoulders and nudged Kitty. 'You must have seen something. You went haring off with Captain Bryant on his motorcycle.'

Miss Hart gave a loud tut and glared disapprovingly at Kitty.

'Really, I didn't see anything at all,' Kitty demurred.

Hattie gave a frustrated sigh. 'Reverend Crabtree was not very well liked. He was rude to everyone at the drinks party. He slighted poor Simon and I saw him arguing with Corny and Victor.'

'I didn't know he argued with Victor or Corny,' Kitty said.

'Well, in Corny's case it wasn't really an argument, honey,' Delilah cut in. 'Corny heard the vicar say something, I forget what now, that absolutely wasn't true. Well, Corny corrected him and the man insisted he was right. He wasn't and he didn't like Corny pointing it out.' Delilah sipped her coffee. 'It was nothing at all really.'

Kitty looked at Juliet who was seated on the low stool playing with Muffy.

'What did the vicar argue with Victor about?' Kitty asked her.

Juliet continued to stroke Muffy. 'I don't think it was an argument.' She frowned as if trying to remember. 'It was after Miss Plenderleith came back from sponging her dress. She spoke to Reverend Crabtree and then just before Miss Plenderleith left the vicar said something to Victor. I assumed it was something tactless, perhaps about my country. Victor was annoyed I think, but really I don't know if it was an argument.'

The gentlemen rejoined the ladies although Simon was not among them.

'Is Mr Frobisher all right?' Lady Medford asked.

'He has gone upstairs. I think the events of the day have distressed him rather,' Lord Medford said as he took one of the wooden framed more upright occasional seats near his wife.

'Have we heard any more from the inspector and Captain Bryant?' Lady Medford picked up her tapestry work.

'They've not long come back, m'dear. Mrs Jenkinson has arranged for them to dine in the library. I daresay they will join us when they are finished,' Lord Medford said.

Hattie clapped her hands together in glee, her bracelets jangling. 'Oh goody, then we might find out exactly what happened. I wonder if they've made an arrest.'

'Indeed.' Victor had settled himself next to Juliet.

'Well, this is a fun Christmas, isn't it?' Lucy remarked and smiled apologetically at Kitty. 'To think I promised you a Christmas with no murders back when I visited you at the Dolphin.'

Kitty laughed. 'I'd forgotten that. Oh dear.'

'I fail to see the humour, not when poor Miss Plenderleith and the vicar are dead at the hand of some unknown brigand.' Miss Hart's chin wobbled indignantly.

'Really, Miss Hart.' Kitty's aunt glared at her companion.

The door of the drawing room opened once more and Inspector Greville and Matt entered.

Lucy immediately vacated her seat and insisted that Matt take it as it was closer to the fire. The inspector took the armchair and Lucy started to offer drinks from the small bar, pressing a glass of whisky on her father and the inspector.

'We are all simply longing to know what has happened,' Hattie declared as she accepted a gin and orange from Lucy.

'I'm afraid I'm not at liberty to reveal details about the case.' Inspector Greville took a sip of his drink.

Kitty looked at Matt. He appeared tired she thought, and she wondered if his shoulder was troubling him after being out in the cold so much today.

'Whisky?' Lucy offered him a drink.

'Thank you.' He took the cut crystal glass from her cousin.

Hattie wriggled in her seat between them. 'There must be something you can tell us,' she pleaded.

Matt glanced at the inspector.

'Well, I don't know if this is common knowledge but apparently the late reverend had proposed marriage to Mrs Vernon and they were engaged,' Inspector Greville said.

His words had the effect of starting everyone into a burst of surprised chatter.

'Engaged? To Mrs Vernon? Well,' Lady Medford said, with a wealth of feeling in the word well.

'I am most surprised. I would never have believed that someone as well, lively, as Mrs Vernon would consent to marrying someone like Reverend Crabtree. It just goes to show that you never can tell,' Delilah mused.

'Absolutely, honey,' Corny agreed.

'And I must say I pride myself on being able to read people, don't I, honey?' Delilah turned to Corny.

'You sure do, sweetie.'

'Reverend Crabtree and Mrs Vernon were not only engaged, but they had intended leaving tomorrow on the first train,' the inspector announced in a casual tone, his attention seemingly fixed on admiring the play of light coming from the facets of the cuts in his whisky glass.

'They intended to elope?' Hattie's eyes widened.

'It certainly appeared that way. The reverend had packed his bags in preparation and Mrs Vernon said their journey was planned. They intended to marry in London and then to continue on via boat train to the South of France.' Matt took a sip of whisky.

'My goodness.' Delilah pressed her hand against her heart.

'That would no doubt explain why Mrs Vernon appeared so happy when we attended church on Christmas morning.' Lady Medford's tapestry lay untouched in her lap. 'Whatever will Mrs Baker make of all this I wonder?'

'Was Reverend Crabtree close to Mrs Baker too?' the inspector asked.

Lady Medford gave an unladylike snort. 'In my opinion I always thought he was playing the one off against the other, but of course Mrs Vernon is much wealthier than Mrs Baker.'

Kitty could see Inspector Greville filing this piece of information away in his memory. She could see it being a motive perhaps for Mrs Baker to murder Mrs Vernon, there was certainly no love lost between them, but Mrs Baker wouldn't have had enough strength to murder Reverend Crabtree, even if he had been aware of her possibly bigamous marriage. Apart from Miss Plenderleith, Reverend Crabtree and Miss Hart, everyone else seemed unaware of any suspicions regarding Mrs Baker and her marital status. They all seemed to be shocked at the news of the engagement too. How did any of this fit with Miss Plenderleith's death?

Hattie finally decided to move from the centre of the sofa to go and select some music for the gramophone. Matt took the opportunity to move next to Kitty.

'By the way, Kitty m'dear, it's all arranged for my man to take you to Exeter tomorrow and bring you back,' Lord Medford said.

'Thank you, Uncle, that's very generous of you.' Kitty wasn't sure if anything would come from this meeting in the tea room or even if the woman would keep the appointment. It was the best information they had received so far about her mother, however, so it had to be worth a try.

'Are you going shopping tomorrow?' Juliet asked.

'No, I have an appointment in town,' Kitty replied. She knew Delilah was aware of the reason for her errand but saw no reason to tell Juliet as well.

'You should have reminded me, Kitty. I told you my car is also at your disposal.' Victor smiled lazily at her.

'That's very kind of you, I'll keep that in mind if I need to go into town again.' Kitty was pretty sure that the offer Victor was making was for her alone and didn't include Matt.

'Well, if you'll all excuse me. I need to make an early start tomorrow.' Inspector Greville finished his drink and said goodnight.

'Do you think he will catch this murderer?' Juliet asked once the policeman had left the room.

'Greville is a good man and well thought of,' Matt replied.

'I wonder,' Victor mused in a quiet tone.

Kitty glanced at him, startled, and wondered what he had meant by his remark.

CHAPTER SEVENTEEN

Kitty had chosen a popular tea room near the cathedral as her venue to meet Mrs Thomas. She arranged with her uncle's chauffeur for him to collect her and Matt from the high street after a couple of hours.

The city was surprisingly busy given that it was the day after Boxing Day and not all the businesses were open. A few remnants of the snow that had fallen at Christmas now lay frozen, black with city grime in odd corners and doorways.

Kitty took Matt's arm as they made their way from where the car had set them down to walk the short distance to the tea room facing the cathedral green. The wind from the previous evening was still gusting, stinging her cheeks with tiny icy needles.

She was glad to reach the warm, muggy comfort of the tea room. Tinley's was quite famous in the city for offering a delicious lunch and for the quality of their baked goods. If Mrs Thomas did not appear then at least she and Matt would have a delicious tea. It was also nice to escape from the tension at Enderley for a few hours.

The building was old with a flagstone floor and narrow wooden stairs leading to the upper eating area. The whitewashed walls sagged and bulged in places and the air smelled of coffee and sausage rolls. Kitty was relieved to spot a vacant table on the ground floor where she had a good view both of the entrance and the cathedral.

She had stated in her invitation to Mrs Thomas that she would be wearing a navy coat and hat with a crimson trim in the hope that it would make it easy for the woman to see her. She knew Tinley's was quite well known and busy so the woman should know where to come and it should not attract attention by her calling there. The Hammett family seemed to have quite a reputation and she didn't want the woman to be scared off before she could tell them what she knew.

'Do you think she will come, Matt?' She took another quick glance at her wristwatch while they waited for the waitress to bring their tea to the table.

'We are a little early yet. Relax, Kitty. It's in her interests to meet you if she can, especially if the information she gives us helps us to track down this Hammett fellow.'

Kitty blew out a sigh. 'You're right of course. It's just I think with these recent murders, that horrid letter, and then feeling that there is someone possibly hanging about the Hall spying on us, it's horribly unsettling.'

'I think Inspector Greville intended to interview Mrs Baker this morning and he was waiting for information from Reverend Crabtree's bank.' Matt stopped speaking when the waitress approached with a tray containing their tea.

The girl carefully set down the small china teapot, milk jug and cups and saucers before placing teaspoons and a sugar bowl before them.

'Thank you.' Kitty smiled at the girl as she left before continuing with the conversation.

'What are your thoughts on these murders? Are they connected to each other? And are they somehow connected with the guests staying with my aunt and uncle?' Kitty placed the metal tea strainer over the cup and poured the tea for them both.

'Quite honestly, Kitty, I don't know. I thought perhaps the vicar had either killed Miss Plenderleith or that he had been the one to perhaps take advantage of her death by disturbing the accounts.' Matt added milk to his tea.

'Do you think he took the money?' Kitty asked.

'Inspector Greville discovered a large bundle of banknotes in the reverend's bag. That money is now in your uncle's safe until the source of it can be determined. It seems possible though that the vicar may have cycled to Miss Plenderleith's and taken advantage of her death before the milkman discovered her. We discovered the burnt remains of the missing accounts pages in the grate of Reverend Crabtree's bedroom. The inspector wanted to confirm the story you heard about Mrs Baker with her. I believe he thinks the vicar may have been indulging in a spot of blackmail amongst his other nefarious activities.' Matt stirred his tea with his spoon.

'Hence the inspector's visit to Reverend Crabtree's bank?' Kitty tried to resist glancing at her watch once more.

'He also wanted to examine the deposits made in the church accounts, I believe.'

'I expect he will ask Mrs Baker about her marriage. Miss Hart and Miss Plenderleith both seemed to think she had committed bigamy and that the reverend knew about it. It would explain that odd remark that Mrs Vernon made to Mrs Baker at the church door if the vicar had confided in her. He may well have tried blackmailing Mrs Baker to buy his silence.' She couldn't help feeling a little smug that she had uncovered Mrs Baker's secret.

'What are your thoughts on Frobisher?' Matt asked.

'Simon Frobisher clearly had no time for his uncle, but I can't see that he would harm him,' Kitty said thoughtfully.

'I agree. I don't think Frobisher is a man who likes violence. He was an ambulance driver during the war, and he flinched each time the guns were fired at the clay shoot. And he had no reason that we know of to harm Miss Plenderleith.' Matt drank some of his tea and rested the white china cup back on its saucer.

Kitty played with the teaspoon resting on her saucer as she considered what Matt had said. 'Unless he wanted to frame his uncle. What if the vicar killed Miss Plenderleith because he was taking money but then someone else killed Reverend Crabtree?'

'Possible I suppose but I don't know, it doesn't feel right,' Matt said.

'The annoying part about it all is that if the vicar was killed so early during the morning it would have been before the shoot, so anyone could have done it.' Kitty had given a great deal of thought to this and she knew the inspector must have done so too. Alice had said the staff had been asked if they had seen anyone out and about early that morning.

Kitty straightened in her seat as an older woman in a worn brown coat and hat approached the tea room door. Over her arm she had a large wicker shopping basket and she glanced around as she pushed the door open as if to check if anyone might be watching her.

Kitty had given her name to the waitress and explained that they were expecting a lady to join them. The woman looked around the tea room as the waitress came to meet her. After a second's conversation the woman approached the table.

Matt immediately stood to greet her.

'Miss Underhay?' the woman asked, looking at Kitty.

'I presume you must be Mrs Thomas. This is Captain Bryant. Thank you so much for meeting us today, please take a seat and the girl will bring you some tea.' Kitty signalled to the waitress and ordered tea for the woman and a selection of cakes.

Mrs Thomas set down her basket and took a seat on one of the plain wooden chairs. It was obvious to Kitty that the woman was ill at ease and nervous. She kept looking around the tea room as if afraid someone might see her.

Once the girl had bought more tea and a delicate, small, tiered stand with an array of cakes and pastries, Kitty encouraged the woman to help herself and waited to hear what she had to say.

Mrs Thomas set aside her shabby leather gloves and tentatively selected a cream cake from the stand with Kitty's smiling encouragement.

'I take it that you know the Hammett family?' Kitty asked once the woman had a cup of tea in front of her and had started to consume her cake.

'Yes, miss, all of Exeter knows the Hammetts. There were the old man, he took the Glass Bottle on from a relative of his mother's. He come to a bad end. He were set upon one night down by the river when he were roaring drunk and he got tossed in the water and drowned. They never found who done it.' The woman paused to glance nervously about the tea room as if checking that no one was listening.

'How awful. Was that when his son took on the public house?' Kitty asked.

'There was talk at the time as it were the young one as had killed his father. Tired of the old man drinking the profits and frightened he might let his tongue run off with him. It were a few years after your ma went missing when that happened. After the end of the war like.' Mrs Thomas licked her lips as if to wet lips that had grown dry during her story. 'The lad didn't enlist because he had some kind of medical problem so they wouldn't have him. Something to do with his leg it were. He walked a bit funny, club foot I think. His brother Denzil were quite a bit younger but they didn't get on. Ezekiel were jealous of his brother, Denzil were a good-looking lad. I'm not surprised as he killed him in the end.' Mrs Thomas sighed.

'I heard there was a sister too. Esther?' Kitty prompted as she encouraged Mrs Thomas to take another cake.

The woman's face changed, her eyes widened with fear. 'She was worse than the lads, she was. She were always the brains behind everything. When Ezekiel used to disappear from time to time everyone used to say as it was to see her for his orders. Lived up on the moors her did. Hard faced lass.' Mrs Thomas shivered as she spoke. 'I had heard tell as she kept a house of ill repute in Torquay and one in Brixham.'

'What happened the day Kitty's mother disappeared?' Matt asked.

'I were only fourteen and in my first job. I remember it because it were in the newspapers a few days after and I said to my employer as I thought as I'd seen your ma. The description seemed to match see. Not as that did me much good as her cuffed me round the head and told me to keep my mouth shut.' She looked apologetically at Kitty. 'I'm so sorry, miss, but I were only a lass and I needed my job. I remember seeing that lady because she were dressed nice. A pretty pink two-piece she had, and she were walking quick and confident like. I think she'd come out from Jacky Daw's Emporium as that were one of the only places open. She come quite close to where I were sweeping so I saw she had one of those suffrage brooches on her lapel. It shone in the light and I remember thinking as she was brave to be wearing that round town.'

Kitty swallowed hard. She could picture the scene the woman was describing quite clearly. She had vague, much faded memories of being towed along by her mother as a small child as she had swept along at a brisk pace. That same pin was now on the collar of her coat hidden today by her scarf.

'What happened next?' Matt asked.

Kitty gave him a small, grateful smile. He had clearly noticed that she was temporarily too overcome by emotion to speak.

'I were out front near the window sweeping when the lady walked past me. Weren't many people about.' Mrs Thomas' brow creased up in concentration as she tried to recall the events of the day. 'There were some kids hanging about playing with marbles and a woman pushing a pram further down the street. Your ma had gone almost to the corner by the lamp post when she suddenly picked up her skirts at the front and took off running.'

'And you didn't hear anything or see a reason why she might have started to run?' Kitty asked. She knew which corner the woman meant, it was the one by the Glass Bottle.

Mrs Thomas shook her head. 'Her didn't shout out or anything.'

'Did anyone follow after her?' Matt asked.

Kitty held her breath waiting for Mrs Thomas' reply. Jack Dawkins had said that he thought perhaps someone had followed her mother so this could be an important clue.

Mrs Thomas' frown deepened. 'I watched your ma run around the corner out of my sight. Then just as I started a sweeping again Ezekiel, the young'un, come walking up the street, hands in his pockets and a face like thunder going in the same direction as her. I'm so sorry, miss. It must have been hard for you all these years.'

Kitty let out her breath, her hands were shaking, and she rested them on her lap for a moment beneath the table while she composed herself. Matt exchanged a glance with her as Mrs Thomas sipped her tea appearing relieved now that she had unburdened herself of her recollections.

'Thank you, Mrs Thomas, you have been very helpful. I wonder, did you ever see or hear anything later that might be connected in some way to Mrs Underhay's disappearance?' Matt looked at the woman.

'The war was on and, well, I don't know how well you know the streets around the Glass Bottle, but there was a lot going on as shouldn't have been. There were a funny atmosphere, and everybody were scared of summat. My employer warned me I was to see, hear and say nothing to nobody. There was a lot of things a being brung up from the river after dark.' Mrs Thomas paused, seemingly lost in the past. 'I remember her a coming, Esther Hammett. Dressed up like a fashion plate she was and there was rumours of a big row at the pub, then her went away again.'

Mrs Thomas' information seemed to match what they knew already from Jack Dawkins. It was clear that Esther Hammett was somehow connected in some way to all of this. If she was still Esther Hammett since Cook had seemed to think the girl had married.

'Mrs Thomas, I am very grateful to you for coming forward with all of this information. Should it lead to an arrest or conviction then you can be sure we shall pay the reward that was offered in the newspapers. In the meantime, we would like to give you something to compensate you for your time.' Kitty took out her purse and passed a folded white five-pound banknote to Mrs Thomas.

She had no doubt from the woman's shabby appearance that this was a sum that could make quite a difference to Mrs Thomas. It was clear that she had taken a risk in writing and meeting them at the tea room.

'Thank you, Miss Underhay. I do feel better now as I've finally said what I saw that day. It's lay on my mind a good many years now.' The woman quickly pocketed the money, secreting it away inside her coat.

Mrs Thomas glanced around the room once more and collected up her gloves. 'I wish you well, miss, but be careful. Them Hammetts are dangerous folk and have eyes and ears everywhere.'

'I promise we shall be careful,' Kitty said.

'Good luck, miss, sir.' Mrs Thomas collected up her basket and walked briskly out of the tea room as if eager to distance herself from any connection with Matt or Kitty.

Matt checked the time on his wristwatch. 'We have half an hour or so before your uncle's car will be waiting to collect us. Would you like more tea?'

Kitty shook her head. 'No, I think I need to walk and clear my thoughts a little.'

They paid the waitress for their refreshments and started to stroll around the green opposite the cathedral.

Kitty slipped her arm through Matt's. 'Would you mind terribly if we stepped inside the cathedral?'

He patted her gloved hand where it was resting on his arm. 'Of course not, old thing.'

They made their way through the arched doorway at the front of the cathedral below the great window into the main body of the church. Kitty had only visited there a couple of times before with her grandmother. Once for a funeral and once because it was raining, and they had been killing time before returning to Dartmouth.

She took a seat near the back, uncertain of why she had felt she needed to be there except that talking about her mother had disturbed her. She closed her eyes and said a quick prayer for her mother, for Jack Dawkins and for Miss Plenderleith and Reverend Crabtree.

Kitty was conscious of Matt sitting quietly beside her, his presence a source of calming strength. She opened her eyes to see him watching her, a look of tender concern on his face.

'All right now?' he asked.

Kitty nodded. 'We'd better set off to find the car and get back to Enderley.'

Matt stood and offered her his arm once more and they walked back out onto the green.

*

Once safely ensconced on the roomy rear seat of the Bentley Kitty snuggled under the travel rug. The thin stream of cold air from the barely cracked open window next to Matt was enough to stop him from feeling claustrophobic without chilling Kitty.

'I wonder if Inspector Greville has made any progress today?' Kitty adjusted the plaid rug over her knees.

'It's a difficult case and they are short of manpower.' Matt had been wondering the same thing.

Listening to Mrs Thomas in the tea room he'd been increasingly concerned over the note that Kitty had received. From what they had learned so far Ezekiel could well be in hiding much closer to Enderley than they had anticipated. Then there was this sister, Esther. They knew so little about her, but Mrs Thomas had seemed more afraid of her than of the brother. The EH could just as easily refer to Esther as well as her brother, Ezekiel.

He glanced over at Kitty and knew she was thinking. He could see her pretty elfin face reflected on the glass window of the car as she stared out into the darkness surrounding the car now that they had left the city. Sleet hit the windshield and the chauffeur was forced to slow down as he used the wipers to try and see the unlit country road.

The deterioration in the weather made the journey take longer.

'I hope we shall be back in time to change for dinner. You know Aunt Hortense is a stickler for prompt attendance at the table,' Kitty said as the sleet turned into hail. For a few minutes the balls of ice drummed relentlessly against the metal body of the motor and they were compelled to slow to a virtual crawl.

Matt leaned forward to address the driver, a youngish man in his late twenties wearing dark green livery.

'Have we much further to go?'

'No, sir, less than three miles, I reckon. Hopefully this will abate soon,' the man assured him.

Matt sat back in his seat. 'At least there are unlikely to be any miscreants abroad with the weather like this.'

'That at least gives me some reassurance.' She smiled at him and his spirits rose.

At last the gatehouse came in view and the car turned up the long drive to the Hall. Matt looked out at the dark, rain-soaked grounds and hoped he was correct.

CHAPTER EIGHTEEN

The chauffeur pulled as close to the front door as possible. Matt jumped out into the wind and sleet, crossing around the back of the car to assist Kitty. They hurried inside the house out of the weather, shaking droplets of water from their coats onto the black and white tiles of the hall floor.

Kitty took off her outdoor things and went to hang them in the cloakroom. She took a few moments longer than Matt as she wanted to ensure that her hat had not been too badly affected by the sleet. She tidied her hair in the mirror and looked for a peg to hook her knitted scarf on so it would dry properly. The end hook next to the nail where the spare key for the garden gate was was free so she placed it there. She stared at the key for a moment as something tugged at the edge of her mind and vanished before she could examine it too closely.

'Would you like a quick drink to warm up before changing for dinner?' Matt asked as he straightened his tie. 'Sherry? Or a cocktail?'

'Why not?' She did feel rather cold and with Alice helping her she could be ready much more quickly than when she had to manage by herself.

The drawing room was deserted apart from Juliet who was seated beside the fireside staring into the coals. She startled as they entered the room and half rose from her seat as if to leave.

'Please don't go on our account. We were about to have a pre-dinner drink, won't you join us?' Quite why Kitty felt compelled to ask Juliet to stay she couldn't say.

Juliet looked doubtful at first but then subsided back on her seat. 'Thank you, a sherry would be nice.'

'Kitty?' Matt asked, his hand on the sherry bottle.

'Thank you, I'll have the same.' Kitty smiled at Juliet.

Matt carried two glasses of sherry over and offered them to Kitty and Juliet before returning to the bar trolley to pour himself a small glass of whisky.

'You live with your grandmother I believe?' Juliet asked, looking at Kitty with her piercing blue eyes.

'Yes, I moved to the Dolphin with my mother at the start of the war. My father was in America,' Kitty explained. Edgar Underhay had used his dual nationality to avoid conscription, but she preferred to keep that information quiet where possible.

Juliet's lips lifted in a small sad smile. 'My parents were killed when Victor and I were quite young. Victor was only just of age. I was still at finishing school. There was an accident with their boat, and they drowned. Ever since then it has been just Victor and I.'

'I'm sorry.' Kitty knew what it was like to be without a parent even though she adored her grandmother and knew her grandmother loved her. Her father had only recently come back into her life and until the summer she hadn't known of her aunt, uncle and Lucy's existence.

Matt came to join them taking a seat a little further away from Kitty.

Juliet looked sad and Kitty wondered what her childhood had been like after the death of her parents. It certainly shed some light on her brother's strange possessiveness.

'Family is very important.' Juliet had turned her attention back towards staring at the fire once more.

'Yes, I know I'm very glad to have been able to meet my family here at Enderley. I wasn't aware of my father's side of the family at all until this year,' Kitty explained. 'Do you and your brother have any other family?'

A tear trickled slowly down Juliet's cheek. 'No, there is just us. I was engaged once to an Englishman, but he died.'

Kitty was mortified that she had inadvertently upset the other girl and looked at Matt for some kind of help.

'I hadn't realised that you and Charles had actually been engaged?' Matt leaned forward in his chair; his gaze locked on Juliet.

Kitty knew there was something going on between them that she knew nothing about.

'Yes, he had asked me right before he was killed. We were so happy.' Her voice trailed away, and she dashed the tear from her face with the back of her hand.

'I remember you dancing together at the embassy party.' Matt's tone was gentle. 'I'm sorry about Charles. He was a good man.'

Juliet seemed to snap out of her reverie. 'Yes, he was. I don't think I will ever forget that terrible night in Alexandria or what you did for me.'

Matt looked uncomfortable. 'It was no more than anyone would have done.'

Juliet finished her sherry and placed her glass down on the side table before getting up from her seat. 'No, it was more than that and I have a debt of honour that I will repay.'

Her gaze locked with Matt's and it felt to Kitty that they had forgotten for a moment that she was still there. The clock on the mantelpiece struck the hour.

'You will please excuse me I must go and change.' Juliet exited the room leaving an awkward silence behind her.

'Well that was strange.' Kitty looked to Matt wondering if he planned to explain anything about what had just happened.

She was surprised when he rose and went to the bar to top up his glass of whisky before returning to take a seat next to her. Kitty waited for Matt to take a drink before she spoke.

'What was that about? Who was Charles and what happened to him?'

Matt sighed and raked a stray lock of hair back from his brow. 'Charles was a junior attaché at the embassy. He and I were good friends. He met Juliet and they fell in love.' He stopped and took another sip of whisky.

'What happened?' Kitty asked.

'I knew that Charles was head over heels for Juliet, but I didn't realise they were actually engaged. Probably no one did, unless of course she had told Victor. Then one evening Charles was supposed to meet her, they were going out to dinner. He didn't appear so she went to find him. The door of his apartment was unlocked so she let herself in. She found him dead at his desk, a single shot through his head. The local police said it was suicide.'

'Juliet clearly doesn't believe that,' Kitty said. Juliet had said Charles was killed and her whole demeanour had told Kitty that she didn't believe the suicide verdict.

Matt gave a tight, humourless smile. 'No, she doesn't and neither do I. They said he had money worries, but Charles was not the kind of man who worried about anything. He was in love, he was happy.'

'What did you do for Juliet?' Perhaps now she might understand the connection between them.

'Juliet went to pieces. The shock of finding Charles like that destroyed her. Victor had gone away for a couple of days when it happened, so she was alone.' Matt glanced at Kitty and then drained his glass.

Kitty sensed there was much more to this story and that Matt was downplaying his part in it.

'We had better hurry and change. The others will be down here soon for dinner.' Matt placed his empty glass next to Juliet's.

Kitty finished her own drink and decided to try and get the rest of the story from him some other time. Perhaps when they were back in Dartmouth away from Enderley and this strange Christmas.

Alice was waiting anxiously for her when she let herself into her bedroom. 'Blimey, miss, I was starting to get worried. The weather is really nasty now outside and I thought as you might have had trouble getting back from Exeter.'

'Sorry, Alice, it did take longer to drive back, and we were freezing cold, so I stopped for a quick sherry downstairs.' Kitty perched on the fireside chair and took off her shoes.

'I've put your frock all ready for you, miss, but I don't think as you'll have time to have a bath.' Alice frowned at the small travel clock on the dressing table.

'I was talking to Juliet in the drawing room. She seems so terribly unhappy.' Kitty rolled down her thick stockings ready to replace them with a sheer pair more suited to evenings.

Alice tutted sympathetically. 'That maid of hers, Maria, she as good as admitted as Miss Juliet's brother pays her to keep tabs on his sister. She tells him everything, what letters she has, where she goes, the lot. Must be like being a prisoner I reckon. I told you as she gives Miss Juliet medicine. Mind you that's nothing as to what that Maria gives the count, if you catch my meaning, miss.'

'Alice, really.' She wasn't certain which was most shocking. That Maria was having some kind of liaison with the count or Victor's manipulation of his sister. 'Poor Juliet.' Kitty turned obediently for Alice to assist her with the fastening on her skirt.

'Them Cornwells is peculiar too, so Gladys says.' Alice whisked Kitty's shoes into the wardrobe and reached down for the black evening dress that she'd re-pressed ready for Kitty to wear.

'Why does Gladys think they are peculiar?' Kitty asked. She thought they seemed rather sickly sweet with their constant endearments and catching Delilah searching through other people's possessions had been distinctly odd. She was keen to hear what the young housemaid's thoughts were about the Cornwells.

Alice carefully slipped her evening dress off the hanger and helped Kitty into it. 'Well Gladys says as she's heard them when they're in company being all lovey-dovey and stuff but when there in't anybody about – they don't notice Gladys a doing the fires and that – she said as how they'm totally different.'

Kitty paused in her dressing. 'How different?'

The young maid wrinkled her nose. 'Sort of brusque and businesslike, not at all like when anyone else is about. He like gives her orders as if he's her boss. Gladys says it's like they'm acting a part.'

'Hmm.' Kitty didn't like the sound of this. It could be tied in with the conversation she'd overheard when she'd been eavesdropping on Matt and her uncle.

Alice's swift fingers tackled Kitty's buttons. 'Gladys reckons as Simon Frobisher is sweet on Miss Juliet an all. That Maria hasn't said nothing about that, so I don't know as she knows. He could be her secret lover. Ooh, I saw a lovely film like that earlier this year. *Forbidden* it were called.'

Kitty sat down in front of her dressing table. 'I'd thought the same thing, but they'd make an odd pair.'

'There's a lid for every pot, miss.' Alice selected some simple diamanté hair clips and dressed Kitty's hair.

Kitty added a touch of lipstick and a dab of her favourite perfume.

'I reckon as there's five minutes till Mr Harmon bangs that dinner gong, miss. You'd best get downstairs.' Alice handed her an emerald green velvet shawl.

'Thank you, Alice.' Kitty gave her reflection a last quick check in the mirror and hurried along the landing.

*

Matt had loitered deliberately on the landing waiting for Kitty to emerge. He knew the others had already gone downstairs as he'd watched them all leave from a hidden spot on the gallery.

Kitty smiled at him and he caught the faint rose scent of her perfume. 'Were you waiting for me?'

'Actually, yes.' He dropped a kiss on her lips as her eyes widened in surprise. 'We don't have much time before dinner, but I wanted to warn you.'

'Warn me? What about?' He could see he had her interest.

'Please don't mention Charles or anything about the conversation we had with Juliet to Victor. It's really complicated, and I promise I'll explain the rest of the story when I can. There are a lot of things going on here that I can't tell you about. I just need you to trust me.' He wished he could tell her everything, but he had no way of knowing how much danger she might be placed in if he did.

He half expected her to argue with him. Kitty hated not knowing things. It took him by surprise when she looked into his eyes and nodded her head, the jewelled clips either side of her forehead winking in the light.

'Very well. I could see Juliet was very distressed and there are so many odd things occurring here.'

The sound of the gong reverberated up from the hall. Kitty took hold of his arm. 'Come on, let's go to dinner before my aunt has apoplexy at our being late.'

He was both relieved and puzzled by her ready acquiescence. In his experience Kitty didn't usually simply roll over when she thought there was something going on that she was unaware of. He had the horrid feeling that she was up to something.

They were last into the dining room but fortunately not late. Juliet looked pale and her eyes were rimmed with pink as if she had been crying. He hoped the conversation they had held in the drawing room had not stirred up bad memories for her. Simon Frobisher also looked pale but composed after the shocking events of yesterday. Hattie was her usual exuberant self, chattering away ninety to the dozen with everyone around her.

Miss Hart scarcely spoke during the meal and contented herself with glaring at Lucy who was discussing her upcoming visit to

Thurscomb to see Rupert while slipping titbits of meat from her dinner under the table to Muffy.

Once the ladies had withdrawn for coffee Matt fell into step with Inspector Greville as the gentlemen made their way to the library for port. Lord Medford poured liberal glasses from the cut-glass decanter as they each found a comfortable armchair.

'Cigar?' His host then proffered around a box of cigars. The inspector, Victor and Corny took him up on his offer. Matt refused as did Simon who had wandered away to the far end of the room to study the shelves.

'Any news, Greville?' Lord Medford asked as he lit up his cigar and blew an aromatic stream of smoke into the air.

'As it happens, Lord Medford, it's been quite a productive day thanks to your daughter, sir.'

'Lucy? What has Lucy to do with this?' Lord Medford instantly became alert.

'I asked her not to say anything until we had investigated further but thanks to her little dog the church candlesticks have been recovered.' The inspector appeared pleased with the astonished response this piece of news provoked.

'What, Lucy's dog found the candlesticks? My word, where were they?' Corny was seated nearby.

The inspector took a puff of his cigar. 'That's the odd thing, sir. They were wrapped up in the missing altar cloth and bundled into an evergreen hedge. Muffy sniffed them out. It was inside the estate walls not far from the gate leading to the lane.'

'How on earth? That gate is always kept locked.' Lord Medford's complexion developed a purplish-red hue.

'Exactly, sir. We are testing for fingerprints but with this rain and them being wrapped up…' The inspector didn't sound hopeful.

Matt frowned. 'Why bring them inside the estate and hide them in a bush? Do you suspect one of the staff or do you think whoever took them might have stashed them hoping to collect them at a later date?'

It seemed to Matt as if the murders were increasingly looking like an inside job. The only key to the gate that he knew of was hanging inside the cloakroom, which any of the house party or servants could have utilised. There were always people at the gatehouse but the gates were kept locked until later in the morning with the keepers letting tradespeople in and out so the culprit was unlikely to have entered that way.

'Perhaps Mr Frobisher may have some ideas. He knew more of his uncle's character than the rest of us and so perhaps may know of any friendships Reverend Crabtree may have made?' Victor looked towards the far end of the library where Simon stood, thumbing idly through a book.

'What was that? No, sorry. I know little of any of my uncle's personal connections. He wasn't a man to have friends so far as I know. I was surprised when I heard that he and Mrs Vernon were to be married. He had a history of extracting money from women but he had escaped matrimony.' Simon blinked and pushed his spectacles higher on the bridge of his nose.

'You are surely not implying that any of my staff, or my head gardener and his brother are somehow involved in these heinous crimes, Inspector?' Lord Medford asked. 'The Golightly family has served my family for generations. They are as honest and trustworthy as the day is long.'

Inspector Greville rushed to soothe Lord Medford's obviously distressed feelings that his trusted servants could possibly be implicated in the vicar's murder. 'No, sir, the verger and his brother both have excellent alibis for the times when the murders must have been committed. I can assure you, sir, the Golightlys are not amongst my suspects.'

'Should bally well think so,' his lordship muttered.

'May we ask who is on your suspect list, Inspector?' Victor crossed his legs, settling back in the leather armchair.

'I'm sure you'll understand that I would prefer not to disclose that information at this point in time, sir. There are however a number of points that we are working upon.' The inspector eyed the count with a level gaze.

'It sounds, Inspector, as if you may suspect all of us.' The count grinned, clearly satisfied with the response.

Simon Frobisher fumbled with the book he was holding, dropping it on the floor. 'So sorry, clumsy of me.' He bent and picked it up his complexion reddening under the watchful gaze of the others.

Lord Medford extinguished his cigar in the large crystal ashtray. 'Better go and rejoin the ladies. Greville, are you intending to make them aware of this find?'

'I think it would be wise to inform them. They may have seen someone perhaps behaving suspiciously and have information that could aid the enquiry.'

CHAPTER NINETEEN

Kitty was seated beside Lucy next to the gramophone when the men entered the drawing room. Lucy had taken her to one side and whispered the story of her afternoon's adventures, including Muffy's find in the rhododendrons.

Matt sauntered over to join them, taking a seat on a nearby stool. 'I can guess what you two are busy whispering about.'

'I take it Inspector Greville has shared news of the discovery with you then?' Kitty's brow arched.

'A few moments ago. I got the impression he wished to see how people responded. He will no doubt do the same thing now,' Matt said.

Even as he finished it was apparent the inspector was doing exactly that. A wave of disbelief and chatter broke out immediately.

'My dear Lucy, why on earth didn't you tell me? And why were you and Muffy out scampering about the grounds alone with a murderer on the loose?' Lady Medford demanded.

'I'm afraid I asked Miss Medford to refrain from telling you all about the find, your ladyship.' Inspector Greville gave Lucy an apologetic glance.

'My dear, were you aware of this?' Kitty's aunt turned to Lord Medford.

'The inspector informed me only a moment ago, m'dear.'

Miss Hart dabbed at her eyes with her handkerchief. 'I knew it. First poor dear Miss Plenderleith, then the vicar, we are none of us safe I tell you, none of us.'

Lady Medford glared at her companion. 'Oh don't be so ridiculous, Miss Hart. I am quite sure that inside the Hall we are perfectly secure. The inspector is staying under the same roof. The grounds however are a different matter. Lucy, you and Kitty must not go out alone until this man is caught.'

Delilah Cornwell stared at Lady Medford. 'Oh my goodness, why I declare I am relieved that the inspector is with us and all but my, I never expected this kind of adventure here in England.'

Her husband patted her hand. 'There, there, honey. I'm sure the inspector has it all under control.'

'I must admit, Inspector, I'm quite confused. If the vicar was murdered for the candlesticks, then why would the miscreant risk bringing them inside the estate grounds? Surely it would have been simpler and safer to hide them somewhere in the environs of the church or even further along the lane if he did have to come back for them?' Kitty asked.

Corny's brow furrowed as he looked at Kitty. 'The little lady has a point there, Inspector.'

'And I can assure you that it's been noted, Mr Cornwell,' Inspector Greville replied.

Miss Hart was still sniffling into her handkerchief much to Lady Medford's displeasure. 'Really, Miss Hart, do pull yourself together.'

'I keep thinking of dear Miss Plenderleith. She was so intelligent and cultured. Such a genteel lady and well travelled. She had that little foible about the pixies, of course, leaving them little gifts at first light at the end of her garden. But she wouldn't harm a fly and now, to think this has happened.' Miss Hart gulped.

'You were good friends with Miss Plenderleith, weren't you, Miss Hart?' Kitty asked. She knew Miss Hart had been greatly affected by the other woman's death and she had the germ of an idea taking shape in her head. Things the woman had mentioned in conversation were triggering a chain of thought.

'Indeed, Miss Underhay. We used to take tea together on my half day off. She had such interesting stories about her travels with her father. He was a professor of folklore at the university and she used to accompany him and take his notes. She spoke many languages; Spanish, French, Portuguese, Italian and German. She was terribly accomplished, and we got along together so very well.' Miss Hart sniffed and dabbed her eyes once more as Lord Medford proffered her a sherry.

Kitty knew she had to pick her way carefully in order to test the various strands of her theory to see if they were correct. She was about to ask another question when Matt spoke.

'I can see why many people perhaps might wish to murder Reverend Crabtree, but not Miss Plenderleith.' He halted and looked at Simon. 'I'm sorry, Mr Frobisher.'

Simon was slumped in one of the armchairs near the Christmas tree. 'Oh, please don't worry about offending me. I assure you that I am well aware of my uncle's true character. Sadly, I'm surprised he wasn't murdered before.'

Matt templed his hands together and looked at Kitty. 'It seems to me, Inspector, that if we assume the same fellow that murdered Miss Plenderleith also murdered the vicar, then perhaps it is the first murder that might hold the key.'

Kitty bit back a smile. She knew that Matt's mind was working along similar lines to her own.

Hattie clapped her hands together in delight. 'Oh, that is so clever, Captain Bryant.' She nudged Victor with her elbow. He had taken the seat next to her on the sofa, close to Juliet.

Inspector Greville's moustache quivered indignantly. 'Precisely the point I was about to make. Miss Plenderleith was murdered at a similar time of day to Reverend Crabtree. A time when few people would be up and about. Now I don't believe the lady would open her door to someone she didn't know.'

'She would have opened it for her cat or if she were about to make her morning gift to the pixies.' Miss Hart's chin trembled. 'She loved that cat.'

'Everyone knew she was in the habit of rising early to do that. She was even talking about it at the party. That was why she wished to leave early. She said the wretched cat would wake her up before the dawn.' Lady Medford glared at her hapless companion.

'That is true, I heard her say this when she was explaining the story of these pixies. We have similar legends in my country too from Bavaria and in the remote villages,' Juliet agreed.

Kitty noticed a trace of a frown on Victor's brow as he looked at his sister.

'It did strike me as a little odd that she suddenly wanted to leave the party when she did. I know she was annoyed that Mrs Baker had spilled her drink on her dress, but she wasn't in a bad humour about it.' Lucy frowned. 'And she knew about her cat's habits so I rather think she was making an excuse to leave over something else.' She turned to Kitty. 'What do you think, Kitty?'

Kitty had been trying to recall the sequence of events after Mrs Baker had spilled her drink. Attention had all been focused on Mrs Vernon as the most obviously injured party.

'I remember she left the room to go to the cloakroom. She wished to sponge her dress quickly before the stain could set. We were all assisting Mrs Vernon.' She decided not to mention for the moment that Victor had not been present in the room when the spill happened. She wanted to see if anyone else had noticed or mentioned it.

'That's right, then she came back in and said everything was just fine.' Delilah nodded. 'I know because I asked her myself.'

'She seemed a bit odd though. Pale and shaky. I thought it was probably the shock of having half of Mrs Baker's drink land on her lap, sherry can be frightfully sticky,' Hattie said.

'I asked her too,' Miss Hart agreed.

'She went and said something to the vicar. You must have noticed that, Count Vanderstrafen, you came back into the room then I think, and she and Reverend Crabtree were looking in your direction.' Kitty was quite pleased with the way she phrased her question. Now he knew that she had noticed that he had been missing.

His ice-blue gaze rested on her for a moment. 'Perhaps, I cannot be certain.'

Matt's leg rested against her thigh for a moment. The slight pressure warning her.

'It occurs to me that perhaps Miss Plenderleith saw or heard something at the party that she was not intended to see or hear and that might be why she wanted to leave early.' Kitty had everyone's attention upon her now.

'Kitty my dear, what do you mean?' her aunt asked.

She noticed her uncle had straightened and the inspector was giving her his full notice.

'Miss Plenderleith was an intelligent woman. She was well aware of my uncle's work and that he might well have documents or items here at Enderley that could have value to someone who was not a friend to this country or its allies. It wouldn't be the first time this had happened.' Her heart was beating against the wall of her chest like a drum. Matt had stilled next to her and she knew he must be wondering what she knew of his real role in the house.

'Please do continue, Miss Underhay, this is quite a theory,' Corny drawled. He too had straightened; his hands were in his trouser pockets and his full attention was on her.

'I believe when Miss Plenderleith left the drawing room to sponge her dress she saw and heard someone doing something that she considered strange, perhaps wrong. Miss Hart has reminded us that Miss Plenderleith spoke five or more languages. I'm sure,

Inspector, you could get a record from the exchange of telephone calls made from this house on the night of the party.' She wasn't certain if that was possible but thought it worth the bluff.

'Indeed, Miss Underhay. Someone made a telephone call from here to the vicarage early in the morning the day the vicar was murdered.' Inspector Greville's voice was silky smooth, and she wondered if he too were now beginning to connect the pieces of the puzzle in the same way she herself had done.

'I believe that Miss Plenderleith left the drawing room to sponge her dress and perhaps saw someone either entering or leaving my uncle's study. That at first didn't concern her. My uncle may have been in the study or could have asked this person to collect something from there.' Kitty took a deep breath.

Juliet's face was as pale as milk.

'I think it was when she was returning to the drawing room that the significance became clear to her of what she had seen. I think she heard this person using the telephone. Miss Plenderleith was a linguist. She understood enough of the conversation, although it was in another language, to frighten her.' Kitty tilted her chin upwards to meet the count's gaze.

'Please do continue with your fascinating fairy tale,' Victor drawled.

'Miss Plenderleith was shocked. This person was a guest of Lord Medford's and of a higher social status. She didn't know what to do so, although she disliked and distrusted the vicar, she confided her concern to him. She knew he would be in a better position to broach the matter with either my uncle or with the person concerned. After all, perhaps it was a mistake and a man could deal with the situation better than she herself could.' Kitty was sure her tone conveyed that this was not a belief that she herself shared with the late Miss Plenderleith.

Inspector Greville's eyes gleamed and his moustache twitched.

'That was when you re-entered the drawing room, wasn't it, Count Vanderstrafen? You came in and saw they had their heads together. They looked at you and you knew that Miss Plenderleith had heard and understood you. Reverend Crabtree told her to make an excuse and go home. He would deal with the matter.' Kitty waited for Victor's response. Her palms were clammy, and her pulse hammered.

'And then what, Miss Underhay?' Victor asked.

The rest of the room was silent, even Hattie hadn't spoken to interrupt. The logs burning in the grate crackled and the mantelpiece clock's tick was magnified by the silence.

'I think that after Miss Plenderleith left, her fate was sealed. You had to silence her. You had heard her say that she rose early and performed her little ritual. You took the key from the cloakroom and went to her cottage.' Kitty swallowed.

Miss Hart gasped and gave a strangled sob.

'I suppose I took the money and destroyed her cottage to muddy the waters as you English say?' Victor's tone was light, but Kitty wasn't fooled.

'No, I think luck played a part in this. I think the vicar, who was not averse to making the most of an opportunity, had cycled early to Miss Plenderleith's to ensure he had all the information he required at his disposal in order to try a spot of blackmail. He saw Miss Plenderleith was dead and spied his chance to acquire some money and bury his misdeeds with the accounts. He cycled back then to the vicarage and was busy having breakfast when the milkman arrived to use the telephone to report the murder.' This was speculation on Kitty's part, but it was the only thing that seemed to fit.

'Yes, you must have believed you were in the clear now. What a stroke of luck. The vicar was under suspicion or Miss Plenderleith's murder could be laid at the door of a mysterious stranger,' Matt added to Kitty's story.

Inspector Greville took up the tale. 'But then I suppose Reverend Crabtree showed his hand. Some extra money for his impending nuptials would come in very handy. He had quite a history of blackmail. There would be little danger to himself, after all he was packed, ready to leave. Except you couldn't allow that, could you?'

'You crept out early before the shoot. You'd telephoned the vicar asking to meet him at the church.' Kitty's hands trembled and she pressed them together on her lap so that Victor couldn't see. 'You took the candlesticks hoping the police would think it was a robbery, like the one at Miss Plenderleith's. Except you didn't want the candlesticks and couldn't afford to have them discovered in your possession. There wasn't much time before the start of the shoot, so you thrust them into the bushes on your way back to the Hall.'

Victor's mirthless smile changed into a snarl as Kitty finished speaking.

'You think you are so very clever, Miss Underhay, perhaps you, rather than Captain Bryant, should be the detective.' He was on his feet before anyone else in the room could move. A small gun in his hand.

'I suggest you do not make any sudden movements.'

Kitty realised his other hand had a firm hold around Hattie's plump upper arm.

'Miss Merriweather and I are going to leave now. I suggest that no one tries to stop me or tries to follow me.' He tugged Hattie to her feet. 'Juliet!' he commanded.

His sister remained seated on the low stool that she favoured. 'No, Victor. I want nothing to do with this.' Her jaw was set, although her eyes seemed to hold an anguished plea.

Anger flashed in his eyes. 'Get up.' He pushed Hattie away from him and caught hold of Juliet's arm.

'Let her go.' Matt was on his feet.

'Or what, Captain Bryant? Do you think I don't know what happened in Alexandria? You and her? Keeping secrets behind my back.' Victor waved the gun at Matt and Kitty gasped.

Her uncle was poised at the edge of the room from his position beside her aunt. Corny's face was a frozen mask and Simon Frobisher was flushed with anger.

'He saved my life, Victor.' Juliet's voice was icily calm. 'He got me to the hospital in time.'

'Enough.' Victor pulled his sister towards the door causing her to stumble.

Matt lunged forward to grab at Victor as Hattie screamed.

Kitty watched in horror as the scene played out in front of her as if in slow motion, although in reality it was over in seconds. Matt pulled out a gun as Victor fired his straight at Matt before Matt had chance to take aim.

Matt staggered but remained upright as another shot was fired and Victor crumpled to the floor. A growing pool of blood stained Victor's immaculate white shirt front. Kitty stared at Corny as he blew on the barrel end of his revolver and calmly stowed it back inside his jacket.

Juliet dropped to her knees beside her brother. 'He's dead.'

Inspector Greville rushed over to verify her statement as Hattie sobbed quietly on the sofa.

'I'm afraid it's true.' He picked up Victor's gun from where it had fallen beside him.

'I don't understand, I should be dead.' Matt looked at Juliet, confusion evident on his face.

'I changed the bullets for blanks. He didn't know.' Juliet rose, tears falling down her beautiful face. 'I promised I would repay my debt to you, a life for a life, and it is done.'

Matt wrapped his arm around Kitty's shoulders, holding her close to him. Her heart raced and she was thankful for Matt's solid warmth. For a horrific moment she had believed him to be dead. Thank heavens Juliet had exchanged the bullets for blanks. She felt quite shaken and sick thinking about what the outcome would have been otherwise.

'I rather think we should adjourn to the library. Lucy, bring the brandy and the glasses. Miss Hart, pull yourself together and make yourself useful for once.' Lady Medford rose and swept out of the room.

Lucy obeyed her mother and collected the items from the trolley. Mr Harmon met the party in the doorway.

'I'm sorry, my lord, I thought I heard gunshots.' Harmon's professional demeanour slipped as he caught sight of Victor's prone body.

'Absolutely right, Harmon, please go and assist the ladies in the library. Better leave everything else to your chaps, eh, Greville?' Kitty's uncle looked at the inspector.

'Quite so, sir. Mrs Cornwell, perhaps you should go and join the other ladies. Mr Frobisher will escort you.' The inspector signalled to Simon to lead Delilah from the room. Mr Harmon followed after them.

'I think I need to have a chat with you, sir.' Inspector Greville looked at Corny.

Juliet had sunk down on a nearby armchair and Kitty could see she was shaking.

'Juliet, may I get you a drink?' Kitty asked as she sat back down with Matt, his arm still around her.

The girl shook her head. 'I will be all right. It was a shock but not a shock, if you understand me.' She glanced at her brother's still form and shuddered. 'I knew always that it would end this way. We argued many times that he was doing bad things, but he would not listen. Always he liked the danger, the risk of being caught and, of course, the money.'

The inspector had been in muttered, discreet conversation with Lord Medford. Kitty watched as her uncle nodded and left the room. She surmised he had been entrusted to make the relevant telephone calls on the inspector's behalf.

'Do you always carry a gun, Mr Cornwell?' Inspector Greville asked as Corny helped himself to a glass of whisky. He held out his hand to take the gun.

'Only when I sense trouble in the air. I've been to some mighty dangerous places in my time. I like to protect myself. I could say the same to you, Captain Bryant.' Corny swallowed a sip of Scotch and passed the weapon across.

Kitty wouldn't have minded a nip of whisky herself. She still felt quite shaky despite the comforting support of Matt's arm around her.

Matt nodded his assent at Corny's comment and passed his own gun to the inspector.

'I'm so sorry, Miss Vanderstrafen, but you do see that I had to shoot.' Corny turned to Juliet.

'No, I understand completely. My brother—' She broke off, shaking her head.

'I'll need statements from all of you,' Inspector Greville warned.

'Of course, may I go to my wife now, sir?' Corny asked as he drained the last of his whisky in one gulp.

'Very well.' Inspector Greville gave his consent as Lord Medford re-entered the room. 'Miss Vanderstrafen, may I speak with you?'

'Feel free to use my study, Greville. Reinforcements are on the way,' Lord Medford announced.

CHAPTER TWENTY

Kitty was a little surprised that her uncle hadn't banished her to the library with the others. She presumed that Doctor Carter had been sent for and some more constables from Exeter.

'Drop of Scotch needed all around I think, eh?' Lord Medford poured a drink for the three of them and handed them each a glass.

Matt still looked quite shaken by his brush with death and took a large gulp from his glass causing her uncle's bushy eyebrows to rise slightly.

'What did happen in Alexandria, Matt?' Kitty asked. 'The rest of the story.'

Matt sighed and stared into the remainder of his Scotch. 'I told you about Charles.'

Kitty nodded. Her uncle walked away to stand beside the fire.

'After Charles died and Juliet found him, she took an overdose. Victor was still away, or so we believed. I found her just in time. I got her to the local hospital, and they pumped her stomach.' He paused to take another, smaller sip from his glass. 'She didn't want Victor to know. We bribed the hospital staff to say nothing and carried on as normal when Victor returned.'

Colour had begun to return to Matt's cheeks while he had been recounting his story much to Kitty's relief.

'You think he murdered Charles, don't you?' she asked.

Matt nodded. 'I discovered that Victor hadn't been where he had said when Charles was killed. I knew he didn't want Juliet to be involved with him and he certainly wouldn't have agreed to them marrying. He knew that I knew but couldn't prove it.'

Kitty sighed. 'That's why he hated you. I saw it when you first arrived but then he seemed to hide it, so I was confused.'

Her uncle turned from his inspection of the fireplace to look towards Victor's lifeless form. 'Dashed villain.'

'And now,' Kitty said, 'are you able to tell me what else has been going on here?' She looked at her uncle and then at Matt. 'Why you had a gun, Matt?'

Lord Medford immediately began to shuffle awkwardly on the spot. 'Not quite certain what you mean, m'dear.'

'Matthew?' Kitty turned her gaze to Matt.

'I wish I could, Kitty.' He failed to meet her eyes.

'I see.' She rose and swallowed the last nip of whisky for courage. 'Official secrets I expect. I rather think Victor was in the espionage business, selling secrets to whoever would pay the most for them. A small tip, if I were you, I would ensure that Maria, Juliet's maid, is held and questioned. She may have quite a lot of information for you. Now, if you'll excuse me, if you want me I'll be in the library.'

Kitty walked out with her head held high and went to join the rest of the party in the library.

*

Lord Medford waited until Kitty was out of sight. 'I'm getting too old for this game, Bryant.' He poured himself another drink and waved the decanter at Matt. 'Spot more? Been one hell of a night.'

Matt considered that something of an understatement. His shoulder ached from where the blank bullet had found its target. He held out his glass and accepted the offer of more Scotch. He would almost certainly regret it in the morning but at least it seemed now his job here was complete. Or almost complete.

Inspector Greville re-entered the drawing room. 'The men should be here soon to collect the count. I've arranged for Miss Vanderstrafen to be questioned further at the police station in Exeter.'

Lord Medford exchanged a glance with Matt. 'My niece also suggested that you question Maria, Miss Vanderstrafen's maid.'

'Hmm, did she now?' The inspector turned back to the door and called to someone in the hall.

A moment later a series of loud thumps and bangs came from somewhere above their heads followed by a woman's voice shrieking. The three men left the drawing room and entered the hall in time to see Maria being half carried down the staircase between two burly constables.

Alice was hot on their heels with her lace cap askew brandishing the copper bed-warmer from their bedroom.

'Doing a runner she was, had her bag packed and Miss Juliet's jewellery in her pockets,' Alice explained to Kitty who had emerged from the library with Lucy to see what the commotion was about.

'She struck me! She is a mad woman!' Maria yelled as the constables forcibly removed her from the building and into a police vehicle.

'I may have hit her with the warmer.' Alice attempted to adjust her cap with her free hand. 'But it's all right, miss, I didn't damage it.'

'Thank you, Alice. That was most enterprising of you.' Kitty beamed at her friend and the girl vanished back up the stairs.

Kitty and Lucy returned inside the library to answer questions from the others about what was happening. Doctor Carter's men arrived to collect Count Vanderstrafen's body with Inspector Greville supervising.

'Come to my study a moment.' Lord Medford opened the door for Matt to follow him inside.

Lord Medford took his place behind the imposing desk and selected a cigar from his humidor. 'Want one?' he asked.

'No, thank you, sir.'

'Cuban, the good ones. The ones in the box in the library are all right but these are the best,' Lord Medford explained as he went through the ritual of preparing, then lighting the cigar. 'Now then.' He leaned back in his chair and surveyed Matt through a haze of blue aromatic cigar smoke.

'I need to telephone and report to the brigadier,' Matt replied.

Lord Medford nodded. 'My niece seems to have been investigating this matter as well as Reverend Crabtree's murder.'

'I can assure you, sir, I have said nothing.' Matt flushed indignantly. He had wanted to tell Kitty. She had done a pretty thorough job of exposing Victor. No doubt if she had been privy to the same information as he and her uncle had, then she may have worked it out even more quickly.

Lord Medford blew out another plume of smoke. 'I don't doubt you, m'boy. My niece is as sharp as a knife. I daresay she's worked a fair bit out for herself. It certainly sounded as if she knew what Victor's game was.'

There was a rap on the study door and Matt rose to open it.

'Thought I should stop by before Delilah and I retire for the night.' Corny entered the room.

'Mrs Cornwell is not too distressed by the events this evening I hope?' Lord Medford enquired.

Corny grinned. 'No, sir, Delilah isn't easily shocked. I hope you won't take offence if, after I've cleared things with the inspector, my wife and I return to London to see the New Year in there. Got a suite at the Dorchester that we use when we're in town.'

Lord Medford nodded. 'Not at all, old chap. Quite understand.'

Corny turned to leave.

'Sir, may I ask you a question? You are of course at liberty not to reply,' Matt asked.

The American turned around, a wary expression on his usually genial face. 'Why certainly, Captain Bryant.'

'Miss Underhay confided in me that she had some questions about yourself and Mrs Cornwell. A small matter of her room being searched, as was mine. Then the events of this evening. Your work takes you to many places and I seem to recall latterly they have coincided with the same destinations as the Vanderstrafens.' Matt looked Corny square in the eyes.

'Your question, Captain Bryant,' Corny said.

'Whose side are you on?' Matt asked. He was certain that Corny and Delilah were working on behalf of someone.

'I'm always on the side of the angels.' Corny winked at him and slipped out of the study.

*

Kitty was sitting up in bed having her morning tea and talking with Alice when there was a knock at her door.

Lucy popped her head in. 'Am I disturbing you?'

'No, of course not.' Kitty smiled at her cousin.

Muffy ran in ahead of Lucy and jumped onto the bed ignoring the scolding he received.

'Delilah and Corny are leaving today and so is Simon Frobisher.' Lucy perched herself on the edge of the bed. 'Simon is going to London with the Cornwells. Apparently, Juliet is to be sent there with her maid for further questioning and Simon wants to get her a solicitor.'

'He is smitten with her then?' Kitty remarked.

'It seems so. I don't know if it's reciprocated to the same degree, but one can never tell with these things.' Lucy made a show of inspecting her fingernails. 'Um, what of you and Matt? Are you both staying on for New Year? Please say you are. If I have to listen to Hattie murdering "Auld Lang Syne" without some sane company, I swear I shall die.'

'Of course, I'd love to stay.' Kitty didn't feel she could answer for Matt. She was still a little cross with him that he couldn't or wouldn't confide in her about whatever else he had been up to at Enderley. Even more so now she knew he had been carrying a gun around and she had worked out what Victor was up to. She knew now that it was connected with the count and his sister and she wasn't stupid.

She also could make a good guess about why the Cornwells were leaving.

Lucy enveloped her in a peach satin pyjamaed hug. 'Oh, thank you. I promise we shall have some fun. Papa will arrange for some more people to come and we shall have music, dancing and lovely food, I promise.' Her cousin leapt from the bed and called to her dog. Before disappearing, presumably to dress for breakfast.

'You have no objections to staying on, do you, Alice?' Kitty asked. She was well aware that Alice's mother might if she heard about Count Vanderstrafen. Kitty had already had to soothe Mrs Miller's concerns that her daughter kept being involved with the police in dangerous situations.

'No, miss, not at all. Gladys says as the staff always has a party on New Year's. Mr Golightly brings his fiddle.'

'That sounds like fun.' Kitty grinned at her maid as Alice flushed.

The dining room was deserted when she arrived downstairs. She helped herself to coffee and scrambled egg and took her place at the table. Hattie arrived soon after and sat opposite her.

'Well, Kitty, wasn't that exciting last night? I have bruises on my arm where that brute grabbed hold of me. I had to get some arnica from Mrs Jenkinson. So terribly brave of Captain Bryant and Mr Cornwell. Poor Miss Vanderstrafen, she seemed such a nice girl. It just goes to show one can never tell.' Hattie ladled marmalade onto her toast as she talked.

Kitty didn't need to reply as Hattie never ceased talking long enough for her to get a word in edgeways.

'Have you heard Miss Hart is leaving too? Your aunt has dismissed her, or Miss Hart has resigned. I must confess I'm not certain which way round it was. Anyway she is leaving today and going to some cousin of hers in Norfolk.'

Matt entered the room and came to sit beside her. She could tell from his face that he had slept badly, and she wondered if the events of yesterday had triggered the violent nightmares that plagued him from time to time.

'Coffee?' she asked as she poured him a cup from her pot.

'Thank you.'

'Bad night?' Kitty asked quietly as Hattie continued to chatter away in between bites of toast.

He nodded.

'Lucy has asked us to stay for New Year. Everyone else apart from Hattie is leaving,' Kitty said.

'Are you happy to stay?' Matt took a sip of coffee.

'Yes. Why not?'

Matt nodded once more, wincing at both the movement and at Hattie's continuous stream of chatter.

After breakfast they managed to escape from Hattie. The drawing room was restored to normal. The only trace that anything untoward had occurred was a damp spot on the rug where Gladys had been scrubbing out the bloodstain.

'Kitty, I wish I could tell you everything but I took an oath.' Matt's expression was troubled as he took her hands in his as they stood beside the Christmas tree. Juliet's origami swan swirled in a slight draught.

'It's all right. I know you and my uncle have your reasons. I'm just glad that Juliet swapped those bullets for blanks. Please though, no more guns,' Kitty said.

'I must confess, I thought I was about to meet my maker.' Matt attempted a smile.

'It's over now at least. Now all we have to do is track down Ezekiel Hammett and his sister.' Kitty gave an involuntary shiver. Beyond the Christmas tree she could see the terrace and sunken gardens leading to the grounds beyond.

Out there somewhere was the man who held some of the answers to what had happened to her mother and she was determined she would bring him to justice if it was the last thing she ever did.

It was almost 1934 and the New Year would bring new opportunities. She smiled up at Matt. The dimple in his cheek flashed as he returned her smile and suddenly the New Year seemed full of promise.

A LETTER FROM HELENA

I want to say thank you for choosing to read *Murder in the Belltower*. If you enjoyed it and want to keep up to date with all my latest releases, just sign up at the following link. Your email address will never be shared and of course you can unsubscribe at any time.

www.bookouture.com/helena-dixon

If you read the first book in the series, *Murder at the Dolphin Hotel*, you can find out how Kitty and Matt first met and began their sleuthing adventures. I always enjoy meeting characters again as a series reader, which is why I love writing this series so much. I hope you enjoy their exploits as much as I love creating them. It was a joy to revisit Enderley Hall and Kitty's family again, especially Cook and her tea leaves. My great-great-aunt Lizzy was a noted reader of tea leaves and palms during the Edwardian and post-World War II era.

I hope you loved *Murder in the Belltower* and if you did, I would be very grateful if you could write a review. I'd love to hear what you think, and it makes such a difference helping new readers to discover one of my books for the first time.

I love hearing from my readers – you can get in touch on my Facebook page, through Twitter, Goodreads or my website.

Thanks,
Helena Dixon

nelldixonauthor

@NellDixon

www.nelldixon.com

ACKNOWLEDGEMENTS

My thanks as always go to the wonderful residents of Torbay who generously allow me to fictionalise their beautiful towns and give me so much support. Many thanks to everyone who supplied me with old photographs of Paignton, Cockington and Torquay. I'd also like to thank the residents of Newton St Cyres and Crockernwell who have also given me a great deal of assistance during my research.

Dartmoor is a wonderful place to visit with rugged scenery, wild ponies and tumbling streams. It's always a few degrees cooler on the moors than down at the coast, hence the differences in the weather conditions. I have taken a few liberties with the weather, but it wouldn't be a wintery book without snow.

My thanks as always go to the coffee crew, Elizabeth Hanbury and Phillipa Ashley, for their unstinting support. My hard-working agent, Kate Nash. To everyone at Bookouture, my incredible editor, Emily Gowers, my very patient copy editor, Jane Eastgate, my fabulous proofreader, Shirley Khan, and talented cover designer, Debbie Clement, plus all the many unseen people who do so much to help 'birth' these books.

Milton Keynes UK
Ingram Content Group UK Ltd.
UKHW011815050923
428107UK00005B/182